MW01635916

Hard Currency

To Gordon,

Hard Currency

Thank you for your dramaturgical wisdom.

Steven Owad

FIVE STAR
A part of Gale, Cengage Learning

– Steve

Detroit • New York • San Francisco • New Haven, Conn • Waterville, Maine • London

Five Star Publishing, a part of Gale, Cengage Learning.

Set in 11 pt. Plantin.

LIBRARY OF CONGRESS CATALOGING-IN-PUBLICATION DATA

Owad, Steven, 1967–
Hard currency / Steven Owad. — 1st ed.
p. cm.
ISBN 978-1-4328-2579-9 (hardcover) — ISBN 1-4328-2579-8 (hardcover) 1. Murder—Investigation—Fiction. 2. Warsaw (Poland)—Fiction. I. Title.
PR9199.4.0946H37 2012
813'.6—dc23 2011051006

First Edition. First Printing: June 2012.
Published in 2012 in conjunction with Tekno Books and Ed Gorman.

Printed in Mexico
1 2 3 4 5 6 7 16 15 14 13 12

For Sara Owad—for remembering to step toward the target when throwing the ball.
And for Ola—for giving us Sara.

ACKNOWLEDGMENTS

This book had the best of all possible editorial journeys. The late Knox Burger was not just a top-notch agent who mentored me through the early drafts; he also helped countless other young writers find their way in the world of publishing.

Various drafts of this story received valuable contributions from Katharine Sprague, Gordon Kato, Laura Hruska, and Laura Klos Sokol (though the latter's input waned as the *piwo* count grew).

The characters and events in ***Hard Currency*** are fictional, but the post-Communist milieu was introduced to me through my work at *The Warsaw Voice*. Thanks to Andrzej Jonas and Bartlomiej Bartoszek for allowing me to experience their country from an insider's position.

Prologue

Poznan, Poland, 1983

Between the train station and the shoe factory stood reminders of why Julian had brought Krystyna here: a butcher shop without meat; a line of people outside a bakery that wouldn't open for an hour; bottles in gutters; listless men lolling on park benches, the morning hours grinding by in slow motion.

"Shortages are worse here than in Warsaw," Julian said.

Krystyna cinched up her textbook bag and kept up with him. "They won't line up for meat?"

"They know there's none coming."

"Maybe it'll come later," she said hopefully.

"They don't seem confident."

Krystyna shook her head in dismay. Whenever she did that (and she did it often), she looked to Julian like a grown woman, complete with a wise woman's remorse; she ceased for a moment to be the eternally curious teenager that she was. She asked, "How come our shop in Warsaw has meat?"

"Because I helped our butcher get distribution."

They reached the factory and walked around back, where Julian opened a metal door and took split-second inventory. Most or all of the twenty-nine workers were there, along with their rep, who scampered up to Julian as if wasted time would translate into lost lives. All eyes zeroed in on Julian and Krystyna—mainly on Krystyna.

"Who's this?" the rep asked.

"My sister," Julian said.

"Why's she here?"

"She'll sit at the back," Julian said, "do homework while we do this."

"Homework?" the rep said. "You brought her *here* to do homework?"

Settling into a chair, Krystyna said across to them, "Ignore me. I'm cramming for a history test."

Julian scanned the workers again. Something was wrong. The lack of chatter. The glum, dead-eyed expressions. The smoke-filled air held a scent of musty inevitability—made this feel more like a mass execution than an illegal union meeting.

Julian recognized one of the faces but couldn't place it. The guy sat slightly apart from the others, arms folded. A pained frown suggested an upset stomach. Julian walked to the table at the front and felt the guy's stare burning a hole in the back of his neck.

The rep followed close behind. "You gotta be crazy, bringing a young girl here."

"I couldn't not bring her," Julian said. "She has to know these kinds of things go on."

"But what is she," the rep said, "thirteen, fourteen?" When Julian didn't answer, the rep said, "It's like religion with you people, isn't it?"

"Maybe let's just do this," Julian said.

"Thanks to you, she'll get her name on a dozen Security Services lists."

Julian's eyes were back on the guy with the upset stomach. *That's where I've seen you. You're a Security Services agent.*

The agent held Julian's gaze for a few seconds before looking away.

"What's wrong?" the rep asked. "You're white as a ghost."

Julian crossed the floor to Krystyna. Up close, he whispered, "Pack up, walk out, don't stop for anyone."

She looked up at him and blinked.

"Don't wait for me outside," Julian said, "and don't take the train. They'll send someone to the station. Buy a bus ticket. Once you get home, just wait."

She affirmed without nodding, gave nothing away. Julian strode back to the rep and looked over at where the agent had been sitting. The chair was empty.

He knows you made him. They're coming.

"That guy who just left," Julian said, "how long has he worked here?"

The rep looked at the empty chair. "Why?"

Julian glanced back at Krystyna. She had stuffed the textbook into her backpack and was now marching past the workers in an impressively casual-seeming bid for the exit. When she got there, the door flew open from the other side and a line of riot cops marched in, truncheons raised, gear clacking.

The workers scattered, but there was only the one exit. A cop put a choke hold on Krystyna, helmet askew. Krystyna kicked and tried to bite him. He dragged her out the door, and Julian leapt over a chair and charged into the teeth of the assault.

A voice cried out, "Don't let that one go!" and a swarm of black uniforms descended. Julian lashed out, but too many hands pulled him in too many directions. Clubs flailed. Sudden pain blurred his thoughts. He fought toward the door, toward Krystyna, but felt himself being dragged back.

A raid had been bound to happen, sooner or later, at one of these places. But not today. Not here or now. Julian had thought he could sniff out danger.

He'd thought a lot of things, but the rep had been right: bringing Krystyna had been a mistake. At fifteen, she was too young to be painted with a stripe of "political provocation." She wouldn't do time, wouldn't be severely punished, but what would happen was hardly an inconsequential alternative: she would be "re-socialized." And would be watched. For the rest of her life. Or the rest of the Communists' lives, if she was lucky.

A third possibility would not occur to Julian for almost a decade. The "rest of her life" might unfold at the mercy of something more perilous than even this heartless, soul-squashing regime. Krystyna's real struggle might not yet have begun. The Communists were, in fact, lurching toward their demise, but a new kind of foe was crouching in the shadows, sharpening its blade, steely glare fixed squarely on Krystyna. And all the courage and conviction in the world would not prepare her—or him—for the challenges that were about to come.

CHAPTER 1

Warsaw, July 1992

Julian strolled into the Gazeta Warszawy building, seized his key from old Jurek the doorkeeper, and sized up the two cops down the hall. They were the most starched things since Communism, and they were clearly there for him, sentries at the door to the politics reporters' room, with taxidermied postures and vacant eyes.

Julian crossed the floor and asked if he could help them.

"They said you'd be here at nine," said the first cop, a florid man with jowls.

"And who are 'they'?" Julian asked.

The cop started to answer, but stopped himself when he realized Julian's tone was offhand rather than inquisitive. Julian slid his key into the lock and turned to the second cop, a Rottweiler with an often-broken nose.

"I'm sorry," Julian said.

"For what?"

"Not sure yet. You'll tell me, right?"

"It's not like that," the Rottweiler said.

"Then my paper hasn't maligned the *polciji* in print again? You haven't been sent down here to 'correct' us?"

The cops exchanged a glance—a touch of uncertainty. The Rottweiler cleared his throat and flipped through a notepad. "Krystyna Krol. Your sister, correct?"

The tone was wrong. The word itself—*sister*—felt wrong. Julian had not seen her for three years—not since a relationship-killing clash of wills in 1989. He swallowed hard and nodded.

"It is our duty to inform you that she has passed."

Now a buzzing sound clogged his ears, a honeycomb drone. The traffic in the hallway drifted in slow motion. The jowly cop's mouth moved, but the words got lost in transmission.

"What?" Julian finally said without hearing his own voice.

"I said it appears to have been a suicide. She was found yesterday."

"No," Julian said, but their expressions said yes. *Yesterday.* Another wrong word, finality in three syllables. Like *abandoned* or *discarded.*

His mind leapt everywhere at once, toward the bleakness of empty shops, toward protests against the *nomenklatura.* To *yesterday.* Everything that had happened—everything apart from right now was yesterday.

The Rottweiler said something about an apartment on Wilcza Street.

"You are aware of her address?" he asked.

Julian said with a lot of breath, "Last I knew, she was in Cracow."

"She moved to Wilcza Street three weeks ago."

Overdose, the other cop added. Amphetamines. And as the deceased's brother, Julian could identify the body. It was necessary.

For a long while Julian couldn't move or speak. The cops exchanged another glance. Neither of them could make eye contact with him, which meant they felt this; they weren't machines. The glimpse of compassion felt cruel.

Julian followed them out to their squad car. The ride to the morgue was slowed by traffic. He looked out at Warsaw and processed only things that suited head-to-toe numbness. The sun poured stifling heat onto the crowds in the streets. The elderly were absent, indoors, sipping cold soups and eating blueberry-filled *pierogi,* recalling other impossible summers. The swarm on the sidewalks moved both quickly and slowly, some people fighting the heat, others submitting to it. The roads melted under articulated buses and delivery trucks. A rust-coated streetcar had jumped its tracks and now blocked an intersection on Jerusalem Avenue, keeping cars from turning to park at the Warsaw Stock Exchange, former headquarters of the Communists' United Workers' Party. Horns honked and smog-spewing traffic crawled along congested arteries. The city was obnoxious, insistent in its cacophony. It went on, irrespective.

The morgue was in the basement of the Banacha Hospital, in a clean area with houses and verdant yards instead of post-war tenements. The cops led Julian down a darkened stairwell, past a snaking line of people waiting to register for beds. They passed through dim corridors and stopped at a paint-flaked door. The jowly cop knocked on the door, a buzzer sounded, and they stepped into a small room with a large window that looked into a darkened second room.

The officers sat on each side of him. Julian caught a pale reflection of himself in the glass, then sniffed the chlorine in the air, the cresol disinfectants that had been slopped into the cracked floors and walls.

"The examiner?" Julian asked.

"No need for him at this point," the Rottweiler said, and a fluorescent light went on in the other room.

The light didn't stay on. It flickered, a nervous tic, barely working, like everything else. Krystyna was on a table close to the window, a sheet pulled up to her neck. Her face was chalk, her eyes dark and closed and sunk deeply in their sockets. She looked cold and old, Krystyna but not Krystyna. Julian managed to nod.

The cops rose and said something about an interview at the Centrum Borough Komisariat. Procedural. Then the fat one lumbered away and the Rottweiler said he would wait for Julian outside, but not for long, because there were things to do, formalities at the komisariat. Then he, too, walked out, and Julian stayed locked in the chair, staring at Krystyna, comforted somehow by the blinking light.

Until she became more remnant than real, like a statue. Maybe *all of this* wasn't real. That wasn't Krystyna on the metal slab. He, Julian, wasn't here. He was home in bed, asleep, digging through some knotted ball of subconscious angst.

The light in Krystyna's room blipped off and he squinted at his reflection in the glass. This, too, was wrong, the brief show followed by darkness. The last words he had ever spoken to her bubbled up: *I won't help you, Krystyna. You want to ruin your life, do it alone.*

He avoided the cops, picked up the death certificate, and left the hospital through a side door.

The walk back to the city center brought cold sweat and a sense of weightlessness. He drifted past embassies and the presidential palace, through Saski Park and the Tomb of the Unknown Soldier, where goose-stepping soldiers guarded the eternal flame. He entered the Ethnographic Museum and took the mildewy stairs down to the Nottingham Pub in the basement. University students crowded the oak-paneled bar and drank iced coffee, the Nottingham's specialty. A waiter crept up behind him and slapped him on the shoulder.

"How's it going, guy?"

No answer was required. The waiter bustled away with his loaded tray, and Julian drifted toward the billiards room in the back. Someone from the paper would be there. Someone talking shop or playing pool or sitting over an Okocim. Anyone would do. Or no one.

She's dead so what you do is you go to a bar?

He told himself he hadn't come far since Krystyna was a teenager and he was dragging her to illegal union meetings. He still tended to act first and consider the consequences later.

His editor, Henryk Milewski, leaned over a billiard table, drawing a bead for a shot. Julian stayed at the doorway, watched him unseen. Milewski was a tuskless walrus of a man, a guy who ate *smalec*—lard—on his bread at every breakfast. Sweat beaded his beet-red forehead and ringed the armpits of his shirt. The big man's trouble with the heat felt apt. This was how time and peace conspired against youthful energy. This was how a leader of Solidarity and a famously mutinous political prisoner turned out: morbidly obese, in real day-to-day hardship, waiting on something good because the battle had been won and the spoils of victory had yet to present themselves.

Milewski poked at the cue ball and watched it bounce off a cluster of other balls. Before the ball stopped rolling, he poked at it again and said, without looking up, "I didn't get your story. That's the second time this month." Milewski looked up and added, "You do it again, I'm supposed to fire you."

Julian approached him. "How'd you know I was here?"

"I see all and know all," Milewski said. "Why aren't you out somewhere at least pretending to be a reporter?"

Julian stared. Had he ever, before today, taken the time to look at Milewski, truly look at him? The guy was a startling mess.

"What's a matter?" Milewski asked.

"Krystyna just killed herself."

Brittle words, something within them cracking. She was dead and her death was something she had asked him to prevent and he had turned his back on her.

That simple?

In hindsight, yes.

He watched Milewski give him some edgy silence. Finally, someone in the other room laughed and the editor lifted a flabby arm and swabbed a handkerchief across his forehead.

"Sit down," Milewski said, stepping toward a table.

"The thing is," Julian said, "I don't know why it happened."

Milewski nodded.

"I mean, I know nothing. Nothing at all."

Which wasn't true. He did know some things. But they were things he wished he didn't know.

Things that got learned—instantly, brutally—once a person knew he'd just been jolted out of a years-long slumber.

Chapter 2

Lieutenant Daniel Kosinski read the advertisement before getting to the dusty Security Services file beneath it. The glossy yellow paper looked like a chance. Not a sexy one, but a chance anyway to escape the penury of law enforcement. The things needed: a down payment of five million zlotys, then four million zlotys per month over two years, plus the start-up costs of registering the business, outfitting the stall, and paying the local borough three months' sidewalk rent in advance.

Kosinski rocked back in his chair and enjoyed the free moment to consider the investment. Leisure was rare, a blessed snatch of unencumbered time in which to lounge and dream and watch the swaying birch branches outside his barred office window. After thirty-seven years at the Centrum Borough Komisariat, he would take every stolen moment afforded him. He worked sixty-hour weeks and had in his office a desk, a phone, two grainy chairs, and a Lucznik typewriter with a sticking *S*. Also there were carbons in the drawers and a new coat of cold green paint every decade that never killed the must.

So a vegetable stand. The idea, sent by a Sochaczew kiosk manufacturer, was both intriguing and depressing. Selling tomatoes might bring in more money than putting away perps did. Peddling carrots and leeks could actually pay the rent. Civil servants were doing it in droves, chucking once-comfortable careers in order to make ends meet. Engineers and scientists, too—trading hard-earned specialist talents for private-sector scraps. Hyperinflation had pummeled salaries. The government couldn't pay its professionals what they deserved. No, Kosinski told himself, it couldn't pay them what any human being deserved. This wasn't what Poles had had in mind three years ago when they turfed the Commie halfwits and declared themselves utterly, albeit belatedly, free.

He pored over the advertisement again, then crumpled it and tossed it into the wastebasket.

You never did this work for money. Why start now?

Besides, next door in Belarus, some cops hadn't been paid in months. Everything was relative.

He flipped open the Security Services file, a *milicja* instrument from the Communist years. Julian Krol, 29 back then (34 now), resident of Warsaw. A black-and-white snapshot showed piercing eyes and deep thought lines around the eyes and mouth. The text would no doubt show everything else. Kosinski read only the first few sentences, confirming the inkling that had compelled him to request the file. Yes, Krol, the journalist whose sister had committed suicide, was the same Krol who'd been a Solidarity activist during martial law. He'd been jailed twice—once for less than a year, once for three years—for championing unions and inciting worker protests. For the last two years he'd been a reporter at a scandal-mongering tabloid, hired on by editor Henryk Milewski, who had also done time for the euphemistically termed crime of "political provocation." Apparently, this Milewski, nicknamed *paczek*—doughnut—for his corpulent dimensions, had recruited Krol into the movement.

So the fast read on Krol: a one-time social crusader who couldn't find a place in the very system for which he had fought. No dragons left to slay.

Kosinski glanced at his watch, then crossed to the wastebasket and picked out the crumpled yellow ball.

You're sixty-three years old. Younger men are retired. Younger men are easing themselves into blissful infirmity. Think of the sun and the fresh air. What about the time to read on those long summer evenings? How many books have you promised yourself?

With his palm, he smoothed the glossy paper against his desktop, ironing the stall-maker's address into readability. Then the door opened and the man from the file appeared in the doorway.

Julian Krol crossed the floor and introduced himself. Kosinski offered his hand and tried to look sympathetic. "Thank you for coming," he said. "I know this is hard, so I'll make it fast. Would you like some coffee?"

Krol shook his head and Kosinski sat down opposite him.

"We know almost nothing about her. We need some information on her past."

"Information on a suicide?" Krol said. "To what end?"

The curt tone was familiar. It was one that much of the population reserved for the state-sanctioned gangsters otherwise known as police officers. Today's beleaguered police force was paying the price for yesterday's iron-fisted *milicja.* Kosinski had made peace with this fact.

He said, "I'll tell you what we have and what we're after. Then maybe you can help me." He pulled from a drawer a list of statements from the dead woman's neighbors. "She was renting an apartment down the block from here. Fourth floor of this same building, at the end overlooking Krucza Street. Does that sound right to you?"

At first Krol didn't answer. Then: "I'd thought she was in Cracow."

"Neighbors say she was in this apartment only three weeks, doing her . . . work. Her dates were coming and going nightly."

"Her what?" Krol said.

"Her dates. Her johns."

Krol leaned forward. "Krystyna *Krol?*" He looked slightly ill.

"I'm sorry," Kosinski said, "I assumed you knew." He pressed on so the moment wouldn't bog them down. "When the officers arrived at the scene, a rock station on the radio was turned up loud. She'd had a cardiac arrest. According to the medical examiner, it was caused by what's known on the street as Angel Fire, a methamphetamine produced in Gdansk. She ingested four times the lethal amount for a person of her size."

Krol now had his head in his hands.

"Are you okay?" Kosinski asked.

"I'm fabulous. I'm thinking of throwing a party."

"I know how hard this must be."

"You don't," Krol said, "trust me. I don't even know. I start catching up with it, it jumps ahead of me."

Kosinski let a few seconds pass. "Angel Fire is one of the worst drugs out there, cheaper than other street drugs, with a higher rate of addiction." Lowering his tone, he said, "Two weeks ago a man in Lublin decapitated his four-year-old son. Amphetamine psychosis."

Krol said, "Krystyna never took drugs."

"Well, my problem here—our very own Poland is Europe's top producer of this stuff. We've been seeking leads to the producer, but without success."

"So you're after her supplier," Julian said.

"We're after—"

"We're not talking about Krystyna. Krystyna is background to something else."

"I'm not sure I'd put it that way."

"Then how would you put it? You're hoping her ex-con brother knows some players in the drug world? Maybe I'm even the one who hooked her up? Or am I missing the point here?"

Joyful cries of children filtered in through the window. Kosinski broke off eye contact, rose from his creaky seat, stepped over to look out. On the narrow street below, kids were playing soccer, using parked cars as goal posts.

"What I was thinking of asking," Kosinski said, "I want to know who her friends were, where she lived before moving into that apartment. Her identity card has her at your address in Ursynow."

"And I told you," Julian said, "I thought she was in Cracow."

"You thought but you didn't know?"

"I haven't seen her in three years."

Kosinski waited for him to continue. When he didn't: "You became her legal guardian when your parents died. When she was fourteen. That was . . . nineteen eighty-two, right?"

"Yes."

"Why did you cease to have contact with her?"

"Vice versa," Krol said. "She ceased contact with me."

"Was she working back then?" Kosinski asked.

"You mean hooking?"

"I mean working."

"She was waiting tables," Krol said.

"Where?"

"Cracow."

"So what came between you?"

Krol pulled out some cigarettes and lit one. The mechanics of the movement, the distressed coaxing of smoke deep into his lungs—Kosinski knew it would help.

"Julian?"

Krol blew out a calming stream of smoke and appeared to make a decision. He looked Kosinski in the eyes and began to spill a story. The issue had been school. Krystyna had been finishing a Master's degree in philology at Jagiellonian University in Cracow. Four languages. Dropped out, though, without telling him. When she finally came home with the news, halfway into the fall semester, she said it was because she needed to slow down, do some thinking without the pressures of school. She would wait tables in Cracow for a while, use the time to deal with some disappointments. Alone.

"She was finishing a Master's degree at twenty-two?" Kosinski said. "Isn't that a little young?"

"She finished high school early."

"Why would she walk away from her studies?"

"It's just what I told you," Krol said. "She wanted to be alone. She wanted to try something other than school."

"And you have no idea what?"

Krol shook his head.

"Did you ask her?"

"A million times and in a million ways."

"So you knew something or someone was troubling her, but you didn't know what."

Krol said, "Is that a question or narration?"

Kosinski glanced down at the soccer game. A boy ricocheted the ball off a Fiat Uno and did a little goal dance. "Where was she waiting tables?"

"A restaurant in the Cracow Old Town. Holst's."

"How long did she work there?"

"Not long. After she left, I tried calling there, but they said she'd moved out, didn't leave a forwarding address."

Krol gave himself over to some memory before spotting the wrinkled vegetable-stall advertisement. Kosinski watched him give the brochure a curious look.

"The autopsy," Krol said. "Did it indicate she took meth habitually?"

"The examiner can't determine that. Only recent use is detectable. She also ingested a substantial amount of hashish."

Krol's whole body seemed to freeze, then tense up with an adrenal rush. "She what?"

"There was pathology from it," Kosinski said, "though she

ingested only a small amount. She was allergic to it, wasn't she?"

"Moraceous herbs," Julian said. "Mulberries, hops, also hemp. There's no way she would go near hashish."

"We found the drug in her pocket and in a dresser drawer. Apparently, she used it as a form of insurance, drank some in a tea. Do you know where her old friends might have purchased their hashish? Someone who dealt it back when your sister—"

"They weren't a drug crowd," Julian said. "Few of them even drank."

"But surely some of them—"

"There's something terribly wrong here," Krol said.

Kosinski sighed. Denial was common among victims' relatives. Solace was sought in the realm of disbelief. "Mr. Krol, she was—"

"Forget the 'Mr. Krol.' You've been reading up on me. Might as well address me informally."

Kosinski peered down at the desk. The Security Services file had been in view since Krol had moved the vegetable-stall leaflet.

"Hash would have made her too sick to kill herself. She wouldn't carry the stuff, let alone take it. Her friends knew that. One sniff and she'd be on her back."

"Not if she kept it—"

"If she kept it under wraps, she'd still have to open it to drink it or eat it or whatever else. Trust me, I saw her get sick. She once spent two days in the hospital after being near a hemp handbag." Krol looked half a foot taller now. "Maybe she *was* hooking. You say that's true, you've got no reason to lie. But she didn't buy herself hashish. It's a physical impossibility."

Kosinski said, "The examiner concluded it was taken voluntarily."

"What else did he conclude? I want a copy of his report."

Kosinski nodded. "You'll get one. We don't have to jump into opposite corners."

"We've already jumped," Krol said.

Kosinski took up the Security Services file. "I know what you're thinking."

"Do you?"

"But the old days are gone. Today's police force is not yesterday's militia."

"Must be why you're holding that file."

"I checked you out because your name rang a bell. We'll find where she got the meth, but we need your cooperation. As she had no other family, and as we have nothing on her—"

"We've moved on to another point," Krol said. "If hashish put her in the morgue, then she had some help taking it."

Kosinski told himself not to push. What Krol was seeking, what he really needed, was a kind of unasked-for bond, an understanding that the death of his sister was tragic and painful beyond all telling. Beyond reason or expression.

Krol asked, "Was the stuff in her pocket hermetically sealed?"

"It was in foil."

"You think she held her breath while she carried it around?"

Kosinski didn't answer.

"And mixed the tea?"

Again.

"Any scenario you come up with, it's impossible."

Julian rose from the chair.

"Where you going?" Kosinski asked.

"I can't lead you to any drug dealers, but if you want anything from me, just let me know. I'll be happy to help." Krol opened the door and pointed to the file. "I take it you know where to reach me?"

Kosinski held up a hand. "All her languages. Was that four of them apart from Polish?"

"English, Hindi, Urdu, and Pashto. Why?"

"What would a girl from Warsaw want with Pashto?"

"Travel. This was during Communism. Jagiellonian had exchange programs in India and Pakistan. Her only other choices were Moscow and Berlin."

"So she went abroad?"

"The programs fell through. Funding. Anything else?"

"We'll find out how this happened, I promise."

"I know you will," Krol said, "because I'll make sure you will."

When he was gone, Kosinski slid the file back into its envelope.

Hated cops. Fine. Thought them incompetent. Nothing new there. Inept cops and corrupt cops were, in fact, legion. Kosinski had spent plenty of time cleaning up their messes. But there was something about Krol—something that made Kosinski sorry he'd interviewed him. There was a kind of rhythm to the guy, an unruly beat that dictated his movements. He was the kind of man who didn't look before leaping.

Kosinski opened another file from his desktop. This one was a beat cop's report on another suicide, a fresh one. A sixteen-year-old girl had loaded up on crank and climbed the old ski-jump in Mokotow, across from General Wojciech Jaruzelski's house. With a friend, she proceeded to spray-paint anti-Communist graffiti on a part of the jump that was visible from Jaruzelski's bedroom window. She plunged to her death while painting the "a" in *swinia*—pig.

Sloppy, Kosinski thought. Sloppy, wasteful, and something that rarely happened just a few years ago.

That vegetable stand wasn't the worst idea ever to come along.

Chapter 3

Something was wrong. Antoni Mirsk stepped from elevator to lobby and the tension in the room felt like a blast of arctic air. Two men were lounging on the leather sofa. They wore tattered jean jackets and smelled of wine and body odor, even from a distance. Cigarettes dangled from their lips. They watched him through intent, bleary eyes.

Across from them sat a woman, who was also smoking. She wore a flowered sundress that clung tightly to her figure. She was also tanned, with light blond hair, maybe a local beach girl who'd been basking in the hottest Gdansk summer in fifty-one years.

These glowering strangers couldn't have been more out of place in this lobby; they had something unpleasant in mind.

Mirsk leaned over his receptionist's desk and whispered, "What's with these three?"

"They've been here since I opened up. I told them they need an appointment, but they insisted on waiting."

"And you didn't call security?"

The woman in the sundress crushed out her cigarette and rose from her chair. "Antoni Mirsk?" she said.

He looked at her without speaking.

"I want a word with you," she added.

"Not without an appointment. I don't just—"

"We don't need an appointment," one of the men said. "You're gonna talk to her."

The man and his partner gained their feet and flexed. They looked drunk enough to fall over. The receptionist scrunched her nose. A deliveryman hefting a bulky water container onto a cooler turned and watched.

"Is this some kind of joke?" Mirsk asked.

"All depends on your definition of funny," the woman said.

Clipped accent, Silesian. Mirsk looked her over, saw that her tan started at her cheeks and faded to white below her hairline. She was using makeup to blanket a turquoise bruise around her left eye. The makeup was so heavy around the eye that she'd padded much of the rest of her face as well, evening things out. The result was somewhat cadaverous.

"Ela," Mirsk told his receptionist, "call security, get these people out of here."

He started down the hall toward his office.

"Give me five minutes," the woman said to his back, "or the world hears some nasty little secrets about you." She'd made sure everyone heard her.

"Ela," Mirsk said without breaking stride, "tell security they might want to wear gloves."

"Want me to share those secrets here and now?" the woman asked. "In front of this prim little secretary who you're probably poking after hours?"

Mirsk stopped and turned.

The woman said, "Wouldn't you rather do it in private?"

He half-expected her bruised eye to blink shut in an audacious wink. "You're not even remotely credible," he said.

"Then go ahead, have Ela call security." She smiled, sucked a little on her upper lip.

Mirsk pointed out the two heavies. "What's with them?"

"Protection."

"From me?"

"It's a dangerous world," she said. "Bad stuff happens."

"Ela?" Mirsk said. "Security?"

"Sure, Ela, pick up that phone. In fact, that's why I'm here: security."

Ela kept her eyes on Mirsk, just short of calling.

Mirsk asked, "What's that mean?"

"It means you're less secure than you think you are. What you're thinking, you're thinking I'm some kind of lowlife. But what you're missing, what you're failing to even *consider*, I'm actually here to help you, you smug bastard. You're so set on passing judgment, you don't have a clue what's going on. So okay, your choice. Call security."

Now she did it. She actually winked—and then turned to leave. Mirsk glanced at Ela and the two goons, then back at the woman.

He found himself saying, "So how can you 'help' me?"

"I thought you'd never ask," the woman said. "I can save you trouble and keep you out of jail in the bargain."

Not a conversation for the lobby. Mirsk led the trio down a hallway to a plush office with Renaissance paintings and a bar stocked with foreign liquor. Mirsk and the woman sat at his rosewood desk. One of the men stood with his back to the door, guarding it. The other one went behind the bar, began pulling bottles from shelves. Mirsk tried to ignore them.

"What's your name?" Mirsk asked.

"Irena Platz."

"And you want from me what?"

"A hundred million zlotys," she said. As an afterthought: "Please."

Mirsk sighed heavily. He'd handled blackmail before. For the newly rich in this country, it came with the territory. So many people craved a fast ticket to the good life, and so many of them had a half-cocked plan for getting it. Mirsk was certain he'd heard every feeble and desperate plot imaginable.

He did the hard-currency math in his mind: one hundred million zlotys was roughly twenty-five thousand U.S. dollars, a fortune for the average Kowalski.

A fortune that, of course, Mirsk was not about to pay.

"Will you take a check," he said, "or do I go open the safe behind the Matejko portrait?"

"A nasty deed has your name on it," she said. "If you don't pay, it gets widely known."

"Are you allergic to the providing of details, Miss Platz?"

She shrugged. "They say you're thinking of Parliament, maybe mayor of Gdansk. Ambitious of you. But news about Antoni Mirsk, family man, tycoon, news of him keeping a confirmed criminal on the payroll, that wouldn't win him many votes, would it?"

"A confirmed criminal?"

"Especially if that guy was running a smuggling operation? Such news might lead to awkward questions, no?"

Smuggling. Sounded colorful. Watching her try to stare him down, Mirsk did some reasoning. Yes, there was muscle in the ranks, and in this pre-rule-of-law jungle, muscle was a force unto itself. You didn't hire poets to keep company executives safe. How far would she go with this?

"That makeup," he said, "only draws attention to your eye."

"My makeup and I will go to the cops and the newspapers if you don't hear me out."

The big man behind the bar pulled a glass from the shelf, filled it with Crown Royal rye whiskey. He sniffed as if it might bite him.

"The cargo comes from Pakistan. Does that ring a bell?"

"Pakistan?" Mirsk said. "*Pakistan?*"

"Well, what you should do right now, you should ask yourself what Pakistan has that Poles might want?"

"I should? Listen. You started poorly and you've managed to

lose steam even from there. Now, I suggest you take all of that very obvious energy of yours and put it to constructive use." He placed a hand on the phone while glancing at the bar. "Just so you know, your two friends over there hurt you more than they help you."

Her second escort was now at the bar pouring a drink of his own.

"Mirek," Platz snapped, "Lukasz. Join the human race for just one second, okay?"

Mirek and Lukasz exchanged glances and went right back at the booze.

Mirsk picked up his phone. "Ela, call security after all. Tell 'em when they get here things might get lively." Recradling the phone, he said, "If you want to shake a man down, Miss Platz, you've got to plan it better."

"One of your employees—"

"There you go again: one of my employees. Shouldn't this wicked felon at least have a name?"

She said, "You mean a name like 'Oskar'?"

Oskar. Man in Cracow. Okay. But if her Oskar was his Oskar, she was talking about simple meat, a bodyguard for local managers.

"Suppose I have an Oskar," he said. "Suppose he's smuggling whatever one might run from Pakistan. You go to the police, you'll be doing me a favor. I learn there's a baddy on the payroll, you make him go away, and society is better off for it. I'm not doing anything illegal."

"Actually, you are," Platz said. "You're not only paying him, you're doing so through a company he's never set foot in. Good money, too. The press would love to hear you explain that."

Mirsk leaned back in his seat. "How would you know how I—"

"How you pay this meathead?"

Mirsk swallowed a lump in his throat.

"A girlfriend told me. She used to work with him."

"In my employ?"

"Nah," Platz said, "she freelanced. Until Oskar killed her."

He watched her watch him. She'd been saving this bombshell, waiting for his confidence to peak, all the better to bring down the hammer.

"Her name's Krystyna Krol," she said. "The newspapers say she died of an overdose. I'll be telling those same papers that Oskar, your illegally paid, smuggling dipshit asshole employee, supplied her with the drugs."

"You have proof he did that?"

"The papers will roast you. You'll lose your career in politics before it even starts."

Appearances. That was the issue here. She could ruin him with appearances. The press, emboldened by a still nonexistent libel law and eager to skewer Commies-turned-capitalists for all evils real and imagined—the whole country would drool over Mirsk's connection to a smuggler and/or *narkoman.* The man in the street, who had trouble getting by while ex-party members like Mirsk got fat, would lap it up. Guilt through newspaper headline. End of political aspirations.

Platz sat back in her chair and crossed her legs. For a moment, Mirsk thought she might prop her feet up on the desk.

"Still think I'm shooting blanks?" she asked.

"No, you appear to have come fully loaded."

She pulled a card from her purse and stood up. "I'll give you some time to get the payment together. Cash, of course. I can be reached at this hotel." She slid the card across the desk. "Room number's on the back. If I don't get a call by two P.M., expect either reporters or cops to come knocking. I still haven't decided which."

She turned around. Her two goons slugged back their latest

shots and awaited instructions.

"Well?" she said. "He's called for security."

One of them belched loudly. The other one wiped his mouth with his sleeve. Irena strode toward the door, but stopped before opening it. She reached behind herself, pulled at her panties through her dress, made something back there more comfortable. She said, "Two o'clock's as long as I'll wait. I don't think you want to test me on this."

Antoni Mirsk took pride in his instincts; in recent years, those instincts had served him exceptionally well. Being on the boards of the Mieltor Salt Mine and the Goleska Petrochemical Plant was all well and good for a man who three years ago had been Communist deputy-minister at the Ministry of Industry. But with Solidarity's democrats snatching power in 1989, and with privatization blooming into a religion, the best way to thrive in this new world order was to worship at the altar of the right to get gaudily rich.

So while politicians wavered, while many freshly minted captains of industry dithered over details and confusing new fine print, Mirsk championed privatization campaigns for the mine and the refinery. He helped set preferential stock prices for employees, knew full well that most workers had trouble buying food and clothing, let alone company stock, which meant shares would gravitate to those insiders who had the money to buy them. When the sale opened, he took out a bank loan and two lines of credit and scooped up seven percent of the mine and six percent of the refinery, cheaply and legally, and then waited for export licenses for salt and gas—which were gimmies thanks to old-school colleagues who never seemed to be too far from post-totalitarian power.

Instincts. The mettle to act boldly, decisively. Everything was available in the early days of so-called freedom. You waved money at your business partners and they sold you their shares, built suburban villas, spent winters in Gran Canaria and Crete. Only a few stayed around to make a bona fide, oligarch-style killing. Only a few had Antoni Mirsk's instincts or long-term perspective.

So he sat in his office and mulled Irena Platz's threat and told himself to follow those instincts.

It didn't take long for priorities to align themselves. There was no guarantee Platz wouldn't take the payoff and run to the papers anyway, so she had to be made to back off. And the so-called smuggling business needed addressing. If what she'd said was true, then serious damage control would be needed.

Mirsk punched auto-dial on the phone.

"Hello," said a voice at the other end.

"I just had a visit," Mirsk said, "a girl with a black eye, Silesian maybe. She knows how we pay some of our security guys."

Chewing sounds filled the line. Martin Figur, head of Mirsk Industries security, was eating something crispy. After a muffled, throat-clearing moment, Figur said, "I'm sure plenty of people know that. So what's the problem?"

"She says one of my guys in Cracow is smuggling something from Pakistan."

"From Pakistan?"

"Or to Pakistan. I don't know. She wants a hundred million zlotys or she'll smear us in the papers, say this Oskar helped a woman have a fatal overdose."

"Well," Figur said, still chewing, "that's a new one, isn't it?" A few chews later: "Who's Oskar?"

"Ret. Oskar Ret."

"Why doesn't that name ring a bell?"

"He wasn't hired through the security department. I had the office in Cracow hire him."

"Without my knowledge?" Figur said.

"Don't take it personally; it was supposed to be without anyone's knowledge."

"Why?" Figur asked. "What exactly"—more chewing—"does he do for you?"

"Just security," Mirsk said, "certainly not smuggling."

"Then why did you hire—"

"Because a couple months ago the Pruszkow Mafia showed up, made extortion demands. At Mieltor. Ret was hired to watch our people while they met with them. You know how it works; they have bulls, so we need bulls. Appearances."

"So what do you want me to do?"

"I'd prefer it," Mirsk said, "if nothing further developed out of this."

"You want me to pay her a visit?"

Mirsk fidgeted with the phone cord. "Whatever this Pakistan is—"

"It's a Muslim country. Used to be in India."

"You think this is funny?"

"Gimme her address," Figur said. "I'll make sure she backs off."

"How?"

"Indeed. How."

"I don't like the sound of that."

"Mr. Mirsk, did she give you any proof that she—"

"She knew the dead woman. She also knows Oskar Ret."

"That's proof? It didn't occur to you that this whole thing's a crock? I thought you understood these people by now. They whip up a scheme, then play it till it hits. They know fat fish like you can't afford bad pub—doesn't matter if she's got anything on you or not. You're supposed to get antsy, offer her a few zlotys."

"That much," Mirsk said, "I figured out all by myself."

"Best way to cool her off, I'll go see her. I'll be persuasive, offer to separate her head from her neck."

"You've got to be kidding," Mirsk said.

"You want this done or not?"

"I don't want anyone getting hurt. I don't want her getting a single grosz, but I most certainly do not want anyone to get hurt."

"I know," Figur said, "you want her to stand down. Little talk with me, she'll lose her friskiness."

Mirsk sat back and gazed at all the bottles on his bar. Not even nine in the morning and he wanted a shot or two. He heard the chewing again.

"What are you eating?"

"Nachos," Figur said brightly.

"Na—what?"

"Mexican corn chips. They just got them in the Marriott. They're big in America. A little cheese, a little hot sauce, mmm mmm."

Mirsk leaned forward, brought a hand to his forehead. "It's not even lunchtime yet."

"That's what the waiter said. I slipped him a couple hundred thousand, got the chef to heat some up. Sounds like this woman cooked up quite a story for you."

"Listen," Mirsk said, checking the card Irena Platz had left him, "she's staying at the Neptun Hotel. Find out if there's anything to this smuggling thing. If one of my guys is involved in—"

"Yeah," Figur said, "I agree a hundred percent."

"And do this alone. Quietly."

Martin Figur paused. Mirsk imagined him probing his teeth with a toothpick, maybe washing down nachos with something Mexican and lime-twisted.

"No problem," Figur said at last, "I do my best work alone."

Chapter 4

Julian Krol left the komisariat and turned toward Krystyna's apartment. A Gypsy boy outside the komisariat held out a leather jacket. "No expensive," he said through gold-capped teeth. "Buy cheap, buy cheap, America make."

The coat was torn at the shoulder and doctored with shoe polish. The boy was gaunt and malnourished.

"How much?" Julian asked.

"One million."

"Half a million," Julian said.

"Seven fifty."

"Half a million."

The boy sucked his teeth and said, "Okay, half a million."

He stepped in close and Julian gave him the money and took the coat—and then looked it over for a second and handed it back.

"You'll sell it faster," Julian said, "if you start at half a million."

He resumed walking, the boy saying, "But you—" and then clamming up and pocketing the money.

Impulsive charity had never been Julian's style. That was precisely why he had to engage in it right now.

The air was heavy and dead, a precursor of a summer storm. Army privates paraded down the road. Their eighteen-month enlistments were over, so it was blow-out time. Draped in "graduation blankets" and swigging vodka, they belted out obscene ditties as they swaggered, arm in arm, between parked cars. The current song: "She's a Whore But I Love Her." Other people on the street gave them a wide berth.

Krystyna had once tossed water balloons at such creatures. It was on the "Wet Monday" following Easter Sunday. Krystyna, nine or ten years old, giggled as she let them fly from the safety of her third-floor balcony. The soldiers cursed her for not filling the balloons with vodka.

Not long after that, he rushed her to the hospital. Back then, such trips occurred almost monthly. When an allergy kicked in, she slumped to her knees and gulped for breath as if drowning. If she was really trying to kill herself, she wouldn't have used hashish. The drug would have laid her out before the meth could be added.

Apart from everything else, she wasn't stupid.

What she *was*—now there was a question. What motivations had Julian missed? What hidden hopes and fears and dreams had kept her up at night? Who, in fact, was she?

What a question to be asking about a dead sister.

Her plan to leave school had come out of nowhere. She was tossing away a lifelong investment. So said Julian Svengali Krol. He'd had hopes for her, had pushed her to apply her ample academic talents. The union thing was a bust, but there were so many other things she could do. He knew she felt pressured by him, and by everyone else who ever watched her breeze through her studies, but he was her father as much as her brother. She had to grow into the things that were best for her. That was the truth, because he was the Big Bro, the anointed shepherd, divine elector.

It had seemed easy and straightforward back then, the nurturing of the potential of youth. Life was black and white; rewards were calculable.

So he'd misread her? Yes. Pushed her too hard? Likely. Was

now—today—a matter of simple human history? The story of a man gaining understanding only after he'd finished doing all of his damage?

The last time he'd seen her alive—funny how time, only three years, could wipe away some memories and yet leave others as crisp and clear as photographs. She was back home from Jagiellonian for the weekend. And she told him, point blank, that she was leaving school. They were sitting down to a dinner of potato dumplings and wild mushrooms when she explained a need to change direction, to "sort some things out," period. No more school, no more following her big brother's lead. She asked for money, needed help setting herself up in Cracow. Her voice faltered, got stuck on the request. She'd already taken a job waitressing, but her salary wouldn't see her through. She would have trouble keeping an apartment for long, assuming she could find one once they kicked her out of the dorms.

The gaps in her logic were astronomical. She wasn't leaving open the option of returning to school later. She was holding something back, wasn't sharing the real reason for this life-altering change.

And when he prodded, she drew further away from him, refused to let him in.

After all he'd done for her.

Finally, he said, "You expect to be happy waiting tables?"

"I expect to be happy somehow, somewhere."

"You could work as an interpreter," Julian said. "Right now, today, without more school, you could be earning double my salary."

"And if interpreting doesn't appeal to me?"

"It has to appeal to you, Krystyna. What have we been doing all these years? Why'd you go through the motions of school if it was so hard to stomach?"

She pushed away her plate. "It wasn't hard. It was so easy it was boring. I thought it could be for me, I thought I could *force* it to be for me, but I couldn't."

"Krystyna. Something bad has happened to you. Or *is* happening to you. Why won't you tell me what it is?"

"What you don't get," she said, "is that I don't have to tell you anything, not anymore. I'm not a child. I'm not your pet project. You've always made demands and I've always fulfilled them. Is it so unreasonable to now make a few decisions for myself?"

"If they're the wrong decisions," he said, "yes."

"Which means you won't even lend me a little rent money?"

The request was easy to weigh. "I won't help you, Krystyna. You want to ruin your life, you'll have to do it alone."

It was a bluff. She would cave in. She had to, faced with a foe of such potent wisdom. But she rose from the table, left the apartment a few minutes later, and basically evaporated. He soon discovered that she'd already packed the few clothes that remained in her bedroom.

Still:

She was his little sister. She'd had precious little experience with the world. She would come back, right? That was how these things turned out.

It took him three days to nudge himself toward reality. By then it was too late; he'd let too much time slip by before stumbling toward the obvious: he *had* been mapping out her triumphs. If she wanted to quit school, who was he to feel wounded? She wasn't a child, he wasn't her supreme fix-all. He wasn't even his own fix-all. His ballyhooed struggle against the Commies—that, too, did not qualify as earth-shattering success; it seemed to succeed only in getting him and most of his co-conspirators-slash-friends thrown in prison for varying lengths of time.

Worse than any of this, he wasn't even central to Krystyna's life. He was central insofar as a lion tamer was central to a broken beast who'd been born into captivity.

So he prepared an apology, phoned her dormitory, but they said she'd moved out. Friends and professors were shocked by her disappearance. A waiter at Holst's Restaurant said she'd stopped showing up for work. No one anywhere had any leads to her whereabouts. A surprisingly small number of people seemed to care.

And in the absence of an obvious next step, Julian then took no steps at all—just waited for her to call or to come home. The normal rhythms of life began to reassert themselves. The knowledge that she was smart enough to take care of herself was a bit of a salve. Krystyna was resilient. She would be okay, eventually. Maybe she'd even thrive.

Before he knew it, three years had passed.

The sound of silence brought him back to the present. The army privates were gone. Julian entered the apartment block on Wilcza Street and ascended the stairs to the fourth floor. The two hallways on each side of the staircase were locked behind glass doors fortified by iron bars. He chose the left hall and rang the buzzer to an apartment. A man answered and Julian told him he lived in four twenty-one and had lost his hallway key. A buzzer sounded and he pushed open the door.

Krystyna's apartment was at the end of the hall, with a yellow notice on the door: "Entrance forbidden by order of the Centrum Borough Komisariat." He turned the door handle, but found it locked. Every apartment in Warsaw had at least two dead bolts and a handle lock. Julian turned to the neighbor's door, knocked, waited, then knocked again. The door finally opened a small crack. A smell of sour cabbage streamed into the hallway. He saw no face in the crack, but heard an old lady's grimy voice:

"Who let you in? I don't know you."

"Good day, ma'am. Can you tell me which apartment is the superintendent's?"

"One eleven," she said. "Go away."

She slammed the door and slapped the dead bolts into place.

He walked down to the first floor and knocked on the superintendent's door. It was beside a garbage chute, with a smell of coffee grounds and moldering fat in the air. A stubble-faced man in an undershirt answered the door. The guy was maybe sixty, but was hunched over and sickly pale, which added a dozen years to his face. His eyes were glazed from drinking and he held himself steady with a hand to the wall.

"What do you want?" he asked.

"I want to see apartment four eleven."

"Four eleven's empty."

"I know," Julian said.

"To rent it, check with the building cooperative. I can't do anything."

"I want to go inside, look around."

"Yeah?" the superintendent said. "No one's allowed."

"I won't tell if you don't."

The superintendent swayed in the doorway and belched into his fist. "It's police orders," he said. "I don't make the rules." He started to close the door.

"Tell you what," Julian said. "Five hundred thousand zlotys."

"Yeah? Normally, I'd mug my own granny for that much. But I've been strictly ordered. A whore killed herself up there and the police are still checking the place. Can't go."

The man pushed the door almost closed. Julian lunged forward and slammed it open, knocking a coat rack to the floor. The superintendent stepped back and peered at him with a raised eyebrow. This stranger breaking into his apartment confused him more than frightened him.

"Make it a million," Julian said, and he reached into his

pocket and pulled out the maroon banknote.

The old man stared at him, at the money. He snapped the bill from Julian's hand, reached behind him, and pulled a key ring from a nail in the wall.

He led Julian up to the fourth floor. The elevator, a two-person contraption installed during post-war reconstruction, was out of order. When they reached the apartment, the old man said, "Don't touch anything. The cops find out about this, they'll fine me or something." He fumbled through keys and opened the various locks.

Dead air greeted them. The superintendent crossed the floor and opened the window.

"This was our first dead whore in a long time," he said, lighting a cigarette. "We had one during the Gierek years, but she hanged herself. They didn't do too many drugs back then. Too hard to get, I guess."

The apartment was small. A living room with an alcove bed, a kitchen, and a bathroom. At most, three hundred square feet. The superintendent stood at the window and blew smoke outside while Julian opened cupboards in the kitchen. He saw salt and sugar, bags of buckwheat, a well-stocked kitchen. The refrigerator had been unplugged and the door left open. It was clean, as was the stovetop and the sink. The dishes were stacked neatly on a rack above the counter. Julian opened the cupboard below the sink, saw a clean plastic bag in the garbage container. In this part of Warsaw, everyone had cockroaches. This apartment, he thought, had never seen one.

"Who cleaned up in here?"

"She did," the super said, "before she killed herself. The cops said they sometimes do that, clean up first."

The living room was clean. Empty vases sat on the window ledge. In the middle of the room, on a red-and-black carpet, strips of tape marked where Krystyna's twisted body had come to rest. She'd died with a knee drawn up to her waist. Whether she'd been on her back or face down, both hands had been at her stomach. The position suggested pain.

"Who found the body?" Julian asked.

"The police. A neighbor called them when she didn't turn off her music. The whore in Gierek's time also liked loud music."

The television held two photographs in cardboard frames. One was of a woman in a winter coat and hat. She was standing before a backdrop of snow-covered hills, waving at the camera with one hand and holding a snowball in the other. Her cheeks were red and she had a wide smile. Like Krystyna, she looked to be in her mid-twenties, attractive and vibrant.

The second photo was a portrait of Julian and Krystyna, taken when he was released from the Rakowiecka Street Prison back in eighty-five. During his sentence, she had lived with her uncle Jozef in Poznan. The government had ruled that Julian, a convicted criminal who had subjected her to subversive political philosophy, was unfit to continue as her legal guardian. Uncle Jozef knew better, though, and when Julian left the lockup and showed up at his door, Krystyna was packed and ready. The photograph showed a smiling Krystyna and a smiling Julian, who was pleased to be on the streets again, dying to reload against the regime. Way back then.

A dresser held a few other photographs, old pictures of their mother and father before a drunk driver took their lives in eighty-one. It also held a textbook in English: *The Fundamentals of the Urdu Language.* She'd been tumbling toward suicide, yet she was boning up on Urdu? Three years after dropping out of school? Under the book was a folded copy of *Gazeta Warszawy,* dated the day she died, July 14, 1992. Julian leafed through the paper. It had one of his stories in it, a piece on the "farming contingent" in Parliament. Forty-one farmers from the Polish Peasants' Party had been voted into Parliament during the last election. Not all of them were big on the protocol of officialdom, which made for lively conflicts and spicy quotes—manna for the editors of *Gazeta Warszawy.*

The superintendent dropped his cigarette butt out the window. "For a whore, what good's a newspaper? She reads the horoscope?" Julian put the paper back and strode into the bathroom. There were towels on the door and the bathtub was clean. The air was stale, but it held a hint of porcelain cleaner. He returned to the living room just as the superintendent was starting to talk, turning his eyes to the sky: "Hard to believe, in a Christian country like this, seems like whores are spreading like the plague."

"You must've known her well," Julian said.

"What do you mean?"

"To hold such a generous view of her. I mean, in a Christian country like this."

With his hand, the superintendent described a cross over his heart. "You're right," he said. "May the mother of Jesus have mercy on my soul."

"What about visitors?" Julian said. "You see any?"

The old guy shook his head. "The neighbors say her visitors were rich. Well dressed, carrying flowers. I guess she was mature for a whore. Had some miles on her. She appears to have been a *biznesman*'s girl."

"Did she pay for the place herself?"

"You'll have to ask the cooperative."

"How much was her rent?"

"The cooperative knows."

"She have any contact with the neighbors?"

"I'm the super. I live four floors down. How would I know?"

The old man closed the window and moved toward the door.

"These days it's better to keep your door closed, don't ask for too much. The people who want too much either become crooks or end up like that." He pointed to the outline of the body. "She probably wanted to get rich. Like everyone else. She probably knocked herself off when she found out it wouldn't happen. That's the way it is with the United Workers Party gone. Money rules, the poor guy gets fucked like a bitch mutt."

Julian asked himself what he was looking for. Some link to her last three years. Some shred of evidence suggesting foul play. If there *was* evidence, it wouldn't be beyond the cops to miss or ignore it. Cops like Lieutenant Daniel Kosinski couldn't find water in a washroom.

Julian turned his back on the old man. "Thanks for the help." When he neared the glass door at the end of the hallway, he heard the superintendent call out again: "Thanks for the money!"

Julian knew that the old man then brought the bill to his lips and kissed it, which was what you did when luck brought you something.

Chapter 5

Ale Kanada!

Irena Platz blinked into a compact mirror and studied her black eye.

Ahhh, Canada!

The country of dreams, the place of comfort. Jobs for everyone, spacious houses with lawns and garages, no more crime or cold apartments or need to paint yourself up and sleep with nauseating morons in order to put food on the table.

Few people invoked the *Ale Kanada!* phrase these days, but Irena had heard it in a movie recently and it had hit her like an epiphany. *Ale Kanada!* Simple. No clouding of the issue. No "but" tacked onto the saying as a discouraging qualifier.

Irena sat at the edge of her moth-eaten hotel bed and dabbed tan face powder around her eye. The bruise, from a Cracow cabbie who chose not to pay for sex, would deepen before disappearing. That was the last time, she told herself, squinting into the mirror. *I've seen my last date. If Mirsk pays, I'll get a visa and get myself across the Atlantic before they even know where to look for me.*

And if I ever hook again, I hope someone puts a bullet between my eyes.

The clock on the nightstand read 14:36. Antoni Mirsk still hadn't called. The bum named Mirek lay snoring on the bedspread, smelling awful. Lukasz, his partner, sat in the room's only chair, pinching a cigarette between yellow fingers and holding a near-empty bottle of cheap cherry spirits. His head lolled against the wall behind him, flirting with sleep.

Maybe Mirsk didn't buy it. Maybe he saw through the threat, tore up the card when she left. There had been something disturbingly smooth about Antoni Mirsk, a confidence that suggested he'd handled blackmail attempts in the past.

Maybe he knew she was basically winging it.

So despite *Kanada,* it was hard to keep from grabbing her purse and running out of the room and forgetting all of this.

She watched the clock and felt her anxiety feed off itself. She wouldn't be here right now; she wouldn't be about to make a hundred million zlotys if her ex-roommate hadn't told her about the smugglers. Krystyna had been cautious in discussing it, said only she was interpreting between Poles and Pakistanis, refused to expand on that. Too dangerous, she said. The only name she ever shared—"Oskar"—was dropped during an unguarded moment, when she learned that Oskar was in Cracow working for that guy from the papers, that Gdansk tycoon, Antoni Moneybags Mirsk. Protection.

And now Krystyna was dead—had killed herself with some back-alley crank.

Irena closed her eyes and recalled the last time she'd seen Krystyna alive. Krystyna was moving out, going back to Warsaw. She would take care of some things, get herself together, stop hooking. It was the kind of promise that a lot of the girls made to themselves, and Irena was pulling for Krystyna to make it happen. Krystyna had had some bad luck, was really too bright and fragile to be a hooker. She deserved a good turn for once.

Yet she ended up at the sad end of the live-until-you-die equation. The news of her death shocked Irena. Krystyna had been tangled in woe, but she never showed signs of wanting to off herself. When she left for Warsaw, she even seemed a little hopeful. But that was what life did to you. It turned your hopes upside down, your dreams inside out. It wrapped its bony fingers around your neck and let go only if you were smart enough to say, "Okay, okay, you're in charge, you bastard; now please just give me a little more *time!*"

The idea of throwing the smuggling story at Mirsk crystallized even before Krystyna moved out of the apartment. If a tycoon in Gdansk was tied to a smuggler, was there an angle to be worked? Would the guy pay to keep the connection quiet? Krystyna's death only strengthened the notion that Mirsk could be blackmailed. Krystyna now couldn't be hurt by any ploy that Irena concocted. And there was no point backing out just because Krystyna had died. Krystyna was a tragedy, but *biznes* was *biznes.* Or at least it was to those who had enough nerve to grab a seat at the table.

Irena fingered the makeup around her eye, decided it didn't look too thick. Turning her gaze upon Lukasz, she decided her hired man looked about as threatening as a tree stump.

"It was real brilliant," she said, "the way you went swimming in his booze."

"Sure," Lukasz said, "much nicer weaseling all that cash out of him. What's that smuggling stuff about, anyway?"

"It's none of your business, that's what it is."

Lukasz blew smoke from his nostrils. "I don't know about that. You said it'd be fast. One meeting, half an hour, and you're out of here and we're back in our courtyard getting wasted."

"You'll be back there soon enough."

"Better be."

The tone gave Irena pause. "What's that mean?"

"This is starting to sound dicey. Anyone in the world could bust through that door."

"You're getting paid, aren't you?"

"Not nearly enough."

The phone rang. The sleeping Mirek stirred and rolled onto his back.

On the second ring, he sat up and rubbed his spider-web eyes. Duty had called. Irena picked up the receiver and said hello.

"I'm calling on behalf of Mr. Mirsk," a lively voice said. "He's thought about your proposal. He'd like to settle."

Irena's pulse started to race. "It's non-negotiable. One hundred million or he's done. Where are you?"

"Right underneath you, in the lobby."

"Your name?"

"Martin Figur. Can I come up so we can go over this?"

"What's to go over?" Irena said. "He's paying or he isn't paying. Are you here to play games, Figur?"

"I'm here to—"

"Because if you are, if you're here to snow me, you might as well go home right now."

"I don't think that would suit Antoni," Figur said with a spryness that made her nervous. "I just need to talk a minute. And if the talking goes well, you'll get your money."

" 'If'?" she said. "There is no 'if' involved."

She waited for him to respond—and realized he was drawing this out for a reason, letting his non-answer worry her.

"You there?" she asked.

"I'm at the reception desk. People are all around me, hearing this. Can I come up, or do I tell Antoni it didn't work out?"

Irena turned and looked at Mirek. The big man yawned and settled back onto his stomach, nuzzling his head into the pillow. A fleck of a past meal clung to the only part of his mustache that was visible.

"I have protection," she said. "Come up alone. You try anything, you'll be sorry."

Slamming down the receiver, she said, "Get up, dummy, he's

coming up here."

She gave Mirek a backhanded clip over the ear. The big man grumbled and sat up again. Lukasz clomped to the door and looked out the peephole.

"Will he be alone?" he asked.

"Yes."

"Beat on him, or are we still acting cultured?"

"Just keep your eyes on him," Irena said. "I'll tell you what to do."

Mirek took a position in the bathroom, peeking out between the door and the wall. Lukasz stayed at the front door, looking out the peephole. The man named Figur approached carrying a black briefcase and wearing a pearl-gray Armani suit and loud silk tie. He was primping himself, flattening his slick black hair with his palm. The nascent middle class in motion.

Lukasz wrapped a hand around the doorknob and turned. Drawing the door open, he kept his body a full step back in case Mr. Nouveau Riche decided to lunge. Figur advanced, and Lukasz raised his hands. Figur was now holding a gun. He was also using the pinkie of his free hand to pick at something between his teeth.

Lukasz backed into the room. "Don't even know you, mister," he said. "I can forget this if you can."

"Leave," Figur replied. "Take the other guy, too."

Mirek bumbled out of the bathroom before Lukasz even lowered his hands. Irena Platz watched without moving. Only one contingency plan could be used at a moment like this. She stopped short of rolling it out just yet.

Lukasz paused at the doorway. "She owes us some money."

"Write it up as a bad debt," Figur said.

"What's that?"

"It's what all the new *biznesmen* say when they know they're not getting paid."

Lukasz shot Irena a hostile look. "Can I at least take my smokes?"

Figur reached down and tossed him the pack. "There are men outside. They'll watch to make sure you leave this hotel fast and don't come back."

Irena watched Lukasz disappear, then trained her eyes on Figur. The guy had a folding cell phone hanging from his coat's breast pocket. His eyes were alert but his body was loose, composed. He was comfortable with that gun; he'd pulled it on people before.

Stick to the demands. If you handled Mirsk, you can handle this guy.

Figur left the briefcase near the door and sank into the chair vacated by the bum Lukasz. He looked slowly around the room, made a point of taking his time, of not looking too terribly impressed.

Finally: "You worried Antoni. Confused him. What part of Silesia you from?"

"How'd you know I'm from there?"

"You sound like you walked off the goat farm. What line of work you in?"

"President of the Republic of Poland."

"Aha," Figur said, "then our new American dream is alive and well." Now he left the gun on his lap, unheld. He stretched his arms and cracked his knuckles.

"Puh-lease," Irena said.

"Do you have any idea what you're doing?"

"A better idea than you can imagine."

"You go after a man like Mirsk, you should plan things. Blundering into his building with two goons, that's just. . . ."

"That's just what?" she asked.

"Were they even deloused?"

Irena looked at the closed door as if Lukasz and Mirek were

still standing there in all their drunken impotence. "Okay, I'll admit it; I've done smarter things."

"I'm interested in this smuggling thing," Figur said.

"I would imagine you are."

"I mean, among other things, what exactly is Oskar Ret running from Pakistan? Or to it?"

"Ask him, he's the one moving it."

Figur took out a comb, began to touch up his already-pristine hair. "Miss Platz, I do plan to ask him. But I need your take on the subject." He pocketed his gun and crossed to the mirror. "You're asking for a lot of money, yet you're not providing one shred of proof? That strikes you as fair?"

"If fair mattered," Irena said, "I wouldn't have gone to Mirsk in the first place."

Figur leaned forward—like he might kiss his reflection in the mirror. Then, abruptly, he snapped the comb into a vest pocket and plucked the gun back out. And pointed it right at her.

"Let's make it simple. You like to talk—*clearly,* you like to talk—so that's what we're going to do right now, have a conversation."

Irena wanted to say *Is that so?* but her throat constricted.

"What's he smuggling?" Figur asked.

The gun barrel looked a meter wide. "You'll be disappointed."

"I don't discourage easily."

"I don't know any more than what I told Mirsk."

"I find that hard to believe."

"My roommate knew some languages. She interpreted for Oskar and his people."

"His people who?"

"You don't run stuff across borders alone," Irena said. "She spoke Urdu. She helped them communicate, that's all. I don't know what Oskar's moving. I just know that when he's not smuggling he's also getting good cash from Mirsk."

"And you figured that out how?"

"Krystyna."

"And what about this drug thing? You told Mirsk that Oskar's drugs killed her."

Irena's fear began to ebb. "I did, didn't I?"

"And?"

"The newspapers would love to hear that. You'd look at Mirsk on the front page and you'd see horns sprouting from his forehead."

Figur mulled it over. "I know all that. I read the papers—even the Warsaw papers. For instance, stories about a woman identified as Krystyna K.?"

Irena looked away. Mirsk was really looking into this.

"Krol, yes? Krystyna Krol? Apparently, she was a fair maiden of the evening?" He paused a moment. "And one look at you and I figure, 'this Irena's also a naughty girl.' You two worked together, didn't you?"

Irena said, "Is that really important?"

"Secondary at best." Figur moved to the phone. Picking up the receiver, he said, "You really should have planned this, Miss Platz. You're out of your league."

She watched him dial, then listened to him talk.

"It's me," he said. "I'm guessing the smuggling is for real, but all she has is hearsay . . . Yeah, from the dead girl."

So he was talking to Mirsk.

"I don't know," Figur continued. "I think so, but I can't be sure." His eyes widened while the man at the other end spoke. "But that's a full day's drive!"

Irena heard a sharp command from the other man, but couldn't make out the words.

"Fine," Figur snapped, "forget I mentioned it."

He slapped the phone down and sulked for a millisecond

before snapping out of it.

"We're going on a trip," he said. "We'll sort this out. If you have packing to do, do it now."

Heat flushed through Irena's body. She had ceded control to Martin Figur. The only thing left now was her feeble contingency plan. "I've left instructions," she said. "If I'm not at a certain place at a certain time, my story will be sent to the police and the newspapers."

Figur filed the gun in his vest pocket and smoothed out his tie, pausing over the soft, silky material.

"Of course it will. Police and newspapers. I'll take that chance."

Chapter 6

The funeral was in a wooden shack in Ursynow, a suburb on the southern outskirts of Warsaw. The real church, next door, was under reconstruction. It had been built in 1790, when the district was countryside and the parishioners were peasants. It survived the Nazi blitzkriegs, served as a tire maker's warehouse during Communism, and was now into its third year of renovations. The construction workers were from a state cooperative that had ancient equipment, huge debts, and a high rate of alcoholism. But also safe jobs. The cooperative would continue to lose money until the government decided the beleaguered job market could absorb more unemployed without a backlash come election time.

Julian sat through the ceremony as if watching a ho-hum movie trailer before the feature presentation. That was another thing—religion—that had come and gone without so much as a tussle. He decided he was probably the first Pole in history to leave the Church without agonizing over it.

While the priest spoke, he recalled snippets of the past, episodes that had meant nothing at the time: a cross-town trip to her dentist when she was nine; Krystyna begging for a cigarette when she was eleven or twelve. Just snatches of her. The rare times she confided in him, sought his guidance, defended him when people called him an anarchy-peddling agitator. Maybe he'd have retained her trust if he hadn't worked so hard—too hard—for her success in school. Less ambition and more affection might have helped. There'd never been a shortage of affection. The shortage had been in its mode of expression.

Hindsight, he decided. Things are less daunting once you're able to look back on them.

The reception was in his two-bedroom apartment, which had gone up along with 20,000 other concrete pillboxes in Ursynow during the housing crisis of the seventies. Once most of the guests had arrived and offered condolences, he retreated into her bedroom. Dark red curtains covered the window, bookcases lined the wall. He briefly considered boxing up her old textbooks. Maybe the university library could use them. Leaving the light off, he took up the phone and called the hospital.

"Banacha Hospital morgue," a woman answered.

"I want to request an autopsy report. The deceased's name is Krystyna Krol. I'm her brother."

"Okay, sir. You'll need to come down in person, fill out some forms. You'll need agreement from the medical examiner, as well as from the morgue administrator."

"Any reason they'd refuse?"

"Just formalities, Mr. Krol. Was the autopsy performed before today?"

"Yes. How soon can I expect it?"

"If the medical examiner is on duty, we can have him sign it today and you can pick it up tomorrow. I can check to see if he's scheduled to come in."

"I'd appreciate that," Julian said. "The name again was Krol. Krystyna."

"One moment."

Sounds from outside the bedroom filtered in. There were maybe twenty people out there. There had been twice that many at the church. Few of them were relatives. Many were his parents' friends, most of whom he'd seen only rarely since

Helena and Marek Krol's deaths eleven years ago.

The woman's voice returned. "Mr. Krol, I'm afraid the examiner isn't scheduled to work today or tomorrow."

"When is he scheduled?"

"He's on holiday."

"That's not what I asked."

"Next week," the woman said coldly. "It's been suggested to me that you call back in a week."

"Any chance the boss might waive the need for the ME's signature?"

"He's the one who said next week. I'm afraid you'll have to wait, Mr. Krol. There's nothing I can do."

No, there was one thing. "Can you put me through to the administrator?"

"I'm not to put any calls through. He's busy."

"Then how about—"

"I'm sorry. Next week."

The line went dead, and the sudden silence in the bedroom was a hammer ready to fall. He dragged himself out to the living room, where the mourners conversed in hushed tones. The swarm of darkly clothed semi-strangers seemed a little perfunctory. Julian walked through the crowd, shook hands, spoke when he had to. They all said the same thing: it was such a shock; she'd had such a love of life, so much promise; maybe she was at peace now.

But they didn't know her, not really. He smiled, asked polite questions, thanked them for coming. He also chain-smoked and told himself to stop acting as if this was about him.

Alone by the balcony door was a familiar face, a girl from Krystyna's high-school days. He picked up two glasses and a bottle of vodka and made his way over to her.

The girl saw him coming and smiled brightly.

"Lydia, right? Little Lydia Debkowska."

"Not so little," she said, taking a glass from him. "How's the newspaper world, Julian?"

"Wish I knew. I've been pretty much ignoring it."

"Then why bother with it?"

"I've been pretty much ignoring that, too." He poured into the glasses. "You're older. I thought I'd see more of her friends at the church."

"Not too many people know about it," Lydia said. "It's been a long time. My mom read about it in the obits."

"She didn't keep in touch?"

Lydia shook her head. "Nobody does. People are focused on themselves now, trying to get by. Not many people have time for old friends."

"When was the last time you saw her?"

Lydia looked up at the ceiling, thought about it. "Maybe three, four years ago, when she was at Jagiellonian. Before she dropped out."

"You knew about that?"

"I heard it from Artur."

"Who's that?"

"Salda. A guy she went with back then."

"Artur Salda? How come I never heard that name?"

Lydia shrugged. "Last I talked to him, it must have been a year, a year and a half ago. He moved to the States about the time she dropped out. Won a scholarship. University of Illinois. He's still there."

"You know anyone else who was in touch with her?"

She swirled her drink in her glass. "You sound like a *milicja* heavy."

He looked around the room. "I'm curious about something. You come here alone?"

"I know you and your uncle Jozef, that's it." She clearly wasn't pained by the fact. She leaned in close, cast a confidential look. "What was she doing, Julian? No one seems to know much about her."

"We had a falling-out. She moved away. It's a long story."

"You just stopped seeing her?"

"More like the other way around."

Lydia stared. "I'm so sorry."

"Me too. You know where I can reach him?"

"Artur?"

"Yes."

"God, no. Artur and I were never pals. He was the showy type, an attention-getter. Last time he called me, it was from Chicago. To hit on me. From another continent."

Lydia looked around the room, into the faces of people she didn't know. Julian steered the talk toward Lydia and what she was doing these days. Eventually, she excused herself and the crowd of mourners thinned and Julian was left alone with his uncle Jozef. They reminisced about the bad old days, when Julian was in prison and Krystyna was in Poznan. They drank half a bottle of Wyborowa, got a little maudlin about a few of the right things and a lot of the wrong things. Then Julian walked Jozef downstairs to a taxi.

On the way back into the apartment block, he glanced at the mailboxes, unlocked his own slot, and pulled out a phone bill and a letter. The letter was on an envelope with a return address that was stamped "Lubon A-M," which meant nothing to him. But the address was in familiar handwriting.

Krystyna's handwriting.

The postmark was dated July 11, from Warsaw, two days before she died.

He tore open the flap:

Dear Julian,

I've started a lot of letters, but none of them ever came out right. It's been so long since we spoke. I don't know you anymore, yet I still think about you all the time. Lately I've been going over what you said to me the last time we talked, about how disappointed you were. You made me feel like a failure, like there was nothing I could ever do or achieve without your help or guidance. So I guess this letter is my way of proving you wrong. Here I am, alive and writing you, alive and finally saying what I've long wanted to say.

I'll say it quickly, in case I lose you somewhere along the way:

Goodbye.

Julian glimpsed the rest of the writing. It looked sharp-edged and daunting, a cursive journey to a place of anger and recrimination.

I'm going away, brother. I'm moving to Pakistan and never coming back. I need to leave Poland, to forget everything. I've done terrible things, things I can't get over without a fresh start. I need to live in a different place, where I can be completely and beautifully hidden, where there's a veil for my face and a veil for my past. I'll be a new person. A nonperson. I tell you this in case you decide to try to find me. Don't bother looking, because I'll lose myself completely. The old Krystyna will be gone.

You'll be pleased to know this is happening because I didn't give up translating, not altogether. I've been interpreting for an importer in Cracow. (My Pashto and Urdu function well even though so much else has been lost.) He'll help me move there, to Pakistan. He's done the paperwork. And Julian, how you would disapprove of him! He's not a good man—not in the usual sense of the word. But he helps me escape myself, and for that I love him dearly. He's a man of few demands, unlike you. Once he winds up some business in Mieltor, my papers will arrive. I'll be gone within a week.

Julian leaned against the mailboxes. "Suicide," Lieutenant

Kosinski had said. "Killed herself."

Consider yourself lucky, my brother. You've received this goodbye gesture. My roomies, Teresa and Irena, I'm paying them no such respect. I'm walking out on them, because stopping to say goodbye would be too cruel. Because unlike me, they have no escape. They'll be trapped in their lives forever. Possibly, that's because they had no big brother to feed them fall-back plans.

So maybe this letter is more of a thank you than a goodbye. I know how my tone must sound, but the truth is, I don't bear you ill will. I want you to be happy—happier, even, than I want myself to be.

Because despite everything, you deserve it. We both do. We both tried. That should count for something, shouldn't it?

Krystyna

Julian forced the letter back into the envelope. The last few days had brought numbness, an inability to negotiate emotion. Now there was a kind of white-hot blindness, a defiant taking of inventory.

Going to Pakistan.

Wanting to be happy.

Wanting to live.

Cramming the re-enveloped letter into his mourner's suit pocket, he climbed the stairs to his apartment. He was in the living room, collecting plates and glasses, when the world cracked down its axis and everything blew apart. A kind of blackness descended, a force he'd never encountered—and when the here and now finally returned, he found himself standing in his living room and massaging his left hand. He had shattered two panes of balcony-door glass with what must have been a childishly cathartic punch. He didn't recall doing it, and his hand hurt like hell.

★ ★ ★ ★ ★

The next afternoon he took a streetcar to the Banacha Hospital. Again the hospital was crowded. Gurneys and beds lined the halls. The heat wave was killing the old and tormenting the fragile. It was lunchtime. Kitchen staff wheeled carts of *befsztyk* and boiled potatoes from room to room. Julian found the stairs to the morgue and located administration. The door was locked, controlled by a buzzer and a hydraulic door check. He rang the buzzer, heard a click, and let himself in. A receptionist sat behind a high counter, jabbering on the phone, jotting something on a pad. She had a gaunt face and a neck streaked by knotted veins.

A small tray of pencils and erasers sat next to her typewriter. He glanced at her writing:

2 Cracow sausage
2 ham/cheese
3 Cola Light
1 orange juice.

Finally, she slapped down the receiver and asked him what he wanted.

"I'm Julian Krol. We spoke on the phone yesterday."

"Yes," she said, "I remember."

"The Krystyna Krol autopsy report. I was hoping—"

"I told you, regulations don't permit me—"

"But surely the regulation's minor. I'm her brother. The family has a right to the report."

"Yes, but not until the ME has signed off. I can't ignore the rules. You'll have to wait."

Julian looked around the empty office. "Is the morgue director in?"

She gave him a hostile look. "Mr. Krol, the director was clear yesterday. Without the ME's signature, he, too, would be breaking a rule. These rules are designed for your own benefit, so only the police and the deceased's relatives can access—"

"I am her relative—her only relative. That's the point."

"If you want to see Mr. Durski, I can make an appointment. Though with the heat wave, with all the related deaths, he's a very busy man."

Good old state bureaucracy. The good-old bad-old years were still around. All decisions, big and small, were made by the man at the top, as the man at the top was the only person who was trusted to think properly.

"When can I see him?" Julian asked.

She consulted a notebook. "Day after tomorrow, one o'clock. Unless something comes up."

"Can you give me his phone number?"

"All calls go through me."

"How'd I know you would say that?" Julian scanned the room for a connecting door to the director's office. There wasn't one. "Thank you."

She lowered her head and tapped away at her typewriter. She didn't see him scoop an eraser and paperclip from the tray.

In the hallway, he started checking doorplates for the name "Durski." The search took him around a corner to a door where his knock went unanswered. He pulled out the paper clip and the eraser, bent the clip straight, pushed one end through the eraser. Then he stalked back to the administration room, balanced the eraser at the joint of the door check's two metal arms. Wrapping the rest of the paper clip around the outside arm, he made sure the contraption stayed where it was, with the eraser pushing downward.

He found a bench around the corner and waited. And waited. Finally, the receptionist lumbered out, a warthog trundling to the watering hole. When she started up the stairs, he walked back and checked the door. The eraser had fallen where the bars came to a V, jamming the check and keeping the door from locking.

He tapped down the eraser and stepped inside. Would anyone really care if a man wanted to see his own sister's autopsy file?

A line of filing cabinets stood behind the receptionist's desk. He found the case files on the top row, cataloged according to date. The Krystyna Krol folder was buried behind four other files from 14 July 1992. He splayed it atop the desk and sifted through the documents.

There was a page with Krystyna's fingerprints and a sheet titled Toxicology Findings. There were a dozen photos—photos he couldn't bring himself to look at—and a copy of the death certificate. But there was no autopsy report. Maybe they were cataloged elsewhere. To check, he pulled two other files at random, saw that both contained reports. He went back to Krystyna's folder.

The photographs showed her much as he'd envisioned her back in the apartment on Wilcza Street: stomach down, hands beneath her body. Her face, turned to the left, was covered by a thick spread of flaxen hair. Only her chin and her bloodless, partially open lips peeked out below the hair. It was as if she'd died while trying to utter a last wish or a confession. It wasn't her, yet it was. He gingerly moved the photos aside and started on the toxicology report, which contained chemical jargon he couldn't decipher. He gave up after the third bullet point and turned to the death certificate.

The copy looked the same as the original certificate, which he'd picked up the day he identified her. It had the same information on the decedent, the same informant, the same certifier. It also had the same time of death and the same "PERSON WHO COMPLETED CAUSE OF DEATH"—an ME named Wiktor Debina.

Further down, under Number 27: IMMEDIATE CAUSE (final disease or condition resulting in death):

"Oral consumption of amphetamine (possibly involuntary)."

The last two words leaped off the page. They hadn't been in the family's certificate.

He fought back questions and scanned the rest of it quickly, all the while hearing footsteps that he knew weren't really there.

Number 28: *Other significant conditions* contributing to death but not resulting in the underlying cause given in Number 27: "Oral consumption of hashish (possibly involuntary)."

His body flushed hot. The suggestion of murder was staggering. He reread the words, again tamped down all questions that might sidetrack him.

Number 29a: WAS AN AUTOPSY PERFORMED? Yes.

Number 29b: WERE AUTOPSY FINDINGS AVAILABLE PRIOR TO COMPLETION OF CAUSE OF DEATH? No.

The family's certificate had said yes. Why would the same ME write two different death certificates?

Number 30: MANNER OF DEATH (underline appropriate cause):

Natural	Pending Investigation
Accident	Could Not be Determined
Suicide	
Homicide	

A brief note followed: "Probable homicide."

It took a moment to regain his balance. Homicide. The calculated taking of her life. This was Krystyna dying again—a second time, more cutting than the first, if that was possible. He picked up the phone, asked Information for the number to the Centrum Borough Komisariat. If the first death certificate was bogus, then the cop's copy of the autopsy report might also be bogus. The ME, this Debina—Lieutenant Kosinski would have to find out what he was up to.

A desk sergeant at the komisariat said Lieutenant Daniel Kosinski would be out of the office until the following evening.

"Then tell him I'll call him tomorrow," Julian said. "Tell him it's regarding the Krystyna Krol murder."

"I filed that case three days ago," the sergeant said. "It was a suicide."

"Was," Julian said. "It isn't anymore. Tell him I have something important."

He hung up hoping the call was not a waste of time. More than half of all murders in Poland went unsolved, and invariably they involved victims who were either poor or from the so-called fringes of society, people who nobody important would miss.

People like Krystyna Krol.

Would the police do any better for Krystyna than they'd done for so many other poor souls?

Could Julian force them to do better?

He pocketed the certificate, refiled the folders, and fled the empty room. As he started up the stairs, the receptionist stalked back down toward him holding her sandwiches and sodas.

She gave him a look but didn't say anything.

Chapter 7

Irena Platz took Martin Figur for a BMW kind of guy and she wasn't far off the mark. Antoni Mirsk's head of security led her down the hotel stairs and out to a maroon Mercedes 190E at the curb. She noticed through the window that he had a second cell phone on the dashboard. Two cell phones equaled twice the status. Maybe he had a third one tucked under the band of his underwear.

He told her to hold out a hand, then produced a set of handcuffs and fastened her left wrist to the drink holder on the console. As he stepped around to the driver's side, he adjusted his tie, primped himself, glimpsed his partial profile in the mirror. She had to admit it, he looked good, in a hard-to-describe way.

Driving, he didn't want to talk. While he watched the road, she tugged at the cuff.

"Break the console," he said, eyes still on traffic, "you'll have to take the whole dash with it."

She sat back and fretted while skimming the sights—the leviathan arms of the Gdansk Shipyard cranes, towering and scratching out metallic yawns when they moved; Germanic architecture, with pointed roofs and ornate cupolas; a Bolivian street band strumming guitars and hawking cassettes outside a trailer selling *hotdogi* and *hamburgery.* It was a long way from the coal-dust hills of Silesia to this place in time. It was also a long way from dreaming about *Kanada* to being abducted by a man who'd been sent by Antoni Mirsk to possibly do her harm. *Kanada* now felt farther away than ever.

The Mercedes left the sloping Gdansk outskirts and joined a new expressway cutting through the forest.

"Where we going?" she asked.

He squinted into the sunlight, stayed within the speed limit. "Cracow."

"Cracow?"

"Yeah."

"Why?"

"It's a good six hundred kilometers. I trust you went potty."

"Why?" she repeated.

"Why do you think?" he said. "That's where Oskar is."

"I've never met him. Why would I have to—"

"Because I say so."

"No, because *Mirsk* says so, right? On the phone? I swear, if anything happens to me—"

"I know, I know," Figur said, "all your info gets sent to the cops and the papers. The universe as we know it implodes into microscopic particles."

His confidence was unnerving. She had stared down much trouble in her life, had lived through drug-crazed dates and corrupt, sadistic cops. She had smooth-talked a knife-wielding hooker who was hell-bent on killing her, had extricated herself from countless other scrapes. But Martin Figur operated on an entirely different plane. He wouldn't be duped or stared down and he wouldn't give an inch unless he had a sound reason for giving it.

Eyes on the road, Figur said, "If Oskar's not the little rascal you say he is, you might as well tell me that right now."

"I didn't lie about him."

"Then I guess we're just going for some confirmation."

He held out a pack of Marlboros. She shook her head, then

spied the console again. There would be wood or plastic under the leather. Maybe if she pulled hard enough, she could break free.

Then what? Jump from the speeding car? Or take the other route: sit tight, play it cool, wait for a gas station. They were driving the entire north–south length of Poland, from the Baltic flats to the foothills of the Tatra Mountains. He would have to stop for gas. She could make a scene at the station, get people thinking this lunatic had kidnapped her, which of course was not entirely false.

Maybe, when they stopped, she could put on a victim act, scream to anyone within earshot that he was a raving sexual predator; he was about to defile her and expire her and dump her lifeless remains in the forest.

No. Danger did not mobilize people; it scared them away. And creating a scene wouldn't make Figur eager to treat her with tenderness and love when they were back on the road again.

She glimpsed the rearview mirror. The driver of the Fiat Brava behind them was singing along to his car radio.

Figur reached down and tugged at his crotch. "Key briefs," he muttered. "Three hundred thousand zlotys and they feel like burlap."

She tried not to watch him while he scratched. She thought about Krystyna, tried to tell herself that no matter how bad things were getting, she at least was not where Krystyna was.

And she recalled something—something that hadn't seemed important at the time. A month before moving out, Krystyna phoned home from the Terespol border crossing, said she wouldn't be home for a few days, was a paid plaything for a client who was escorting foreign businessmen into Poland from Belarus. Irena thought nothing of it. The date no doubt dumped Krystyna in a hotel room, went and handled his business at the border, and returned to her in the evening.

But it was the first time Krystyna ever used the word "client" instead of "date" to describe a guy. And Terespol, now that Irena thought of it, was brimming with hookers. They were strung out along the highway like neon signposts, plying their trade for the Russian and Belarussian lorry drivers who poured across the border twenty-four hours a day. It seemed strange that a date would incur the expense of bringing Krystyna along when there was such a smorgasbord of possibilities on-site.

So Krystyna's "client" was her smuggler? And she was there because he needed her there? To translate or interpret?

Figur turned up the air-conditioning and ignored her. By the time they bypassed Warsaw, the fuel gauge was close to empty. She dozed off for a while, surprised that fear did not keep her awake. By the time they reached Kalisz, three hundred kilometers south of Gdansk but still more than two hundred kilometers from Cracow, the fuel light started to blink.

Figur pulled onto the roadside, popped the trunk, and brought out a canister. So much for a gas station. So much for the chance to escape. He filled the tank, then hiked off to the bushes to urinate, keeping his back to her.

She yanked at the handcuff but the console wouldn't budge. She opened the glove compartment, saw an operator's manual for a Mercedes 190E, a cluster of napkins, a map, a cigarette lighter. She felt inside the door panel, searched for lord knew what. Then she tugged at the cuff again, which only hurt her wrist. Finally, Figur returned. She told him that she, too, had to relieve herself.

"You can wait," he said.

"Until what?"

"Cracow."

"That's what, three hours? You want me to do it in your nice new car?"

Figur hesitated, glanced up and down the road.

"It's not a threat," she said, "it's a prediction."

So he opened her door, pulled the handcuff key from a coat pocket, and released the cuff from the dashboard. When she was out of the car, stretching her legs, he closed the cuff around his right wrist and slid the key back into his pocket.

"You're kidding," she said. "You're not coming with me."

He started walking, pulled her along. "We don't have all day."

"I won't do it like this."

"Did I offer you a choice?"

"Where would I run? We're in the middle of nowhere. You don't think you'd be able to catch me?"

"You're a hooker. You do all sorts of things for men. What's so off-putting about making a little *siusiu?*"

She stopped near some bushes and he stopped with her. He looked away from her, did her the courtesy. Considerate. Real gentleman. She hiked up her dress and went.

Standing up again, she said, "You enjoyed that, didn't you? Felt a little tingle down there."

He led her back to the car without answering. For a split second, when he unfastened the cuff and had yet to reclose it around the console, a move was possible. Hit him. Drive the cuff through his lip, bust his goddamn glaringly white teeth, run for it.

But she waited too long, wrestled her adrenaline, gave him time to reseat her.

When they were back up to speed, he fed a cassette into the car stereo. The band was *Big Tits,* players of protest music for the post-Commie times. They belted out their signature song, "Pornola," and Figur sang along under his breath and soon the day digressed into evening and Irena realized she was starving. The car clock read "21:34" when Figur turned the Mercedes onto a dirt road west of Cracow. He pulled up in front of a white Skoda Favorit, its high beams sharp in the darkness.

A man climbed out of the Skoda and walked into the glare of the lights, bisecting the beams with his massive frame. He had ginger skin and curly black hair, looked Armenian, maybe Georgian, though there was something Polish about his high cheekbones and generous nose.

"Well, I'll be," Figur said, "the guy's a *mieszaniec.*"

"Go ahead," Irena said, "call him a half-breed to his face."

Reaching over, Figur unlocked the cuff from the console and left it dangling from her wrist.

"Let's do this."

She pawed open the door and stepped onto the dirt road. The night wind was brisk. Her legs had stiffened. In the distance, two peasants were stringing swaths of hay together by hand. For light, they had a flickering kerosene lantern and a waning gibbous moon made misty by the summer-evening haze. The ginger-skinned man looked even larger walking toward her. His face showed quiet concern.

"Martin Figur?" he asked.

"That's right." Figur grabbed Irena by the arm. "You know her?"

Oskar Ret looked her over and shook his head. He looked confused.

"She says you run a smuggling business," Figur said. "The man who pays you is concerned about that."

The big man's eyes gave Irena another onceover. "Smuggling? She said that?"

"Antoni needs his people to fly straight," Figur said. "He's strange that way. He knows the importance of appearances."

Ret stepped forward. Irena tried to look him off but broke the stare before he did.

"Have we met?" Ret asked.

"You knew my roommate," she told him.

"Who?"

"Krystyna."

The big man froze. "Krystyna Krol? Lives on Powisle Street?"

"Lived," Irena corrected him.

Figur was slapping his car keys against a thigh. "Miss Platz here tried to blackmail Antoni."

"She what?"

"Wanted a payoff. Or she'd blab to the press about you. Which makes you one of Antoni's least-favorite employees."

Again Ret stared at Irena.

"What?" she finally said. "What's wrong with you?"

But she knew what was wrong; he was piecing this together. He turned to Figur. "I didn't expect this."

"So it's true?" Figur said. "You *are* smuggling?"

"It's not as if—"

"Smuggling what?"

Ret shook his head. "Don't try to come down on me, friend."

"Oh?" Figur said. "Personally, I don't care how you make your living. Run drugs, sell guns, pawn off Russian trinkets. But surely you can understand my concern. When guys like you are under Antoni's employ, he is only one phone call away from a world of unpleasantness."

Oskar appeared to think the statement over, looked to Irena to maybe be a little slow.

"What I need from you," Figur said, "I need you to assure me that phone call won't be made. Put my mind at ease."

"How?"

"By telling me that whatever you're doing is relatively tame. Tell me it's *not* drugs. Tell me it's sugar beets or knock-off Head & Shoulders. And while you're at it, tell me no one else from Mirsk Industries is involved in it."

Ret nudged dirt with his foot.

"And I mean now," Figur said. "There's no time to play hard to get."

Ret still wouldn't meet his gaze—couldn't. "I don't know you. You're just some guy from Gdansk."

"Are you mentally challenged?" Figur said. "I brought this girl down here in handcuffs. Do I look like someone who wants your story to get out? I need assurances, that's all. I need to know that Antoni won't be embarrassed by you. Whatever you say stays between us."

Irena didn't like the sound of the word "us." She peered across the road. A forest of pines stretched into the night. The closest trees were maybe twenty yards away. Figur's gun was in his belt. If this Ret had a gun, it was concealed.

"Mr. Figur," Ret said, "please don't take this the wrong way, but you can go to hell."

Figur shoved Irena toward him. "She told Antoni you killed a girl. Now, the way she put it, I'm thinking it's a lie. But lies can be as damning as the truth if they're told right. Can you maybe, possibly, get that through your half-breed head?"

With the word "half-breed," everything about Ret changed—the look on his face, the alertness in his eyes, the now-rigid posture. This sent a chill down Irena's spine. His next move could be directed at Figur or at Irena or at both of them.

"Jesus," Figur said, also catching it, "we're gonna be here till sunrise."

He reached into a vest pocket for a cigarette. Seeing this, Irena acted without thinking. She raised her left arm, raked his face with the handcuff. Swinging the arm back down, she bounced the cuff off his eye socket and tore into his cheek.

When she broke into a run, her legs moved almost too fast for her body to keep up—stumbling, lurching. Having the cuffs on and having her heart work at roughly one thousand beats per minute made it hard to maintain balance and choose a direction.

"My face," she heard Figur say behind her.

There was little light to guide her. She dove into the cover of the trees before the first gunshot rang out. Two more shots came before she realized Figur was not only chasing her, he was coming fast. She stumbled, groped the air blindly as bullets chipped bark off of nearby trees. Her legs hit branches and stumps. Adrenaline propelled her forward, but she felt—she knew—she wasn't going fast enough. She glanced back to gauge the pursuit. Figur was there, but Oskar remained at the car, oddly detached, as if he saw such chaos every day.

She fell, but regained her feet in a single bound. Her leather soles gave poor footing on the crackling, pine-needle forest. Figur fired his gun every few seconds. He seemed to have a lot of bullets.

CHAPTER 8

Julian slotted a token into the pay phone and dialed a number in Cracow. The clock on the Warsaw Central Station wall read 8:30 A. M. There were still ten minutes until the InterCity to Cracow.

Belarussian traders swarmed the next platform for the nine o'clock to Minsk. They moved in slow motion, lugged around bundles of cheap clothes, smoked pungent Russian cigarettes. They kept apart from the Poles, and the Poles returned the favor.

"Hello," a voice in Cracow said, "Holst's Restaurant."

"Hi," Julian said, "I'd like to speak with the manager."

"He's not in."

"When will he be in?"

"He won't be," the voice said. "Not today. Mr. Markat is coming in for him."

"Who's that?"

"Mr. Markat is the owner."

"You mean Jacek?"

"Konrad. Konrad Markat."

"Of course," Julian said, making a mental note of the name. "When do you expect him?"

"I don't know."

"Can you check?"

"Sure," the voice said, "hold on."

Julian waited, watched a traveler ponder over a new business-card machine next to the ticket windows.

"Yeah," the voice said, "he'll be here about one."

"You're on the Old Town Square, right?"

"That's right."

"Thanks."

When the line was free, he slid another token into the slot and dialed Henryk Milewski's number at *Gazeta Warszawy.* Henryk, old-buddy-old-pal, would help him now. He didn't know it yet, but he would. He had saved Julian's job more than once, covering for deadline misses, shielding him from an editor-in-chief who wanted to replace him with a gung-ho kid fresh off the plane from America.

Milewski answered the phone sounding like a sea lion with sleep apnea.

"Do me a favor," Julian said. "Call the Cracow cops. Get a list of prostitutes they've arrested in the last year or so."

"What for?"

Julian checked the clock again. "I'll tell you what's going on later. I have to catch a train."

"They don't just give those names out," Milewski said.

"They will for you. You've done harder digging. Find out if Krystyna's been arrested, plus whatever else there is on her. An address, if possible."

"They'd want a bribe," Milewski said. "What's all this—"

"Then use your expense account. Be a good *biznesman.*"

Milewski paused. "Julian, the way it works, the editor gives the order, the reporter beats the path. You know, chain of command? Results-oriented capitalism?"

"Just proves you can buck convention," Julian said. "I'm going to Cracow to meet someone. I'll be back tomorrow to talk to this *milicja* dinosaur at the Centrum Borough Komisariat. You'll be in the office later today?"

Milewski said he would be.

"Then I'll call you at five-ish. I'll give you the whole story then."

Milewski paused, no doubt puffing on a cigarette between labored breaths. He said, "You're supposed to be in mourning."

"I am," Julian said.

"Doesn't sound like it."

"My train'll be here any—"

"In fact," Milewski said, "you don't sound like yourself. You sound . . . awake."

Probably true—for the first time since Krystyna's death.

No. For the first time in memory. Now there was a future rather than a present, a tangible goal.

"Awake," Julian said, "is probably a good way of putting it."

"Might be counterproductive," Milewski replied. "You're messed up right now. You might not be firing on all cylinders."

"I also need to find a guy named Salda. Artur Salda. Flew to Chicago three years ago August or September. Check through your guys at the American embassy. See who sponsored him and where he might have—"

"I've been doing this a few years, Julian. I know the drill."

"Good. And make sure you're at your desk at five. Boss." Julian paused and decided to throw in a long shot. "And see if the cops have anything on a Markat. Konrad Markat."

"Who's that?"

"Probably no one. Owns a restaurant Krystyna worked at in Cracow."

"And you figure what? What's he done?"

"I don't figure anything. I need some information before I can start figuring."

"Julian," Milewski said, "I really don't see—"

"Krystyna was murdered," Julian said. "It wasn't suicide."

"Oh," Milewski said, and Julian heard disappointment in the single syllable. Milewski was no doubt thinking his one-time protegé was embracing denial, redesigning the past in order to take the sharp edge off the present.

"I'll tell you more when I call later," Julian said. "And Henryk?"

"What?"

"Try to lay off the cigarettes. At least until the heat wave ends."

The train compartment smelled of burlap and mold. An off-duty cop sat stiffly across from him. Julian watched him yawn and lean back, and recalled the last time he'd had *milicja* trouble. He was unzipping his fly in a washroom of a Warsaw milk bar. A cop blackjacked him from behind, leading to eleven stitches and a forty-eight-week prison stay for telling workers at a Mazury Lakes printing cooperative they didn't have to take a wage rollback. The plant's directors had been ordered to make more jobs without increasing the budget, and the workers' duty under the ethos of socialist brotherhood was to tighten their belts and spread the wealth.

The trip south to Cracow would cover three hundred kilometers and take almost four hours. To pass the time, Julian leafed through *Polityka,* one of *Gazeta Warszawy*'s biggest competitors. The lead story was about a SEC, one of the special economic zones that were springing up around the country. Julian had done stories on scandals surrounding the zones. The SECs were designed to boost local economies by offering tax breaks to investors who sited businesses in areas of "high structural unemployment." Big money was at stake and time was precious, because the Europeans were pestering Poland to close the zones in the interest of free-market competition. Once Poland joined the EU, which would happen sometime before the next ice age, the zones would have to go. But in the meantime, the government was having at it, opening as many zones as it could find investors for.

They made abandoned buildings and disused land available for next to nothing. Companies savaged one another for zone permits that would save them billions of zlotys in taxes. This particular *Polityka* story was about a cosmetics manufacturer who accused a soft-drink maker of greasing government palms for a spot in the Gliwice zone. There was a paper trail, incriminating bank transfers, even recorded phone messages. The story had a sadly familiar ring to it. Venality was a hallmark of the new and improved times; it was growing so common as to feel mundane, just another thing among things. Democracy and capitalism were great, but maybe some enforceable rules would have made the so-called system transformations go more smoothly.

The train reached Cracow shortly before noon. The mercury topped out at 34 degrees Celsius, and the crowds in the Central Station's underground walkway and out on the streets moved in slow motion. Gypsies and hawkers languished on dusty station steps. Kiosk attendants sipped colas and fanned themselves with newspapers. Julian had last been to Cracow to meet student demonstrators and organize a May Day protest. That was seven years ago. The gray melancholy of those days was gone. Now the streets held color and verve. Tour guides led groups of camera-wielding Germans into the station. The once-crumbling wall of the Main Post Office now held a billboard thirty feet long. The colossal message: *Always Coca-Cola.* The traffic was denser, more urgent. Taxis disgorged departing fares and picked up new ones without seeming to stop. Smog choked the air.

Julian went straight to the Old Town and sat at a crowded sidewalk cafe. A schoolboy in a uniform and a beanie lit a firecracker, and a flock of pigeons rose in unison and resettled at the other end of Europe's largest market square. The Sukiennice, a 14th-century trading hall, sat in the middle of everything, blocking from view half of the restaurants. Julian looked around but saw no Holst's Restaurant. When the waiter came, Julian asked him where it was.

"This is Holst's," the waiter said. "You're sitting in it."

The sign was blocked by scaffolding.

He walked into the restaurant and asked for the owner. The bartender ignored him. A pretzel-spined bathroom attendant said she wasn't paid to keep track of people. Waiters clipped about with trays. Julian entered the kitchen and approached a chef standing over a grill laden with grease-spluttering pork cutlets.

"I'm looking for Mr. Markat," he said.

"Shipping/receiving room, next to the walk-in freezer." The chef garnished a plate with lettuce. "While you're back there, tell him I quit."

"Oh?"

"I can't handle the heat anymore."

Julian walked past ovens and a dishwashing enclave and knocked on the door. No one answered, but he heard a rustling from the other side. He knocked again and a voice said through the door, "Whoever wants me, tell them I'm not here."

"That won't work," Julian said back, "because I'm the one who wants you."

Silence followed the statement.

"Mr. Markat?" Julian said.

Finally, the door opened a few inches, musty air being sucked out. A man poked his head out and fixed his eyes on Julian. He was maybe fifty and he had a compact body and deep-brown bug-eyes that took up half his face.

"What is it?" he asked.

"I'm here about a waitress who worked for you three years ago. Krystyna Krol."

"Who?" Markat said.

"Krol. If I recall, she didn't stay long. I have a few photos. Maybe they'll—"

"And you are?"

"Julian Krol. Her brother."

Markat watched him awhile, then swung the door open. Despite his dwarfish height, he was well sculpted, like a flyweight. The sleeves of his white dress shirt were rolled up to his elbows. He was holding a fishing reel. A tackle box sat atop the desk, against a stack of invoices. Some of the box's contents—spoons, jigs, spools of monofilament line—had been spread atop various papers and cans of pickled beets and peas. On the wall sat a pair of mounted pike, maybe thirty pounds each. The fish bared needle-thin teeth, poised to chomp at unseen prey.

Markat opened the reel's bale, tugged spiraled clumps of line from the spool. "Three years ago? I can hardly remember three weeks ago."

"It's been awhile."

He held out the last photo he'd ever taken of Krystyna: Krystyna at twenty, smiling, vivacious, hopeful.

Markat looked at it. "Yeah, I think I remember her. She didn't stay long. I think she went to another restaurant."

"You know which one?"

The line-pulling arm got back to work. "I can't even be sure she's the girl I'm thinking of." He stopped to rummage through the tackle box. "You could have just called. You didn't have to come all the way down here."

"How'd you know I'm not local?"

Markat found a pair of needle-nose pliers, snipped the line from the reel. "She was from Warsaw, right? That's the Krystyna you're talking about?"

"Yes."

Markat waved a hand. "Long gone, like so much else when

you get to be my age."

Julian looked him over again. Markat was far from elderly. The way he moved, the way he held himself, he looked as though old age would not take him without hellacious resistance.

"I'm in a rush here," Markat said.

"What's the catch?"

"Catfish. A monster in a catchment of the Bug River. Maybe he'll still be around when I get there." He studied his tackle-box mess, then asked, "You a fisherman, Krol?"

"My dad took me when I was five or six. I could never sit still for it."

Markat humphed as if to say that was too bad. "You're missing the point entirely."

"Am I? What if your catfish isn't there? What if you don't catch anything?"

"Then at least I will have communed with Mother Nature."

Markat tied new line around the now-empty spool. "I'm sorry, if your Krystyna is my Krystyna, she didn't leave a forwarding address."

"You have any idea where she was living?" The door sprang open and a blonde woman clomped in wearing shorts, a tight T-shirt, and pink, floor-pounding clogs. She ignored Julian, stood with her hands at her hips, dripped disgust. "Where's my money, you Jew?"

"For God's sake, Teresa," Markat said, "I have a guest."

She stepped forward. "My money. You promised it and I didn't get it and now I want it. I need it."

She was in her early twenties, pretty without being beautiful. Too much makeup marred her face. Julian's mind flashed back to the photo in the apartment on Wilcza Street. The girl in the hat, with the smile and the snowball. Why hadn't he grabbed that photo?

There was also the "Teresa" in Krystyna's letter, the roommate in Cracow. *This* Teresa?

Markat put down the reel. "Give me five minutes. Go look in a mirror or something, hunt for a wrinkle. I'm in a meeting."

"Why do you have to be like this?" she said. "It's not a lot of money."

Markat sighed. "Wait at the bar for five blessed minutes, until I'm finished with this gentleman. If you can't do that, then leave. Cross the square, find a job selling tourist charms or something."

"If you don't pay me," she said, "I'll tell everyone you're a cheat." She turned and faced Julian. "And if you're smart, you won't do anything with this guy that involves money. I'm giving you fair warning."

If she was the girl from the photo, Krystyna had changed beyond description. Hostility, vulgarity, desperate volume—Krystyna had always steered clear of such evils.

But then Krystyna had stopped being the Krystyna he had known.

"Teresa," Markat said, "I'm asking you to wait for a very short period of time. The request is reasonable."

Teresa finger-twirled the hair by her cheek. "Fine," she said, "but if you blow me off, I swear I'll be out of here. I'll leave you. I'll tell everyone you're a dirty, tight-fisted Jew."

Markat chuckled. "Come on, Teresa, you know I'm a full-fledged *Polak.*"

"Everyone knows you're a Jew."

"Who's everyone?"

"They *say* so. And you're hiding it!"

Markat threw up his hands. "Fine. *L'chaim* then."

"A midget Jew."

He laughed loudly. "I'm found out."

She slammed the door on her way out.

"Farmer's daughter," he explained. "From Opole. Thinks

she's found the big time."

"Why don't you just pay her?" Julian asked.

"Why don't you just mind your own business?" Markat turned back to his fishing gear. "Mr. Krol, the waitresses come and go. Someone offers better wages, they're gone just like that. That's what happened with your sister."

"This Teresa—"

"You're interested in *her* now?"

"How long has she worked here?"

Markat narrowed his eyes, stopped working on the fishing rod. "What's going on here?"

"Maybe she knows where Krystyna—"

"She doesn't know. Teresa's only been here a few months."

"Then maybe someone else from your staff, someone who's been here three years."

"None of them have."

"Not a single one?"

"Go ask around. This is the restaurant business. I'm lucky to get a year out of anyone. I'm sorry, I can't help you."

"Actually, you can," Julian said.

"Look, you're starting to—"

"What about your files?"

"My what?"

"Employment records. Taxes. You'd have an address for her."

"She worked off the books," Markat said.

"Oh?"

"Again, it's the restaurant business. You pay social-insurance charges on salaries, you go broke. Ask anyone. Forty-eight percent on each salary? Every restaurant from here to Szczecin pays people under the table."

Julian knew this, but he'd hoped Holst's might be an exception.

"Thanks for your time," he said, "and good luck with the catfish."

Back in the restaurant, his eyes adjusted slowly to the darkness. At the bar, he took a stool next to the blonde woman named Teresa, who was sipping black currant juice. Premature wrinkles lined her eyes. In this light, her skin looked gaunt, fast-aging. Now—again—she looked like the woman in the photo.

"He's all yours," Julian said, pulling out a cigarette. "Tell him his chef's quitting. I forgot to."

Teresa gave him a sour look and tromped into the kitchen. Despite himself, Julian liked the way she walked, with a bounce that was unself-consciously sexy. When was the last time he'd looked that way at a woman?

He waved the bartender over.

"What'll you drink?"

"Ice water," Julian said, "no bubbles."

When the barman returned with the drink, Julian asked him if he'd like to make a fast two hundred thousand zlotys.

"I'm busy," the barman said. "Make it three hundred. Or something in dollars."

Julian slapped three notes on the counter. "You know that blonde who was just out here?"

"Her name's Teresa. You want a date, ask her yourself."

"I don't want a date."

"That's refreshing," the barman said.

"I'm going to sit in the corner, over there. When she comes back out, all you do is hold out your phone, tell her Krystyna Krol's on the line."

The barman rubbed his nose. "Who?"

"Krystyna Krol."

"That's all?"

"That's all. Easy money."

The barman sucked his teeth. "Am I gonna regret this?"

"Something tells me you'll survive."

Julian took his water to a corner table. There were now four or five vacant tables. Most of the diners were outside on the cobblestones, enjoying the sun. The barman slid the money into his vest pocket.

Julian stirred his ice cubes with a straw and peered out at the crowds in the square. A trumpeter atop the Church of the Virgin Mary blew some crippled notes to mark the hour. The exchange between Teresa and Markat stuck in Julian's mind. If she worked here for him, then the guy ran a loony bin of a restaurant.

When Teresa returned, the barman had the phone off the hook, ready. He said something to her and handed her the phone. She stared briefly at the receiver, seemed to go blank, then raised it and spoke into it. Her voice was inaudible. She looked frightened, not confused or surprised. She looked guilty. After a pause, she spoke into the phone a second time.

Then she saw Julian watching her from a distance. She slammed down the phone and called the barman over. He dutifully leaned over the bar, offered her his face, and she slapped it with one hand and picked up her drink with the other.

"You a cop or a gangster?" she asked across the room. She had looked more appealing walking the other way.

"You knew Krystyna," Julian said.

"I knew who?"

"I need to ask you a few questions."

She lit a cigarette, blew the first smoky exhalation right into his face. "What's going on? It's not every day you get strange phone calls at places you're rarely at."

"Not being here must make it hard to work."

She let out a throaty laugh that made the other diners stare. "You think I wait tables for him? That what the Jew told you?"

"If you don't, then what do you do?"

More laughter—absolutely humorless. She said, "You don't

catch on, do you?"

"Apparently not."

"You want a date? Is this you playing hard to get?"

She air-kissed him. Marlene Dietrich she was not.

So Markat was her *alfons*—her pimp.

"Krystyna worked for him too, didn't she?"

"If you say so," Teresa said.

"I saw a photo of you in her apartment."

"In Krystyna's apartment?"

"You were in the mountains. You were holding a snowball."

Teresa tilted her head, made a show of being intrigued. "You're sure it was me?"

"Yes," Julian lied.

"Then look again. I hate mountains. The thing about snow, it's cold." She took another drag. "Look, whoever you are, I'm just here for my cash. Yes, I made it on my back, and yes, Markat gets a cut. Half of Cracow knows it; I don't see why you shouldn't."

She looked poised to leave.

"Krystyna was my sister," Julian said, and waited a moment before adding, "and she's been murdered."

Her eyes asked a million silent questions at once.

"Drug overdose," Julian said, "a few days ago. The medical examiner calls it a 'probable homicide.' "

She began to rise from her seat. He clamped onto her wrists, guided her back down. "I'm not here to cause trouble."

She tried to jerk away, but he kept a firm grip.

"Stop that, you're hurting me."

Other diners were staring again. Julian looked down at her arms. The tracks and punctures didn't surprise him. She caught his expression, and when he let go, she simultaneously rubbed her arms and hid them from view. She looked jittery, fidgeted with a fork.

"Working girls don't tattle on each other. We just can't do that."

"The police don't even know I'm here," Julian said. "No one does."

She reached for her juice—anything to occupy her hands. She eyed him warily. "I met her only a few times. You're wrong about that picture business, though. You've got me mixed up with another Teresa. Are you gonna tell Markat—"

"I won't tell him we spoke. No."

She reached into her handbag and pulled out an address book. She flipped to the "N" page and turned the book around for him.

Teresa Nowak, Powisle Street. Block 8, apartment 7. Julian jotted it down.

"If he's an *alfons,* what's he doing working in the kitchen?"

"Comes in from time to time," she said. "He keeps tabs on his things, the Jew."

"How long have you worked for him?"

"That's none of your business."

"At least three years?"

"What do you want from me? Markat's been around forever. He had girls back in the seventies. He had them when the dates paid with stuff off their ration cards."

"They did that?"

"Canned ham, rice, things that were hard to come by."

"Is he good to you?" Julian asked.

"You mean does he hit me?" She shrugged. "He's no worse than most. He just doesn't pay sometimes. He strings you along, makes you really need him."

"You have an address I can reach you at?"

She looked away, then rose from the table.

"I don't get it," Julian said.

"What don't you get?"

"First you're calling him names, then suddenly you're afraid of him. Does he have a temper?"

"Good luck with Nowak," she said. "With her, you'll need it."

She clipped out of the restaurant, choppy on her high heels. Julian waited a few seconds, then stepped back into the kitchen. The chef intercepted him at the ovens.

"If you want the boss again," the chef said, "he's gone. He left out the back."

"How long ago?"

"Just after the blonde left."

Julian stepped past him and glanced at the storeroom door. "He take his fishing gear with him?"

"Fishing gear?" the chef said. "No."

"You sure?"

The chef flipped some sizzling meat and grumbled something under his breath.

"I didn't catch that," Julian said.

"Weren't meant to," the chef said, and this time Julian caught his next mumbled words: "We need a fan in here."

Julian left him there to make his peace with the heat. Stepping out of the restaurant, he pulled out his notebook and reread the name and address.

Teresa Nowak, Powisle Street. Block 8, apartment 7.

It was a solid lead, one that Lieutenant Kosinski would have to look at.

Also one that could be followed up without having to wait for cops to start acting like cops.

Right this minute.

Chapter 9

Lieutenant Daniel Kosinski melted into his recliner, undid his belt, and sipped his beer. Death, destruction, corruption, anarchy—be gone all evil that men did to other men, at least for this one hallowed day away from the komisariat. There was a soccer game on TV, Legia Warsaw versus Blackburn Rovers in the Champion's League. His wife Eliza was in the kitchen kneading dough for *pierogi,* Sunday dinner. The phone was disconnected. He'd often considered rigging the doorbell so he could disconnect it too, but that was a bit much. Life was unfolding backwards. Under the Commies, he'd spent years begging to be used correctly. Now he couldn't finagle a free moment. The retirement was over and the real work was starting.

One offside and two corner kicks into the game the doorbell rang. Kosinski sagged into his chair, tried to make no noise, be invisible. But of course a moment later the thing rang again. Eliza hollered at him to stop being a baby, just answer it—so he waited a little longer. After the third ring, he trudged to the door and opened it as if his mother-in-law was on the other side.

Instead, he saw a squat man with pop-bottle glasses and a perpetual look of apology.

"Well," Kosinski said, "what do *you* want?"

"Can I come in?"

He hadn't seen medical examiner Wiktor Debina in four

months—since an appearance in court, when the district prosecutor called upon the ME to swear that yes, the six holes in the victim's chest had been caused by little steel things that came hurtling out of larger, longer steel things at eight hundred yards per second.

Debina was not the type of man to make social calls on cops, so Kosinski knew this visit would lead nowhere good. He ushered him in and offered him tea. He did this because he'd been raised to behave in a *kulturalny* fashion. He also did it because Eliza would have divorced him if he did what he really wanted to do—which was to turn him around, march him down the hall, and stuff him in the garbage chute.

Nothing personal. He knew enough about Debina to respect him. Poor bastard had become a doctor at the blissfully ignorant age of twenty-four, and had been plunged headlong into a pool of stiffs before he even tacked his degree to a wall. And he performed his job for the princely remuneration of a hamburger flipper in London or Paris. The Banacha Hospital, like all hospitals, was broke. It had one mammogram machine, an acute shortage of beds, and a "nutritional budget" of forty thousand zlotys per meal per patient. Prisons, meanwhile, adhered to meal budgets that were three times higher per inmate—in line with European Community human rights guidelines. Apparently, human rights extended to the incarcerated but not to the ill.

All of which was just one more reason to get off the state payroll.

Which men like Debina would never do. Men like Debina persevered despite trifling issues such as the need to pay rent. He threw dogged dedication into cutting open bodies and finding out what had made them dead—this while colleagues were jumping to the private sector, setting up clinics and buying medical equipment from western European countries once the equipment's certifications expired there.

"Warsaw's winning one nothing," Kosinski told Debina. "How's Kasia?"

"Kasia's fine. She sends her best."

"I take it you're not here for the match."

Debina shook his head. "I didn't want to bother you."

"Yet you did."

"I wouldn't be here if it wasn't. . . ."

"You look awful," Kosinski said, "like one of your stiffs."

"I'm not sleeping much. And I'm starting to find gray hairs."

Kosinski nodded, waited for him to come out with it.

Finally: "It's delicate. The Krystyna Krol autopsy. It's your case, correct?"

"Meth overdose."

"Meth overdose. That's where our problem is."

"Our problem?" Kosinski said.

"It was my problem. Now that I'm talking to you, it's yours, too." He looked at his feet, summoned the courage to trot out whatever confession he'd been sitting on. "Krystyna Krol received an improper examination."

"Improper how?"

"I gave her to my intern. I had eight bodies. I hadn't slept in thirty hours. I was getting punchy. I let him do the external examination and write the final report."

"But you did the internal?"

"Yes. But I signed the report without reading it. The report you have in your files, it lists the cause of death as suicide. I've had to change that, write a new protocol."

Kosinski leaned forward in his chair. "Change it to what?"

"Probable homicide."

A Blackburn striker was on a fast break, but Kosinski switched off the tube and turned in his seat to face Debina full on. "You filed a bogus report?"

Debina nodded. "The intern botched it. I was dead on my feet—"

"You already said that. They can take your license for this."

"Not can," Debina said, "will." He had the new report in his blazer pocket. He pulled it out and handed it to Kosinski. "This is the right report. Revised yesterday."

"How do you revise an autopsy report?"

"Based on the original examination and on what I learned subsequent to it." He paused. "Consider my giving you this thing now as my filing it. I guess I'll keep working until the phone rings."

Kosinski glanced at the report. "How'd the intern botch it?"

"Dependent lividity."

"What about it?"

"You know what it is?"

Kosinski did—all cops did—but he said he didn't so he could hear the whole story.

"The body," Debina said, "the blood, you know, settles at the points nearest the ground. Gravity. After an hour, the skin turns blue, looks like it's been air-brushed. My intern didn't notate lividity on the report."

"He didn't see it?"

"He didn't think it germane," Debina said. "He realized the mistake after the report was filed."

There was another pained break in Debina's speech.

"The victim was found stomach-down, with both arms tucked under her body and a knee curled up to her stomach. She should have had lividity on the front of her body, but she had it on her back and her calves and heels. Someone moved the body after lividity was fixed."

Kosinski read the new report while listening.

"I've already filed a new death certificate," Debina said, "but I've kept it out of the protocol. I've been trying to find a way not to file it."

"You could have just ignored it," Kosinski said. "You could have let it go."

"Could you do that?" Debina asked. After receiving no answer, he said, "Me neither."

"And now you feel a need to commit professional suicide?"

"This was the first time I signed off on something I didn't supervise."

"I bet it'll be the last," Kosinski said.

Debina nodded sadly. "And there's more. The victim's brother is asking for a copy. I've had the clerk at administration stall him, but I'll have to give him the new report sooner or later. If I'd left the old one in the protocol, if another doctor ever saw it, the lack of a lividity notation would have jumped right out. And if I gave Krystyna Krol's brother this new report . . ." Debina swallowed the thought, so Kosinski finished his sentence for him.

"You'd unleash a furor on the police force and the hospital."

Debina could only nod again.

Kosinski said, "Lividity means someone moved her. It doesn't mean someone killed her."

"Well, in that respect, remember, I did the internal. There was scalding of the tongue and the esophagus, from a tea laced with hashish. It's possible she simply drank the brew too fast, carrying out the deed without regard for her own pain. But it's also possible she was forced to drink it."

Kosinski shifted in his seat. "You found signs of *that?*"

"No, but the lividity suggests someone was with her at the time of death. That someone could have forced the tea into her."

"Wouldn't there be an indication? Bruising? Trauma of some kind?"

"Not all force is physical, lieutenant. Some force is psychological."

"Oh?"

"Persuasion," Debina said. "Holding a gun would work, as would any other number of non-contact inducements."

"That's an arbitrary conclusion for a man in your profession to reach."

Debina sighed. "Lieutenant, some aspects of an autopsy have more to do with exclusion and deduction than with clear indication of cause. Any assumption we make about this kind of scalding has to depend on the other physical evidence. Given the lividity, it's possible that whoever was with her led her through the process. That's all I'm saying."

"And the methamphetamine?" Kosinski said. "Someone 'persuaded' her to fill herself with poison?"

He thought back to what Julian Krol had said on this point: there was no way Krystyna would have used drugs to kill herself.

Debina pulled out a tissue and honked his nose into it. "She took the pills after the scalding of the esophagus occurred. Roughly one hundred milligrams didn't make it to the stomach, because she went into cardiac arrest while ingesting them. The anomalous thing, she appears to have kept ingesting them even after the onset of cardiac arrest. The last few pills didn't get very far."

"Meaning?"

"Meaning either she was extremely determined to kill herself or someone filled her mouth with pills when she was physically unable to swallow."

Kosinski leaned back in his chair and undid the top two buttons on his shirt. "This heat ever gonna break?"

"Excuse me?" Debina said.

"Until you got here, I was feeling good. I mean, for a moment, I forgot we were living in a sauna. Now I'm back to feeling miserable."

Debina blinked. Kosinski folded the new report into quarters, tore it down the middle, and let the pieces fall to the floor.

Debina looked shocked. "But you'll have to investigate. What if there's a trial? You'll need that for court."

"Look," Kosinski said, "I know the kiosk attendant down the street makes more money than you do, but you need your job and your job sure as hell needs you. Write up another report."

"Another—"

"Put a new date on it—the date of the death—and I'll burn the report I have in my files. No one will know it was changed, and I'll still have the right report for court."

"That could get you fired," Debina said.

"I'm assuming your intern didn't tell anyone. If he stays quiet, we're all fine."

"What about the victim's brother? If she was murdered—"

"Let him have a copy," Kosinski said. "I'll have to start an investigation anyway."

"He'll want to know why the first certificate said suicide. This isn't safe."

Kosinski said, "I'll talk to Krol. I'll put it in terms he can relate to. I don't think he's out to have anyone's job."

Debina heaved a long sigh of relief.

Kosinski picked up the remote control and asked, "You like soccer?"

"I don't follow sports."

"That's a shame. Everyone should save time for it. All that energy. All of it so . . . I don't know what." He turned on the TV. The score flashed on the screen: Legia Warsaw: 2, Blackburn Rovers: 0. He let out a cheer. This was the first thing in a long time to coax reflex joy from him.

"Not many examiners would do what you just did. Everyone's

out to save themselves these days. Whether they need saving or not."

"It was a bad mistake," Debina said. "It doesn't warrant compliments."

"Then let's put it in perspective. A doctor at your hospital let a boy die last week. The boy's appendix burst while the doctor was set to go home. There was no operation until the next morning."

"There could have been mitigating circumstances," Debina said.

"There were," Kosinski replied. "The doctor was dog tired and needed to sleep. Sound familiar?"

For the second time, Debina couldn't look Kosinski in the eyes.

"Stay and watch the game with me. We'll drink beer and complain about things."

"I can't," Debina said. "I'm on in half an hour."

"I might have guessed."

"I won't forget this."

"No," Kosinski said, "I bet you won't."

When Debina was gone, Kosinski settled in to watch the rest of the match. But it was no use. Spending time watching soccer felt like a crime, so he donned a proper shirt and stepped through the humid afternoon to the komisariat. On the way, two bums asked him for money. He gave each a ten-thousand-zloty note and hinted that food might be a wiser purchase than wine.

In his office, he sat down with the file on Krystyna Krol, pored over the photos of the corpse and read the statements from the neighbors and the building super. The last time her door was heard opening and closing was at 11:15 P.M. The time of death was established at 11:00 P.M., give or take an hour. At the very least, that left an hour between the time her last customer left and the time her body was moved. Either all of the neighbors had missed something or someone was lying.

And he knew that these days few citizens were eager to share information with the police. Fear of the post-Communist wave of criminals dwarfed interest in good citizenship.

He scanned his notes on the neighbors. The youngest one, a Mrs. Baraniec, was sixty-four years old. The oldest one, a Mr. Rybnik, was eighty-two. Between them was a Mr. and Mrs. Zych, sixty-eight and seventy-two, and a Mr. Zawada, sixty-nine. All of them had been home at the time of death. These people could have been bowled over by a feather.

Chapter 10

Julian strode past the Sukiennice and down a cobblestone back-street. Under the long shadows of Wawel Castle, he felt a vaguely familiar thrill, something he'd once felt almost daily, way back when. It was visceral, a kind of self-propelling energy. There was no choice here; the task was the task; it demanded he follow through.

How? Stake out the restaurant and wait for Markat to return?

Visit Krystyna's old roommate, Teresa Nowak?

Or go back to Warsaw, pass those two names to Lieutenant Kosinski?

There were two hours before his train, so he started toward Powisle Street. Krystyna's letter tugged at his thoughts, that line about interpreting, working for an import business.

He found a phone booth. The glass had been shattered and the receiver melted by a vandal's small-time arson job. Julian listened for a dial tone, then checked the book and found the number to the Pakistani embassy in Warsaw.

A trade counselor answered, sounded pleased to be receiving a call. Julian asked if any Polish companies had called lately requesting Urdu interpreting services.

"We're a purely diplomatic post," the counselor said. "We provide no commercial services to Polish companies. If someone needed an interpreter, we would suggest they try a translation firm."

"Are there any Pakistani companies registered at the embassy?"

"Unfortunately," the counselor said, "our two countries' economic links are confined to trade—mainly cotton textiles and leather. Poland receives less than one percent of our annual exports."

A breeze was skipping off the Vistula River, brief respite from the heat. "What about education? A twin-university program? I know Jagiellonian had one a few years back."

"It would be easier," the counselor said, "if you told me precisely what you're looking for."

What indeed? "I'm doing a story for *Gazeta Warszawy,* for our monthly insert 'Partners.' It's on the Asian economic presence in Poland. We're looking for examples of Polish-Pakistani cooperation."

"Oh." The counselor sounded pleased. "In that case, I'll mail you copies of our recent press releases as well as the journalist's kit we put together for this year's Poznan International Fair. It highlights our trade links and our other contacts with Poland."

"Other contacts?"

"That's right."

"Such as?"

"Registered at our embassy we have two physics professors in Przemysl and a cricket coach at the Poznan Academy of Physical Education. Naturally, we have a handful of other professionals, too."

"But no one who's approached you for interpreting help."

"Not that I remember," the counselor said. "And anyway, we wouldn't keep records of something like that."

"Thanks for your time," Julian said.

"But I—"

He recradled the receiver and continued on toward Powisle Street.

Teresa Nowak's apartment block sat back from a grassy knoll crawling with pigeons picking at bread crusts. She answered the door wearing frayed jeans and a paint-stained sweater. She was the woman from the photo, with almond eyes and an arresting beauty that would outlast middle age. Her fiery-red hair gave her a kind of warmth that couldn't be extinguished. She gave him a onceover look, seemed able to size him up—to size anyone up. He watched her watching him, drawn to her despite his purpose. There were no introductions.

"Come in," she said, and turned and left him to close the door and sit where he might.

He stepped into the living room. The place was clean and fresh, with elm furniture and a Blaupunkt stereo with a collection of Mozart and Mahler on display. If she was a hooker, she was a good one—whatever that meant. The windows were open. Lemon-scented furniture polish mingled with weedy air from the Vistula. Julian sat on the flower-patterned sofa.

"I'm Julian Krol, Krystyna's brother."

"That seemed likely," she said. Like the Teresa at Holst's, she didn't put on airs. Unlike Teresa Kozlow, she carried herself with ease, with the patience of a methodical boxer taking apart a pug. The Adagietto from Mahler's fifth symphony lilted on the air, but horns and engines intruded during the calmer segments.

Okay, Julian thought, *so this is how it'll be.* He said, "Krystyna's been murdered."

She turned her back to him. Maybe this wasn't news to her. Maybe it was stunning news.

"How?" she said, barely above a whisper.

"Drugs. Methamphetamine and hashish. Forced into her."

She crossed to the stereo, turned off the music.

"I haven't seen her for three years," Julian said. "I'm trying to trace her steps."

"Investigating her sordid past?"

"Konrad Markat was her *alfons.*" Receiving no reply, he said, "Right?"

She nodded. "Poor Krystyna. . . ."

"Do you work for him, too?"

"That would be none of your business."

"Krystyna mentioned you in a letter. She also mentioned an Irena. The three of you lived here. I don't know—"

"Krol, could you please just . . ." She raised a hand that said to stop talking. He understood why. She hadn't known Krystyna was dead. She needed a moment.

To give her that time, he crossed to the window and looked outside. At a riverside market, a butcher slapped blocks of pork fat onto metal hooks. Next to the fat sat a fishmonger's table of smoked eel and mackerel.

When Julian turned back to her, she looked different, a little softer. She also looked calm and ready—a pro at the unenviable job of having to digest woe and move on.

He asked her if she or Irena worked for Markat.

"Irena works alone," Teresa said. "I work for an agency. Krystyna works . . . worked for a different agency." She grabbed a pack of cigarettes from the mantel, lit one. "Why aren't the cops asking me this?"

"Because they've called it a suicide. I'm going to make them change that."

He gave her what he knew, told her Krystyna had been in Warsaw, explained the letter and the switching of the death certificates. When he finished, she sat on an ottoman, brought a cup of cold tea to her mouth.

"She moved out two weeks ago," she said. "She was moving

to Warsaw."

"To do what?"

"I don't know, but she said she was done with the life."

"Her letter said she was working for an importer."

"Yeah?"

"An importer who was going to help her move to Pakistan."

Teresa only nodded. So Pakistan was no surprise to her. But she didn't exactly rush to fill in any blanks.

Julian said, "You lived with her a long time. You must have known what she was thinking. You can help me."

She clucked her tongue and suddenly looked weary. "I can?"

After a long pause, Julian asked, "Is it money you want?"

Again she turned her back to him. She lifted her tea, but stopped short of drinking it. "Poor Krystyna. . . ."

The doorbell rang. Teresa crossed the floor and opened the door to two strange men. One of them, a tall and muscular foreigner with dull brown skin, peered past Teresa and Julian and scoped out the room. The other one was dressed in a pearl gray suit—Armani, maybe—and had a red gash running from his right eye to his chin. He locked eyes with Teresa, seemed distrustful, at the ready. The facial gash couldn't have been more than a few hours old. It had been scrubbed clean, which gave the skin around it a pulpy texture.

Teresa looked unfazed by it.

"What?" she demanded.

Armani rolled out a salesman's smile. "I'm a friend of Irena's. I'm looking for her. She around?"

"No, she's not around."

The guy took one step inside and started looking. "When do you expect her?"

"I don't recall inviting you in."

Armani hesitated, then smiled and stepped back, but not far enough so the door could be closed. Julian studied the second guy, the dark-skinned foreigner. Arms crossed, the big man was as sedate as his partner was restless.

"Truth be told," Armani said, "I don't just need her, I *need* her. Understand?"

"No," Teresa said, "I'm afraid I'm a little slow."

"If she's not here, where might she be?"

"She might be out of town," Teresa said.

"Yeah? Until when?"

"How about Sunday?"

"Today's Sunday."

"Then make it Monday." Teresa glanced at her wristwatch. "Did you cut yourself shaving?"

"I've offended you, is that it?"

"You learn fast. Good-bye."

He stepped forward again. "What's the hurry?" He peered inside as if Irena might be hiding behind the sofa.

"You guys better leave," Julian said, thinking, *They could break me in half if they wanted to.*

Armani only raised an eyebrow.

Teresa said, "I don't need your help, Krol."

Mention of the name snapped both men's attention toward Julian. In their shock, they allowed Teresa to gently stiff-arm them both a half step backwards so she could slam the door closed.

Teresa flicked in the dead bolt.

"Irena's had her share of creeps," she said, "but I didn't think they'd start showing up with running sores."

Julian stepped closer to her. "You said Irena works alone, right?"

"Look, Irena *is* visiting a friend in Warsaw. She *will* be back tomorrow. If you want to talk to her, you'll have to—"

"Was Krystyna that friend?"

Teresa sighed heavily.

"She was murdered," Julian said. "Doesn't that bother you?"

"More than you can imagine, but you don't get it."

"What don't I get?"

"I don't *know* why she ended up dead. She and I were never that close."

"You lived together," Julian said.

"We shared a flat; we weren't joined at the hip. We got along, looked out for each other, but there was a line there. Krystyna had trouble trusting people, didn't handle hard times well. I don't know where she went or why, just that she was getting out of the life. That's all she told me, and that's all I *wanted* her to tell me." Her tone softened, maybe tinged by guilt. "I wished her well, then went on with things. Which was exactly how we both wanted it, at arm's length."

Now her thoughts seemed to drift to a hazy distance.

Julian stepped in even closer. "Listen, Teresa—"

"No, you listen. You want to talk, you should talk to Irena."

"I will."

"She was closer to Krystyna. I can't. . . ."

"Can't or won't?" Julian said—and then watched her roll her eyes at his persistence. "Those two guys"—he motioned toward the door—"with them showing up, I'm thinking Irena's in some kind of trouble."

Teresa nodded, seemed to think about it. Reaching a decision, she told him a story. Since moving in eight months ago, Platz had been one surprise after another. She was full of reckless ambition, a small-town girl with big-city dreams, determined to make it, to get out of the life, to get money, real money—somehow. She had a new hopped-up cash-earning plan for every day of the week. She did things like pay people to start up pyramid schemes, like that Russian politician. She tried setting up a mail-order lingerie company, lost three million zlotys.

But she paid the rent on time, and Krystyna drew a kind of

strength from her, no doubt because Irena *did* have energy—which Krystyna did not. Though a year younger than Krystyna, Irena was a kind of big sister. Which was a shame, given that she was also a colossal screw-up.

"Can I make a request?" Teresa asked.

"What's that?"

"Leave me out of this."

"I don't even know what 'this' is," Julian said.

"Leave me out of it anyway."

"Why?"

"The police and I are not on good terms."

She gained her feet and went back to polishing furniture. Julian glanced down the hallway, saw two bedrooms. He started toward them.

"What are you doing?"

"Which room was Krystyna's?"

"You have no right—"

"No," he said, "I probably don't."

He continued into the first of the two rooms, expected her to follow, but she stayed where she was, stuck between forces that he suspected he would need to understand before this was over.

The bed was stripped. A small nightstand held a phone. Julian opened the closet, saw a few dresses, some short, some more formal, nothing loud or tawdry. The nightstand drawers were empty: no notebooks, no letters or papers or business cards, not even a pad and pencil by the phone. The bottom drawer held a two-year-old phone book. The front and back covers were coated with idle doodlings. A corner of the back cover held the words "Lubon, 7:30"—and the name sounded familiar. But from where?

Next to the time was an inscription of a few words in what must have been Urdu or Pashto. Under that, a short notation:

"zakat" - USD 100 per

Hindi? Urdu? He tore the page from the book, set the book on his lap, and leafed through it in search of "Lubon" listings. One was circled in pencil. He dialed the number and the phone at the other end rang nine or ten times. Sunday. No answer. He scribbled the address under the "zakat," pocketed the paper, and left the room.

Teresa was standing right where he'd left her. He stepped into her bedroom and pulled the door closed. The room was as well kept as the living room, with jewelry boxes and cosmetics on the dresser, magazines and photo albums stacked neatly on the shelves. A novel sat on the nightstand. Kundera.

He yanked open drawers. The second one produced a pistol, a Mauser that looked like Third Reich issue. He squinted down the barrel, ejected the bullets, and pocketed the gun. Then he leafed through one of the photo albums. Smiling strangers looked up at him. There was a fragile, elderly couple; a few young, well-dressed men; a stream of people who could have been anyone. There was no Krystyna, no Markat, nothing that looked like anything.

He peeked out of the room and saw an empty quarter of the living room. When he returned, Teresa was on the sofa, legs crossed, posture straight, no more anger in her eyes.

"Put back whatever you took," she said coolly. "Krystyna gave me the gun, if that means anything."

Julian felt the weapon in his pocket. "Where'd she get it?"

"I don't know."

He pulled out the scrap of phone-book cover, held it up for her. "What's this mean?"

"Krol, you strike me as a guy who has trouble making friends."

She opened her hand for the gun and he walked over and held it out for her. She snatched it away before he fully released it.

He thought back to Warsaw, to Krystyna's funeral. It felt like years ago. "You ever meet a friend of hers? A guy named Artur Salda? Went to school in Chicago?"

She stared death rays at him. "It's time for you to leave."

"I'll be phoning you from Warsaw."

"Lucky me," she said.

"You're right, I'm not a nice guy. But someone's getting away with Krystyna's murder. And you're wearing this mask. You're trying to look above it all, divorced from it. But you're not. You're in the middle of it, and you know it. You can't just wish it away." He started to leave, but stopped at the door. "When I call you from Warsaw, be here to answer it."

"Or else?" she said.

"There is no 'or else.' Just be here. Stop pretending you don't care."

He left her standing there, holding her cold tea, assessing him. He closed the door behind him and was barely onto the street, looking left, feeling a little guilty, when a fist came from the right and caught him in the ribs. Two pairs of hands pushed him into a car. On the way in, he glanced up and saw Teresa at the window, watching him, gripping a gun that no longer had any bullets.

A blanket was thrown over his head, snuffing out the light. Someone pounced on top of him, digging knees into his ribs.

"Hold him," said a voice just outside the car. "I'll go get the girl."

It was the same voice from a few minutes ago. Hamburger-face, the guy in the Armani suit. He sounded determined.

Chapter 11

Irena Platz rolled over in the grass and awoke to a sound of snuffling canine curiosity. A gangling German shepherd stood over her, his snout inches from her face. She blinked twice and tugged at the handcuff around her left wrist. It still pinched the skin and the hand was now numb and blue, with shards of pain shooting up the arm.

She rose to her feet and looked around. The dog panted and pranced, wanted to play.

She was in a farmyard. The angle of the sun and the shadows said she'd slept through a good piece of the morning. A horse stood next to its plow, hitched to an iron bar jutting from the wall of a rickety barn. She slogged her way to the front of the barn and saw a small farmhouse with a chimney puffing smoke. There was no one in sight.

First thought: get home, warn Teresa that Figur and Ret might show up.

But she didn't know where she was, only that Cracow wasn't far.

Jittery, she couldn't not search for Martin Figur and Oskar Ret among the trees and hay bales. The fear was new to her. Whatever else was true about the last twelve hours, however close she'd come to getting killed, Mirsk and Figur were going to great lengths over this thing. But why exactly? To protect what? It must have been as Figur had guessed: Oskar Ret was moving drugs or guns. Witnesses were not wanted.

She stepped around the barn. The dog followed her, nudged her hand with its snout. She petted the damn thing, envied its simplicity.

Then she creaked open the barn door and saw a big peasant holding a leather horse halter.

He froze, stared at the handcuff.

"Hello," she said.

"Miss?"

"I need help. I was kidnapped."

He stiffened, didn't seem to trust that. She held out her blue hand.

"They'll be looking for me," she said. "They're looking right now."

Which was probably true. Still, the farmer couldn't speak. With broad shoulders and strong, gnarled hands, he was good country stock, older than his years but hardy-looking. Judging from the leafy debris in the area, his crop was cabbage.

"Come here," he finally said, waving her toward him, "in here."

She stepped into the barn. The dog tried to follow, but the farmer kicked it in the ribs. It yelped and ran in circles before fleeing.

The barn interior was dark and foul-smelling. A sty at the far wall held nine or ten pigs. Hay sat piled near the door, a pitchfork atop it. Teresa scanned the area for tools.

"Who's the ones who did you this?" the farmer asked, studying the cuff.

"My father has money. They kidnapped me for ransom."

She tried to close her hand but felt nothing.

He crossed to an oily bench and took up a pair of bolt cutters. "Come here. I'll have to nip a bit of skin."

The cutters looked like mutant forceps, with wide handles and a heavy, pug nose. Made in the Soviet Union.

"*Those* things?"

"You got any other ideas, Miss?"

She walked to the bench and let him lay her arm flat.

"Don't let the pressure move it," he said.

When the jaws closed over the cuffs, they pushed back the flesh, added more pressure. He squeezed the arms, and after a brief, sinewy struggle, the cuff sprang off. Blood pumped back into her hand, bringing delayed pain.

"Jesus Christ," she said, her hand slowly catching fire—and she saw from the farmer's expression she wasn't supposed to use that name in that way. She rubbed at the wrist, fought the pain, held her arm to her chest, told herself to just take it, it would die down soon.

"Where's the nearest phone?" she asked.

"In town. Go start north up the—"

"Take me there," she said. "I have to call home."

"My wife and I, we don't want trouble."

"Trouble's what you'll get if they come here and find me in your barn."

She waited, knew he wouldn't refuse her. Finally, he said, "I have a truck. I have to tell the wife I'm going."

She followed him out to a canvas-backed delivery truck. The cab smelled like rotten produce. The farmer strode to the house, and the dog pranced over and hopped into the truck's bed. When the farmer returned, it took him a while to get the engine to turn over. Lying on her side, below the window, Irena worried about Figur and Ret's next moves after she'd lost them. Ret had known Krystyna. Did he know where she lived? Would they drop by and find Teresa there?

The Polonez pitched and sputtered them into Rudawa, eleven klicks west of Cracow. The phone was outside a post office, with four people standing in line to use it. Two peasant women were there with carrots and turnips spread out on coarse blankets.

Irena cut to the front of the line, ignored the complaints behind her, told a man twice her size to stuff himself. She dialed her home phone number twice, each time receiving no answer. With doubt fading to dark presentiment, she tried a third time, then returned the phone to its cradle, told one particularly loud complainer to get cancer, and crossed back to the truck.

She tried to stay positive, recalled an advertisement she'd read in *Kurier Krakowski.* The Canadian government was guaranteeing swift immigration for anyone who would bring one hundred thousand dollars with them to the True North Strong and Free. She'd memorized the advertisement word for salty word. But now where would she get that kind of money?

She pulled herself up and into the idling Polonez. "Cracow," she said.

"There's a komisariat just down the—"

"The one I need's in Cracow. It's not far."

Again, the farmer couldn't refuse a lady in need—just wasn't an option. She told him the komisariat was close to Wawel Castle, on Powisle Street.

The drive was slow and rocky, with cars and trucks passing the sputtering truck.

They were two blocks from the Old Town, idling on a street where an odor of sewage seeped up into the air, when she saw the first billows of smoke. The truck drew parallel to the Wawel Castle parking lot, and the flames became visible, roaring from her bedroom window, stabbing the sky like orange pitchforks. The fire trucks had yet to arrive and a crowd had gathered outside the building. The place was fast becoming a burnt-out shell. Everything inside was no doubt gone.

She did a fast scan of faces—and slowed her mind and did a second, more judicious scan.

Teresa Nowak was not in the crowd.

Chapter 12

"I'll be there," Lieutenant Daniel Kosinski said into the phone.

After hanging up, he jotted down the appointment: two o'clock tomorrow, 21 Roza Avenue. The job: area manager, Warsaw, of a new magazine distributor.

He sat back in the recliner and thought about it. It was strange; he'd forgotten applying for the job, weeks ago, in a moment of I-can't-take-it-anymore vexation, after learning there wasn't one single carbon left in the entire komisariat—which forced him to put everything aside, run out to an office-supply shop, and buy them himself.

The new job would be a cinch. Hire drivers, supervise returns, make sure money went where it should. Double the salary. Evenings and weekends at home. A chance to finally start acting his age. Only a fool would pass it up.

Still. . . .

He stepped into his bedroom and opened the closet in search of old clothes, the older the better. Only two people were on the books for selling Angel Fire in Warsaw. One was Marion Nadulski, a twenty-one-year-old chemistry student who cooked the stuff in his rented bedroom and tried to sell a batch to his landlord, a card-carrying member of the Christian National Union political party. Nadulski was now in Warsaw's Wola prison, had been for seven months.

The second one was Fryderyk Hryczuk, a Ukrainian citizen who'd been naturalized in eighty-nine. An undercover cop in the Old Town had caught Hryczuk smoking hash and had found on him 9.7 grams of Angel Fire. Citing a "potential threat to society," the prosecutor pushed for a prison term for trafficking.

But failed to get a conviction.

The law was against him, thanks to the days of old. Legally, the Ukrainian could carry ten grams of meth without any problem whatsoever. Communist legislators had decided drug abuse could only affect the decadent West, and had consequently found no reason to ban possession of small amounts. Post-Communist legislators had not yet gotten around to fixing that. The judge sympathized with the prosecutor, lauded him for his socially responsible determination, and freed Hryczuk after two months in jail.

Kosinski found Hryczuk's last listed address by phoning the arresting officer. The small time *narkoman* lived in a room over the Bar Bartek, a dive down on Krakowskie Przedmiescie. Maybe he knew who was moving Angel Fire. Maybe he could be persuaded to talk about it. It was a long shot, but then so was the TotoLotek lottery, and Kosinski purchased three tickets every Wednesday afternoon.

He dug from the closet some polyester pants and a lime-green blazer. The clothes had last been in style when Brezhnev was still in borscht. The blazer's lapel had a small tear in it, so Kosinski tugged on a couple of threads and created some raggedness. Then he looked at himself in the mirror and wondered if he still looked like a cop.

Yeah, he decided. *You're a cop no matter what.*

He headed for Krakowskie Przedmiescie Street.

Bar Bartek sat across from the Old Town, a hundred yards from the Royal Castle, a building with golden tapestries and artworks by European masters. The Bartek was shabby, uncared for, smelling of stale beer and urine; the castle was sparkling and stainless, assiduously tended to. The Bartek was crime and disorder, a dingy den for world-beaten old-timers and addicts of all shapes and sizes; the castle was ordered history, where the past was recalled in terms of crystal chandeliers and drawing rooms where kings and courtiers relaxed after dinners of pheasant and wine sauce. Tourists and locals ignored the Bartek on their way to the castle; the Bartek's patrons looked out at the castle only when there was a concert or a rally in the sprawling square out front.

If anyone was winning the battle of the opposites, it was the Bartek. The castle was opulence incarnate, but in the last two years, three of the bars around the Bartek had morphed from expensive tourist restaurants to hangouts for the dispossessed. The underclass was moving in for the simple reason that it was growing; it was falling hard and it needed space upon which to land.

The place was near empty when Kosinski arrived. A bewhiskered bum lay passed out on a table in the corner. In front of him sat a plastic bowl of sourbread soup and two dry halves of a bun, his temporary license to keep the table. Kosinski asked a bartender if he knew a "Fryderyk," and the bartender said "the Uke" was at a table by the window.

Hryczuk looked pretty much as Kosinski had expected. He had needle-pocked arms and caked saliva at the corners of his mouth. He was small, a wisp of a man with thin bones and fragile features. His clothes were almost as old as Kosinski's.

Kosinski ordered a buffalo-grass vodka and waited for the addict to leave. Then he sat down opposite the Ukrainian.

"I was told you can help me," he said.

The drug dealer sighed and pulled a cigarette from an ashtray. He stood up, walked around the table, and bent over as if to tie a shoelace. He froze like that, bending over.

"What are you doing?" Kosinski asked.

"It's my ass, cop. Go ahead, kick it."

His voice was high-pitched and his speech heavily accented, with the edge of a serrated knife.

"Thanks anyway," Kosinski said.

Hryczuk stood back up. "You sure? My parents were murderers. They helped Hitler invade. They made *kaszanka* sausage from the blood of Polish babies. Plus, I'm a leech on your hospitality. Became a citizen, then turned around and sold crank. Come on, you won't get this offer again."

So he enjoyed talking. That was promising.

Kosinski said, "I'm not much on the Poland-for-Poles business. And I know you'd earn more money in a Polish prison laundry than in parliament in Ukraine, but I'm not the jealous type, either. I just want to talk."

Hryczuk sat down and sipped from his glass. Carbonated water. "You're too old to be on the streets like this."

"You get to be my age, you realize there's a lot of things you're too old for. You're one of two people charged with selling Angel Fire in Warsaw. A woman recently overdosed on it."

Hryczuk snorted back some phlegm in his throat. "Only two guys caught? Everyone sells it."

"Everyone sells crank. Not everyone sells Angel Fire."

"Ah."

"I want to offer you something," Kosinski said.

"I figured. You're not here for fun, right?"

"If you tell me who sold you *your* stuff—"

"Sure," Hryczuk said, "very funny."

"—if you do that, I'll get the cops in the Old Town to steer clear of you."

Hryczuk stubbed out his cigarette. "Snitching is bad for the health. Besides, the cops are already clear. Haven't hassled me in months."

"But you've seen plenty around, right? Plain clothes? They think no one recognizes them?"

"You'd call them off just like that?"

Kosinski leaned forward. "That's how important this is. I'll let you make all the petty *kompot* and pot deals you like."

Hryczuk drummed the table with his fingertips.

"Or," Kosinski said, "we can go the other way."

"How's that?"

"I can make your life miserable."

"You don't waste time, do you?"

"Like you said, I'm old. I don't have much time to waste."

Indecision played on the Ukrainian's face. Kosinski sipped his vodka, let him think it over.

"I hate to tell you, cop, but I haven't touched meth since prison."

"Okay." Kosinski rose from his seat. "Your choice."

"No, sit down, I mean, it's true. It's too hard to get and not common enough to keep me anonymous. Someone kills himself, the cops come down like locusts. Which you're proving right now. Your girl—your overdose—she bought the stuff on the coast, up where they deal it in every courtyard."

"What makes you say that?"

"Or she bought it here. Or someone gave it to her. Her boss, her boyfriend, maybe her priest. You never know these days. Maybe she got it from someone in her building. Someone who—"

"I get the point," Kosinski said.

"Or she mixed it herself. It's easy, you know. A barrel of BMK, a few beakers, a fire extinguisher for when things get hot. I don't know anyone selling these days. Like you said, I'm kind of petty. I don't do anything that could put me in the Wola for too long."

"But you remember your old supplier's name," Kosinski said.

"No. I never met my supplier. All I met was a courier."

"Named?"

"Walesa."

"Walesa?"

"What can I say, he's unoriginal."

A pale man skittered up to the table. He stared at Hryczuk, jittery need burning in his eyes.

"*Jezus Maria,* Karol, a heat wave outside and you look like a block of ice. Can't you see I'm talking with the cop? Take a fall, I'll see you in a bit."

Karol retreated to another table and stared with wide eyes.

Hryczuk continued: "I haven't seen Walesa since before I was busted. Word has it he was picked up himself, though that's just a rumor. He hasn't been on the street in months."

Hryczuk glanced toward the bartender, who was pouring tea from a rusted samovar. *Tea,* Kosinski thought, *in this heat.*

The Ukrainian wiped his nose with the back of his hand. "The cops would really leave me alone?"

"If I tell them to. What's Walesa look like?"

"Short and fat, graying hair, handlebar mustache."

"The meth dealer, not the president."

"Short hair, bad acne, looks like a flattened pomegranate. Good luck finding him. I just described half the *narkomen* in Warsaw."

"What about friends?" Kosinski said. "Other customers who purchased from him?"

Hryczuk dug a finger into his ear, twisted it. "They'd tell you what I just did. Give him some credit, cop. He doesn't hand out business cards." He looked out the window, then back at Kosinski. "By the way, you know my name, but I don't know yours."

"Kosinski. Centrum Borough. Will you keep your eyes open? Ask around?"

"Tell you what, I don't see any cops sniffing around me, I'll see what I can do."

"Good."

"I've never been a kapo before."

"It's not as bad as you think." Kosinski leaned in close. "There's something else you can do."

"This is a give-and-take relationship. I do the giving."

"We'll work out compensation. Thing is, what I have in mind is . . ."

"What?" Hryczuk said.

There was no way to say it except to say it: "It's not one-hundred-percent legal."

"Oh?"

"I want you to lean on some people."

"You're kidding. Me?" Hryczuk paused to look down at his own unimposing physique. "Do you not see who you're talking to?"

"Size won't matter," Kosinski said. "You have the presence for it. Some elderly folks don't want to tell my officers what they saw or heard one night. I need you to get it out of them, any way short of violence."

Hryczuk said, "Ahhhhh—"

"But steal from them or harm them in any way and I will make you regret it for the rest of your life."

Hryczuk thought it over. "You're a very pleasant man, you know that?"

"I get by."

"I've been reading the papers. You guys are working second jobs to pay the rent."

"Us guys being cops?"

"What I'm saying, I have this feeling you don't have a budget to pay me."

"How would two million zlotys sound?"

"It would sound promising," Hryczuk said, "but what is it, your own money? Word on the street, cops have stopped paying snitches."

"Word on the street is word on the street," Kosinski said. "We'll make it payment upon delivery."

He slid a piece of paper across the table. Hryczuk snapped it up and read the names, ages, and addresses of Krystyna Krol's neighbors on Wilcza Street.

Kosinski said, "My overdose, she was staying in apartment four eleven, died on July 14, between ten and midnight. Find out if anyone came or left around that time. I'll need the best descriptions you can get."

Hryczuk didn't answer.

"What's wrong?" Kosinski asked.

"It sounds like something you could do yourself."

"Some of these people may have seen me at the crime scene. And police officers are not allowed to be as persuasive as they sometimes need to be."

Kosinski rose from the table. The pale man named Karol quickly filled the vacant chair.

"By the way, how'd you get citizenship?"

"My dad was an engineer," Hryczuk said. "Came to work at the heat-and-water plant in Zielona Gora in eighty-six. I haven't seen Donetsk since."

"You ever going back?"

Hryczuk made a spitting motion. "They ate the animals in the zoo last year. I think I'll stay a while."

Chapter 13

Julian listened for sounds as the car whisked him through the streets. The blanket was still over his head. One of the abductors had pushed him flat on the back seat, told him to stay quiet. The other one, Armani, must have been at the wheel. After tossing Julian into the car, Armani had said he would return to the apartment and "get the girl." But that was what, ten minutes ago? And Armani had since returned without saying a word.

Now Armani spoke—to his partner: "You sure this place is okay?"

"I wouldn't suggest it if it wasn't. How's your face?"

"Never mind my face, you asshole."

"Asshole?"

"You still owe me an explanation."

Julian felt the man beside him shift in his seat. The sounds of city driving receded, and the man gave his partner directions: Left here, right here, stop driving like you've never been behind the wheel. The car made fewer turns once it hit the countryside. The scent of summer hay filtered in. The sun burned at the blanket.

A half hour later they stopped for good, and Julian felt himself being pushed and pulled up a sidewalk and into a building.

"You sure no one'll pop by?" Armani asked.

Again his partner told him to relax. They sat Julian down on a chair and placed his left hand in a rough metal object. Julian knew what it was, though he hoped he was wrong. He hoped his hand wasn't in a vise.

His fingers grew white, bloodless. Only his thumb remained free, resting atop the vise's jaws. When they snapped off the blanket, he screwed his eyes shut against a sudden glare. They were in a garage of some sort, a disused place with a few tools on the benches and oily dust in the air. The windows were boarded up. A fluorescent tube overhead provided the light.

Armani reached into Julian's pocket, pulled out his wallet, checked his identification card. Then he returned the wallet and straightened Julian's collar.

"What did you do to Nowak?" Julian asked.

"That's her name? Nowak?" Armani turned to his dark-skinned partner. "Come on, we need a little heart to heart."

They left, locking the door behind them. Julian's ribs ached. He slowed his breathing, listened for sounds to suggest his location. Sparrows chirped, which told him he was in the country, which he already knew.

Whatever they wanted, he doubted he could supply it. He looked around the garage. A rusted, engineless Trabant sat over a mechanic's pit inside a bay door. An interior door led to an office. He freed his hand from the vise, walked to the door, tried the knob. It was locked, but the knob and the area around it were dust free, had been handled recently. From up close, he could make out old stenciled spray paint on the door. The black letters had faded with time, but he filled in a few blanks and read their original message: "Lubon Auto-Mechanik."

Lubon A-M. From the phone book in Krysytna's bedroom.

So these guys knew her. They were the ones she'd worked for?

He was alone for more than an hour, which gave him time to worry. The Security Services had once placed him in a room like this, tied to a chair for half a day. There was always the fear of a beating back then, but there was never fear like this, never anything like a vise. There were rules to the game back them. Commies versus democrats, them against us. Today, the bad guys were cowboys and everyone was out to submarine everyone else in the name of the zloty. Julian felt out of his depth in this scene, untrained for it.

When they returned, he was searching the bench for tools to pry a board off a window. The one with the cheek had doctored his facial laceration with a bandage; he told him to sit down, then crossed the floor and held out a pack of cigarettes. He'd also gelled and combed his hair to a helmet-like sheen and he smelled like cologne—good cologne, but far too much of it.

The brown-skinned man leaned against a workbench at the far wall, looked intent on leaving the interrogation to his partner.

Julian accepted a cigarette and let Armani light it. "So what is it you want?"

"For now, your attention." Armani tugged a paper from his vest pocket. "I had a little research done. You were jailed in eighty-three for organizing a union in Poznan. Jailed again in eighty-seven. For underground publishing. Twice caught defacing monuments."

"They were statues of Lenin," Julian said. "You'd have done the same."

"A Solidarity member. You attended more than sixty meetings and traveled illegally to East Germany in eighty-eight and eighty-nine. The purpose: to disseminate illegal publications and engage in political provocation. One year later, you became a journalist for *Gazeta Warszawy*, membership in Solidarity and all other organizations terminated. Why'd you drop out?"

"Because the Communists did."

"You stopped publishing, continued to raise your sister, though the state technically transferred custody to her uncle Jozef in Poznan. You continued to reside in Ursynow."

He paused again, dabbed at his bandaged cheek. Then:

"You were suspected of having a drinking problem. You traveled only rarely and socialized even less. You did not marry and you pursued women erratically. You were a regular at Legia Warsaw soccer matches, and you sometimes gave to the Equilibre charity."

He stopped and handed the paper to his partner, who filed it in a pocket.

"You still give to Equilibre, Julian? It's tax-deductible."

Julian didn't answer. That Security Services files were still in the ministry was common knowledge. That Armani could access them with a simple phone call was worrying.

Someone would have had to fax him the file. That meant Armani or his partner had a machine nearby. Behind that closed office door?

Armani closed in on Julian, leaned on the armrests of his chair. "You're wondering how we got this, aren't you?"

"Yes," Julian said.

"Tell me where Irena is and I'll let you go."

"I've never met Irena. Before today, I'd never met Teresa Nowak, either."

"Irena came home this morning, didn't she? She stopped by before we did, told you to expect a visitor with a cut face."

"If you say so."

"What were you doing at her apartment?"

The impulse: tell him he was tracking a killer. But then maybe he was talking to the killer—or killers—right now.

"My sister died," he said. "She used to live there. I went to pick up her things."

"Yet you left the apartment a few minutes after we did—empty-handed?"

"I was returning later."

"Krol, Irena's the only thing you have to bargain with. I suggest you use her."

"I wish I could, believe me."

Armani glanced at the brown-skinned man, who shrugged.

"You comfortable?" Armani asked him. "Want some tea and cookies or something?"

Slowly, the brown-skinned man made his way toward them.

"His hand," Armani instructed, and his partner obeyed, grabbing Julian's left arm. "Back where it was," Armani said.

This time the brown-skinned man hesitated.

"Do it," Armani said.

The big guy put Julian's hand back in the vise. Julian instinctively clutched at the handle, but Armani said, "Touch it and I'll shoot your fingers off."

"We never agreed on this," the dark-skinned man said.

"No one gets hurt who doesn't want to. He doesn't have to."

The dark-skinned man looked like he needed a washroom.

"Hold his free arm," Armani said.

It took him a moment, but the big guy stepped forward and grabbed Julian's wrist and pulled it up behind his back. Lightning tore through Julian's shoulder; instantly, it was on the verge of separating.

Armani grabbed the vise handle. "Everyone's got an agenda. I haven't met anyone in the last two days who isn't holding out on me. And I'm getting tired of it."

He stared accusingly at his partner when he said it. He gave Julian a few seconds, then moved to turn the vise handle.

"Don't do this," Julian said.

Armani was bluffing. It would take a special kind of monster to torture a guy like this. Armani gave Julian a few more seconds, then cursed under his breath and looked away. The vise's jaws closed imperceptibly, adding a crushing pressure.

Julian jerked forward, tried to pull free.

"Krol, please, there are no options here."

Julian tried to pull away, tearing skin on the palm. "My sister died," he said. "That's all."

"And you've never met Platz or Nowak before?"

"Jesus. No."

Armani turned the vise again, but this time there was no new pressure. Julian opened his eyes, saw his tormentor puzzling over the vise. The guy turned the handle again, and again the jaws didn't contract.

"It's stripped," he said with more breath than voice. "What a fucking nightmare."

Armani stood up straight, sucked in a deep and calming lungful of air. He glanced around the room, then crossed the floor to the tool bench and picked out a hammer. "What is it with you?" he asked Julian. "You think silence is bravery? You think holding out is gonna help anyone?"

Julian bit into his tongue. Armani swore under his breath, then tapped the vise with the hammer, tried to bring it on line. Nothing.

The brown-skinned man said to his partner, "You're insane."

"Then make a suggestion!" Armani screamed. "Everything's going straight to hell, yet you stand there like a lost little schoolboy. Try helping."

The dark-skinned man held his stare for a moment, but ended up looking away. Armani muttered, "I expected as much. Unbelievable."

He turned and began pacing, muttering something, wrestling with his options. Then a calm—almost serene—look came over him. Julian had seen it before, on the faces of Solidarity activists who knew they were nicked. There was peace in that, peace in being hauled away by the *milicja*—because it meant the doubt and uncertainty could end, at least for the moment.

Armani brought the hammer down on Julian's thumb.

Julian's breath fled in a rush. His teeth freed his tongue, his mouth gulped for air that wouldn't come. The dark-skinned man let go of his other arm, and Julian slumped forward. He looked down at his thumb, which was hanging backward onto his wrist, red bone poking out.

"God almighty!" the brown-skinned man cried. "You're psycho, man!"

Armani still looked peaceful. "I suggest, Oskar, that you not say another word to me. Not until it's something useful."

"Idiot! Don't use my name!"

Julian barely heard them. He tried to lift his free hand, but pain shot through his shoulder. He heard the hammer clatter onto the concrete floor.

"I didn't want to do that," Armani said into his ear. "You left me no. . . ." That he couldn't finish the sentence suggested at least the horrific act was starting to dawn on him. Armani again turned to his partner. "Let's give him a few minutes," he said, starting for the door. "Let's give *me* a few minutes."

The man named Oskar remained transfixed on Julian's thumb.

"You're in this," Armani said. "We're partners now, whether you like it or not." Then, as an afterthought: "So start behaving like it."

The big man didn't answer, but the look on his face said yes, there was no going back from a thing like this.

Oskar followed Armani out of the garage and Julian heard the door lock from the outside. The sounds of the sparrows returned. He tried again to free his hand from the vise, but the shoulder was sprained, useless. He was stuck there. He called out—weakly—and knew that the calling, too, was useless. So he sat still, fought the pain, and hoped—out of nowhere, surprising himself with it—that Teresa Nowak had fled the apartment before these guys torched it.

Eventually, the sounds of the sparrows stopped and everything else stopped with them. The voice in his head grew dizzy, disjointed. He found himself slipping into a dark void free of pain, entering a place he'd never known before.

It was a place of frightening silence. A place he worried he might never leave.

CHAPTER 14

Martin Figur felt tense enough to snap. He willed his thoughts toward the last time he'd let things get as out of hand as they were now. There was no last time. A line had been crossed, a seal broken. There was no going back.

And this was especially troubling because he still didn't know where he was going.

It was time for Oskar Ret to come clean about the smuggling business.

He drove Oskar to the Okay Bar just down rural road 702. Oskar, close-lipped, emphatically stoic, kept up his mute routine. Well, that would have to end. Oskar would have to discover some conversational skills.

At the buffet line, Figur grabbed a tray and said, "What'sa matter, asshole?"

Oskar wore a sour look. He didn't answer. Big surprise.

Figur pushed his tray toward the *babcia* behind the counter, said he wanted fish. Pike-perch.

"Today we're doing pork," the woman said, "breaded cutlet with potatoes and beets."

"Then pull some fish from the fridge, fry it up. I'll pay you for it." Figur yanked out his wallet and flashed a wad of money. Ret, as always, watched like a constipated zombie.

"Do you want the pork or not?" the woman asked.

"Listen, it's not a hard concept. I give you money"—Figur slapped two hundred thousand on his tray—"and you serve me.

It's called *biznes,* in case you've been off grazing or something."

The *babcia* looked right through him, reached up, pulled his tray away, and turned to the next man in line.

Ret pushed his tray forward. "I'll have the pork," he said.

Just like a fucking lemming.

They sat at a window facing the garage, and Oskar felt Figur staring at him. He tried to ignore him, focused on his cutlet, sawed the meat into strips while thinking of Irena Platz. If Platz had any brains, she would be in a nice, safe komisariat right now, telling a story about a kidnapping. Telling them the names Oskar Ret and Martin Figur.

Snatching Julian Krol to get to her had seemed like a good idea at the time, but it wasn't. Krol didn't know where Platz was. Krol was a waste of time. But because of everything that had transpired, he was now also dangerous, a victim and a witness.

Oskar felt his fork leave his hand. Figur had snapped it away, tossed it onto the next table.

"Look at me," Figur said. "There's a hooker out there who knows you're a smuggler."

"And who you kidnapped and tried to shoot in the back."

"Which puts you and me in the same pile of trouble, doesn't it? Time for some of that whaddyacallit, transparency. What happens if Platz gets to the cops? What's she going to tell them about you and Krol's sister?"

Oskar retrieved his fork, wiped it on a pant leg, and speared a potato. "She worked with me, translated, just like Platz told you. Why she ended up dead I don't know, but I had nothing to do with it. She left the job a couple weeks ago."

"Worked with you," Figur said. "What's the cargo?"

"Look," Ret said, "let's just find her. My imports are my business."

" 'Imports,' " Figur said. "Nice word."

Oskar gestured toward the garage. "Did you really have to act like the KGB? You can't go around maiming people."

"And what about this garage?" Figur asked.

"What about it?"

"It's yours or what? How sure can we be no one will show up?"

Oskar slapped down his fork. "If we're partners, I guess I'm the junior partner, huh?"

"Very junior. Apprentice level."

Oskar looked him in the eyes and said, "Then, boss, I quit."

This time Figur pulled Oskar's whole plate away, held it hostage on his side of the table.

"I repeat, what's the cargo? Or I'll shoot you here and now."

Oskar stared. Figur tried to look as if he meant it—and Oskar was sure he did.

Finally, Ret said, "Blue jeans."

"What?"

"The cargo. Blue jeans. You asked."

For a while, Figur looked as if someone had just passed gas. Finally: "So what else do you 'import?' Toilet paper and ration cards?"

"Jeans made in Pakistan," Oskar said. "Ten tonnes of blue jeans is a lot of money when you're paying twenty cents a pair."

"You really expect me to believe—"

"A Japanese factory in Rawalpindi. Company had bad press over child laborers. Protests in Tokyo, so they donated their stock to a local charity. It was a PR move while they pulled out of the country. The charity was supposed to sell the jeans and be saints with the proceeds. But two of their guys turned around and started selling to my guys."

Oskar watched Figur's expression closely. The explanation was so surprising that he had to at least consider it.

"The jeans came cheap," Oskar said. "We have 'Lee' labels sewn on, sell them in Belarus and Ukraine, also in markets in Silesia. We're on the third of four transports."

Figur was hard to gauge, still going over it in his mind. Finally, he said, "How do you handle border crossings?"

"People get paid. Look, you've been asking for my opinion on things, now I'll give it to you. Number one, we go back to Krol. We find out if Irena made it home this morning. If she didn't, we let Krol go, send him back to Warsaw."

"Right. Let him go."

"After your bloodletting, he'll be too scared to make waves. We threaten him before he goes, tell him he's dead if he talks. I'm sure you can do a convincing job of that."

"It would still leave Platz."

"We find her."

"How?" Figur said. "We even know where to look?"

"I used to pick Krystyna up at this apartment, this place rented by an agency."

"What do you mean?"

"Place called Hearts Agency."

"Escort agency?"

Ret nodded.

"She worked there?"

"I think so. If not, a friend of hers did. So we go there and if she's there, great. If not, we ask about her there. We get to Irena, we bite the bullet and throw some cash at her."

"Right," Figur said again.

"We have no choice. She goes to the cops, we're finished."

Figur was a fool if that possibility did not gnaw at him. Things were moving fast, too fast to handle, thanks mainly to Figur and his Wild West stupidity. Why torch the hooker's apartment? Because she'd given them the slip? Because she'd been mouthy? Figur oozed violence, torture, bullyism—evils that Oskar knew and understood much better than he wanted to. Guys like Figur were destined to rage themselves all the way to unfortunate endings. It was obvious to everyone except for those guys themselves.

He watched Figur slug back his raspberry compote. Antoni Mirsk's head of security looked like he was still going over the blue-jean news, still mulling over the proposal to pay Irena Platz.

"Okay," he said at last, "for now we'll do it your way. We'll track down Platz." He swabbed his face with an expensive-looking handkerchief. "But we'll do that after we see what Krol knows."

"We let Krol go," Oskar said. "We scare him, but we let him go. No more vises."

He watched Figur watch him. "Where you from, anyway? You a Gypsy?"

Oskar sighed. "My mother's Romanian."

"Ah, I figured."

"Which doesn't mean Gypsy, dumbass. Gypsies are a different people, came out of northern India. And while we're on the subject, what makes them so bad? They been a plague on your house, Figur? Wronged you somehow?"

Figur slurped up the last raspberries from his compote. "Forget I mentioned it," he said. "But you know what, how about if you show me a pair of those blue jeans?"

"Why?" Oskar said.

"A guy hears about twenty-cent blue jeans, he gets curious as to whether they really exist."

Chapter 15

It would be Legia Warsaw versus Bayer Leverkusen, and the heat smoldered low to the pitch. *Gazeta Warszawy* editor Henryk Milewski stood outside the gates of Legia Stadium and chewed on a leathery piece of fried kielbasa. All the slurping and swallowing made it temporarily hard to breathe. Maybe that was a psychological thing, his body's way of telling him to stop eating—while another part of his body told him to go ahead, the food was right there, smelling great, *available.*

The soccer crowd jostled past him, all elbows and boozy breath. Many of them weren't shy about taking stock of Milewski:

"Look at that poor bastard."

"How'd they get him out of the zoo?"

"*Jezus Maria,* he's gonna have a heart attack!"

Mounted riot police kept restless horses in tight formation. The fans, teenagers draped in the green and red of Legia, jeered the cops, taunted them, dared them to hop down from their get-away ponies.

Milewski scanned the sea of faces for reporter Marek Janicki, the suicidal nitwit who had insisted on meeting here. Milewski had an assignment for the young journalist from America, a job that could be a front page and a career fast-tracker.

Milewski gobbled down the last of the kielbasa and patted his florid face with a sweat-sopped handkerchief. Janicki turned up decked out in Legia green and red and well-worn army boots, just one of the boys.

"For Chrissakes," Milewski said, "why meet here?"

Janicki rubbed his hands together, loving life. "It's an action place. Keeps you on your toes."

"You gotta be kidding."

"Actually," Janicki said, "my cousin plays for these guys. He gave me season tickets soon as I hit Warsaw. He's reserve, but I have a feeling he'll get in today. I mean, man, I haven't seen him play since he left MSL."

Milewski chose to drop it. When he'd first met the kid, the kid shook his hand like some rapper on MTV Europe: a full-finger-lock and a push away at the end. On that first meeting, Janicki showed off his perfect Polish, bragged about being raised in an immigrant family that had made itself stinking rich in the States, and told Milewski what was wrong—exactly, precisely, ad nauseum—with Polish journalism:

"Too many passive sentences. Too much authorial opinion, not enough fact. We gotta cut the writers' ramblings, teach 'em how to structure. We gotta stop publishing press releases as stories. People are gonna think we're a mouthpiece for hire." On and on. He knew his journalism, and Milewski had seen his freelance pieces for *Wprost*, but something about him remained signally wrong.

"How old are you?" Milewski asked him.

"Old enough to know better."

Milewski put him at twenty-two, twenty-three tops.

A gaggle of skinheads neared the entrance. Milewski drew Janicki aside so they could tromp on by.

"Let's go find our seats," Janicki said, and they fell in with some fans heading toward the north side of the field, where there was a partial roof to provide shade.

"What's your cousin's name?" Milewski said.

"Bartocki. Striker. Cross your fingers for him."

The turnstile at the entrance was a tight fit. The cop frisking fans gave Milewski a double take. The fat man was too old to be attending a Legia game. He was also sober, which was a dead giveaway of honorable intentions. The cop waved them both through and they made their way to the top of the grandstand. The fans were already taunting the Leverkusen fans, who were locked away in the eastern corner of the stadium surrounded by a wall of riot police. A chant went up:

Bayer licks
Warsaw pricks!

The German fans responded with an organized raising of middle fingers. The chant soon digressed into a new one:

Bayer scores
With fräulein whores!

When the game started, few people watched it. Firecrackers were lit and rolls of toilet paper were tossed onto the pitch. In the west-side bleachers, neo-Nazis in bright orange shirts started a series of Third-Reich salutes. The non-Nazi hooligans, all eleven thousand of them, ignored them. Milewski lit a cigarette, watched Legia's number 11 play the ball back to his goaltender.

"Here's the thing," he said. "I need a piece that might expose one of Poland's richest men as a crook."

"Yeah?" Janicki said.

"Yeah."

"And you want me for it. Why?"

"Because you're too full of yourself to be afraid of the assignment."

"Who is he, the anti-Christ?"

"Antoni Mirsk," Milewski said. "You've heard of him?"

"*Antoni* Mirsk? Holy shit."

"Yes," Milewski said, "holy shit."

"Guy in Gdansk? Owns salt mines and gas permits?"

"One and the same."

Janicki plucked his reporter's notebook from a jacket pocket, got a pen ready. "Shoot," he said while the fans got a new chant going:

Bayer blood
on Warsaw mud!

Milewski said, "I'll arrange an interview for you at Mirsk Industries. One look at you and Mirsk will think he's dealing with a child. Use that. *Be* a bit of a child. Find out what you can about one of his employees."

"Who?"

"A man named Oskar Ret."

Janicki scribbled the name in the book. A contact at Cracow Main Headquarters had told Milewski that Krystyna Krol was arrested twice in the last year for solicitation for the purpose of prostitution. The person who bailed her out both times: Oskar Ret, who had a record himself.

"What's so interesting about Ret?" Janicki asked.

"Run-of-the-mill low-life. Did three years for knifing a guy in the lobby of the Victoria Hotel. Also two years for stealing a truckload of counterfeit Marlboros and selling them at the Russian market in Bialystok. He's not destined for greatness."

"What's he do for Mirsk?"

"That's the question. I haven't been able to find a phone number or an address for him, but I—"

"Where'd you hear he was working for Mirsk?"

"Listen," Milewski said, "curiosity helps, but would you shut up for one short minute?"

Janicki shrugged.

"Thing is, I haven't been able to track him down. But I did

find his parents. Or at least his parents' number. His mother says he works as a delivery truck driver at the Mieltor Salt Mine."

"You're starting to lose me," Janicki said.

"You've heard of the mine?"

"Course I have. National treasure. Blah."

"The financial controller says Ret pulls in forty million zlotys a month, an upper-management salary, but I called all the department heads and none of them knows him. Ret collects pay without working. He's been on the payroll for three months."

Janicki stopped writing. "Big deal. Half the country's in the gray zone."

"I called the salt mine's parent company in Gdansk," Milewski said. "The owner, Mirsk, you know him. Liberal-Democrats want him in their party. A tycoon paying big money to a felon. We can get mileage out of it. So you'll go to Gdansk, extract a few general but suggestive quotes."

"Sounds pretty soft so far," Janicki said, "just a bunch of circumstance. Isn't exactly Watergate."

"Watergate wasn't Watergate. Not when it started." Milewski mopped his face with his handkerchief, mixed old sweat with new. God, it was hot. "Get just enough from him so we can put Mirsk in bed with a Cracow hoodlum. We know Ret isn't driving salt trucks around for his forty million."

Where was Julian? Milewski had hit on all this thanks to Julian's request to check Krystyna Krol's criminal record. And Julian hadn't called at five o'clock, as he'd said he would. That wasn't like him. If he was down in Cracow knocking on doors, some of those doors might open up on Oskar Ret.

Someone hurled a vodka bottle at a security guard on the field. Three riot cops pulled a guy—any guy, it seemed—from the crowd and roughhoused him toward the exit. A skinhead a row down produced some vodka and took a long swig. Janicki made a *tsk-tsk* sound.

"Booze slows the reflexes," he said. "Takes the wind out of your willy."

Legia scored and the stadium erupted. Someone tossed an empty vodka bottle. Janicki ducked and it smashed against a concrete step. A strange stir spread through the crowd. Everyone was gaping at the Leverkusen section. The German fans had their pants down around their knees and were shaking their privates in a show of contempt for Warsaw.

"Jesus Christ," Milewski said. "What's happening with the world?"

"I wish I had my camera," Janicki said.

The Legia fans started another chant, but a group decided to go one better, inched closer to the wall of riot cops around the Germans. Some threw bottles and full cola cans. Others shouted obscenities, tried to get new chants going. The Germans tugged up their pants and responded with another symphonic raising of middle fingers. Riot police trotted over from other sections of the stadium, weathered the barrage of cans and bottles. Then nine or ten fans hopped the fence and stormed the pitch.

Bedlam had been officially launched.

With fans now running everywhere, Janicki cheered and laughed, while Milewski tried to make himself small. The players gamely played on until there were too many people on the pitch for the security guards to handle. A Bayer player who'd been running for a clearing kick just kept running until he was in the clubhouse. His teammates and the Warsaw players were close behind. A soda-can missile felled a Bayer midfielder. A Legia defender helped him to his feet and the two made it off the pitch before the fans could intercept them.

Milewski stayed where he was, gripping Janicki's shirt in case the reporter took a notion to charge the field. The area around them was now empty, with fans pouring onto the pitch. The neo-Nazis kicked at brittle wooden benches, pulled up jagged slabs with which to battle the cops. There was no escape. The cops were starting a sweep through the stands, coming straight this way.

"Where should we meet next time," Milewski hollered over the tumult, "the bear pit at the zoo?"

"Ooh, bear pit . . ."

The line of riot cops neared them, flushing out whoever was left, clubs flailing. Mounted police charged onto the field, formed a diamond at the east end. Rioters pelted them with parts of torn-up benches. The horses danced and whinnied.

Milewski found himself being jerked down the steps toward the exit. Escaping fans clogged the concourse. Janicki led the way, plunged them into a wave in the crowd to be carried to the exit, where the cops swung their clubs at anyone and everyone. In the dash out the gate, Milewski took a blow to the forearm. Janicki caught one on the crown. Blood trickled from under his Legia cap, but his pace didn't slow.

"If the guys back in Hamtramck saw this," he said.

They stood for a while outside the fence, watched the mayhem. Horses tossed their riders and fans used whatever they could as missiles. The Leverkusen fans scrambled toward their buses. A phalanx of police ordered everyone back from the fences, and people didn't walk away, they ran. The slow ones caught batons on the head. Milewski and Janicki retreated into Ujazdowski Park, a lush, quiet place on the border of the insanity. They sat down at a bench where an elderly couple tossed bread crumbs to pigeons, stoically watching the world fall apart.

Milewski's lungs felt like fire. "How's your head?" he asked.

"Starting to hurt." Janicki probed underneath his cap with his fingers.

"Better get to the hospital now," the old lady said, tossing bread to the birds. "It'll be busy, from the looks of things."

So they started a slow walk through the park. Where the park met a street lined with police cruisers, Janicki stopped. He was wobbly and pale, wasn't walking right.

"I lied," he said. "My cousin doesn't play for Legia."

"What?"

"I just wanted to . . . I've never been to one of these games. Sport in the states, it's a bore. People go just to watch the game."

"You dragged me here," Milewski said, "for the fun of it? You put me at the mercy of twelve thousand Neanderthals . . . for a kick?"

Janicki looked pleased with himself. Milewski hoped the facial expression would soften, but if anything, it deepened.

He decided then and there he wouldn't trust a baboon like Janicki with the piece on Mirsk. He decided to go meet Mirsk himself.

They reached the hospital before the other casualties arrived. Milewski argued with the nurse. Janicki's residence permit had the American living in the Zoliborz district—which meant he should have gone to that hospital. Janicki curled up on a hallway bench and said, "I just need a little nap," and the nurse finally hopped to it.

Milewski found a pay phone and called *Gazeta Warszawy*.

"Any messages?" he asked a copy editor named Wanda.

"I'll say. A cop in Cracow called a few minutes ago. He said you requested a background check on a felon."

"Oskar Ret." Milewski said. "I already got the info on that check."

"Uh uh, a check on a man named Konrad Markat. I wrote it down for you."

Markat. The guy Julian had asked him to look into.

"Markat is an *alfons*," Wanda said. "They say he's been pimping since the seventies. He ran a counterfeit ration-card ring in eighty-three, was arrested in Warsaw but had the charges dropped. He's also been charged with extortion, bribery, assault—three times for assault. Each time, charges were dropped."

"Why?" Milewski asked.

"Because it appears he has friends. He runs companionship agencies in Cracow, moved south from Warsaw just before the Commies got the hoof. He owns a restaurant and four other businesses in Cracow, bought them at cut-rate prices during privatization campaigns. Seems he followed some politicos to Cracow. The cop said he's pretty much untouchable."

It was an old story. The end of the Commie dream, an upheaval for most people, was a mere hiccup for those with connections. Milewski could never have predicted this when the socialist dystopia was considered the worst of all possible nightmares. When the United Workers' Party dispersed, some Party men jumped to the private sector, took foreign-trade concessions with them. Others stayed in politics, while still others settled into management-board posts with state-owned factories and paid themselves huge salaries. The old network remained intact but informal. If this Markat pimped for government or ex-government men, the network could still provide him with all the business he could ever desire. Lucrative business.

Was *Markat's* door one of those that Julian was now knocking on?

"This all sounds promising," Wanda said. "We doing a story on Markat? I think we should get a photo of him and doctor it so he's wearing pink panties and a garter."

"It's too early to print anything," Milewski said.

What did it have to do with Antoni Mirsk and Oskar Ret?

What was Julian doing in Cracow?

Milewski told Wanda to save him her notes; he would be back

at the paper in an hour.

He left the hospital and hefted himself onto a streetcar. Next stop: Warsaw Central Station and a ticket for tonight's train to Gdansk. A familiar feeling began to grow, a seed of exhilaration. Also a vague feeling of fear. He was plunging himself into the unknown—and he was sweating so profusely and his heart was working so hard to feed blood throughout his ample body, that he worried all of this excitement might literally end up killing him.

Chapter 16

Julian stirred. A tinny echo sounded, someone close by, speaking, but the words far away. He fought to open his eyes, but his mind rolled in darkness.

"Come on, Krol," a woman's voice said, "snap out of it. I don't have all day."

Now the eyes opened a bit. He saw a foggy sliver of hospital walls. Teresa Nowak sat perched on the edge of a chair beside his bed. She was still wearing her paint-stained cleaning shirt, still giving him a cautious look. Those eyes never strayed far from distrust.

The room's three other beds were empty. Julian's tongue felt frozen. Anesthetic. He looked down, saw one arm in a sling, resting against his body. The other arm ended in an unwieldy plaster cast, suspended overhead by a metal rod. He felt nothing, not even his back against the bed. They had put him in hospital pajamas, one arm torn to fit over the cast. There was a window, but no sounds from outside. A night table beside him held a paper cup and a rusted water pitcher. An order on the wall read, *Zakaz palenia*—No smoking.

Julian croaked through the brain fog, "They're after Irena."

"And you, apparently. You're in Skawina Hospital."

"The—"

"They've put a pin in your thumb. If you try to use it, they'll have to amputate."

"What happened?"

"You've got a few days in bed," Teresa said. "I told them you were thrown from a horse. The horse stepped on your hand."

"How did you—"

"Across the hall and out the courtyard entrance. I followed you in a taxi. Now just listen to me, because I have something to say and I have to be somewhere else." She swept back her red hair. "This isn't happening to only you, okay? The guy who raced up the stairs to get me . . . my guess is he used my cleaning chemicals. He set fire to my apartment. Why, I don't know, but I have no money and no home. I have nothing, thanks to you."

She was shaking slightly. Julian asked, "Why are you helping me?"

"Shut up and listen." She leaned in closer, her mouth to his ear. "It's me I'm helping by pulling you out of that garage. Whatever Irena's got herself into, I'll figure it out. But far as you're concerned, something else now gets important. After your visit, all I have left in this world is the nine million zlotys I took from your wallet on the way over here. And I'm not letting you out of my sight until we balance things out."

"Balance things out?" Julian asked.

"I need a new home in a nice city, preferably far from here. I want a nice apartment with nice furniture. Just like I had."

"I'm supposed to buy these things?"

"A lump-sum cash payment will do. We'll say twenty thousand U.S."

"And we're just assuming I have that kind of money?"

"We're assuming you can at least get access to it. It's the price for ruining a woman's life." She reached into her purse, pulled out a blue debit card. "I got this from your wallet. I would feel better if we made a few withdrawals right now."

"It's a Warsaw bank," Julian said, "no branches south of Piaseczno. And you'd be disappointed by the withdrawal limit."

She rose from the chair and slid the card into her purse. "We'll check that out once you're healthy enough to move." She stepped toward the door but stopped, checked something else in her purse. "By the way, you won't want to mess with those two guys anymore."

"I didn't want to mess with them in the first place."

She pulled out the scrap of phone-book cover that he'd taken from Krystyna's room. "I made some phone calls, found a language professor at Jagiellonian. 'Zakat' isn't Urdu, it's a Pashto word."

"Pashto?"

"A zakat is a tax on farm produce in Afghanistan."

"A what?"

"Which includes opium. Especially opium, if you ask the professor. The warlords, the Uzbeks, the various groups that control the border crossings, they all levy it, and the smugglers either pay it or they lose their cargo. Krystyna's people were running drugs."

Krystyna's letter. *An importer in Cracow,* she'd said of her boss. *Not a good man—not in the usual sense of the word.* Drugs made sense.

Teresa continued: "This professor, the Golden Crescent, he says, Pakistan, Afghanistan, Iran, he says if Krystyna's smugglers are paying zakats, they're not doing it for corn or honey." She gave him time to respond to that, then said, "I'll be back in a few hours."

And just like that, she got up and left.

He lay still a moment, took some time deciding this new information was useful rather than disturbing. He tried to sit up, but weakness set him back. He called out for a nurse, but no one came. The call button over his bed didn't work.

Now things were clearer. Platz must have known about the dope transports. That's why the two goons wanted her. But why would they think that he, Julian, was working with her? Armani and the brown-skinned man—Oskar? Oliver? No, the first name was correct: Oskar—they had no reason to fear him.

Unhooking the cast from the ring under the metal bar, Julian swung his feet into a pair of tattered hospital slippers. As he tried to stand, the room shifted beneath him. He lurched and stumbled before righting himself. Sweat chilled him as he floundered to the doorway and looked out at the vacant nurses' station across the hallway. The nurses were in the television room at the end of the corridor. The music from the TV sounded game-show chipper. Jurek the doorkeeper at *Gazeta Warszawy* often had it on in his little booth: *Dobra Cena*—The Price Is Right.

Julian made it across the hall by bracing against his IV holder. Cradling the phone between his chin and his good shoulder, he tried a nine and then a zero and found an outside line.

"*Gazeta Warszawy*," he told the operator, "collect. Julian Krol for Henryk Milewski."

He gave the operator the number, and after a short pause someone answered.

"*Gazeta.* Wanda Borowska speaking."

"Hi Wanda, it's Julian. I'm looking for Henryk."

"I'm Henryk today," Wanda said. "Henryk's in Gdansk. He left a message for you, said you'd call."

"What message?"

"Hold on a minute." He heard her sifting through papers. "First thing's a phone number. A guy named Artur Salda. You have a pen handy?"

Julian paused. Salda. He'd forgotten about him. He found a pen atop an ECG printout. "Okay, read it slowly."

Borowska gave him a number in Chicago, then said, "And there's a man named Oskar Ret in Cracow."

"When's Henryk get back?" he asked.

"Tomorrow," Wanda said.

"Where's he staying in Gdansk?"

"I don't know. Julian, it says here you shouldn't interview this Oskar Ret. It's kind of weird, but it says for me to tell you he's there in Cracow, but it says not to interview him—no matter what."

"I know why," Julian said. "He's not pleasant. Will you do me a favor, Wanda? Call a Lieutenant Daniel Kosinski at the Centrum Borough Komisariat. Tell him whatever Henryk told you. And tell him that Oskar Ret and one of his friends just tried to kill me."

Wanda missed a beat before saying, "What?"

"And tell him Oskar Ret's friend has access to Security Services files."

Julian looked down the hall. Shadows crawled the wall of the television room. *Wojciech Barin, zapraszamy do gry!*—Come on down! The hallway light dimmed and Julian's legs buckled. He righted himself, warded off collapse.

"I have to go," he said. "Tell Kosinski I'll call him."

He cut the connection, dialed the number to the operator, recited Artur Salda's phone number. He told the operator to charge the call to *Gazeta Warszawy.*

There was a delay. Someone had changed the channel on the nurses' television. A news anchor was now reporting that the opening of the special economic zone in Chelm would be postponed because of a scandal. A paper producer had tried to bribe its way into the zone.

Salda answered after the sixth or seventh ring, offered a groggy Polish *"Slucham"* instead of the English "Hello."

"Artur Salda?"

"Yes?"

"My name's Julian Krol, Krystyna Krol's brother."

"Who?" Salda asked.

"Julian Krol."

Salda mumbled, "Julian . . . who?"

"Krystyna's been murdered," Julian said.

A woman in a robe hobbled out of a nearby room, took slow, painful steps toward the washroom.

When Salda spoke again, he was in a different world. "Murdered? My God. . . ."

"Lydia Debkowska says you kept in touch with her. With Krystyna. When no one else did."

"Jesus," Salda said.

"When was the last time you spoke with her?"

"Mr. Krol, this is a shock. I mean, I don't even know what you—"

"Look at it this way," Julian said. "For me, it won't ever *stop* being a shock."

After a pause, Salda said, "I haven't seen her for almost three years."

"Okay, but back then she cut contact with everyone she knew in Warsaw. She made a point of getting lost. You were the only exception. Why was that?"

Another pause. Julian was about to continue when Salda said, "Because of the abortion."

The phone slipped from Julian's shoulder. He snapped it back up. "What did you say?"

"I know you didn't know this. She'd had—"

"What did you say?"

"She found out she was pregnant. About a month before she quit school. I'm sorry, Julian. Jesus. What happened? What did she. . . ."

He was still speaking, but the words got lost. An abortion. Krystyna.

It explained a lot. It also hurt almost as much as the news of her death.

"I'm not sure I'm hearing this right," Julian said.

"She didn't want to tell you about it. She said you'd go crazy on her, make her life a living hell. She was scared, and so was I. Neither of us wanted a child, but we couldn't afford to . . . we just couldn't handle it."

"You didn't tell *anybody?*"

"Abortion was illegal. Still is over there, right? And what woman ever discusses such things anyway? If I remember, she *tried* to tell you about it. She tried to because she needed some money to get it done."

"She asked for money, but she—"

"But she was too afraid to tell you why. Right? Ashamed, too. So she simply asked for the cash. For the operation. And to spend some time getting herself together afterwards."

"She said she wanted it to pay the rent," Julian said—and now anger supplanted all other emotion. "Why didn't *you* pay for the damn thing?"

"The operation?" Salda said. "With what? I was broke."

"But rich enough to move to Chicago?"

"On a scholarship and borrowed money. Listen, I went to Chicago a week after the abortion. She only called me a few times after that, wanted nothing to do with me. We left it at that."

The room was starting to spin. Salda's voice was turning to an echo. Julian hoped it would stop altogether.

"I don't really know what you're looking for," Salda said, "but if there's anything I can do, I mean, anything at all—"

"There's nothing," Julian said. Then, softly, as if admitting something horrible, "Thank you for being straight with me."

Hanging up, he fumbled the phone again.

So there it was, the main thing on her mind the last time they'd spoken. He started toward his room, a marathon on now-burning legs. He steadied himself at the doorway, and his brain ordered another step forward, but his muscles didn't respond. It was like standing in the middle of a dream with stuttering gaps. Curious. One moment he felt he could move forward, and then, vaguely, but only vaguely, he saw the ground rising up to meet him.

And felt the floor's cold, hard linoleum against his cheek. He sensed his eyes rolling inward, watched his own dream-like state melt into full-out hallucination. There was now something strange in his world, something that was neither here nor there but that was fundamentally relevant. There were no barriers, no walls or ceilings, only a cold floor and enveloping darkness and an endless wall of china, of all things, the Czechoslovakian china that his mother had once collected—cup after saucer after plate, each piece falling, one by one, onto a shattering floor. And he was down there on that floor, on his knees, grasping after the barrage like an overwhelmed juggler. He was deafened by a million destructions, was a tiny element in the blitz. He couldn't keep up, couldn't hold onto one single piece of china.

Chapter 17

The drug dealer was late. Lieutenant Daniel Kosinski sat on the concrete steps along the Vistula River levy and opened a copy of *Gazeta Warszawy.* The odor from the river was of something dying, of untreated sewage mingling with weedy life. For local fishermen the liquid muck was good news, as the Vistula's chub and pike-perch were drawn to the smorgasbord at the outlets. The shoreline around the sewers was prime real estate, with fishermen angling for the best of the dumping ground's pickings.

A large-font quote on page two of *Gazeta Warszawy* caught Kosinski's eye. *"Unemployment is not a problem. Given the economic indicators, the numbers work out just fine."*

The words were from a young government economist, an ivory-tower genius. There were beggars in the streets, four in ten people scrounging for rent money, violent crime growing by double digits each year. Maybe for the young economist it was easy to see the bottom line because he had no real contact with the bottom.

Kosinski glanced at the fishermen and flipped to another story, a feature on a Starochowice man who had chopped off his friend's head on a drunken bet. *Newsweek* had picked up the story, run it worldwide.

Then he heard the Ukrainian accent behind him:

"Paranoid old bastard. Whacked me in the head with a baseball bat."

Kosinski looked up. Hryczuk was holding a cloth to his forehead.

"What happened?"

Hryczuk sat down gently. He hawked up some phlegm. "Money first. Two million, like you said."

Kosinski pulled from his pocket four golden objects that gleamed in the sun. Hryczuk took them and looked like he wanted to toss them in the water. They were lapel pins, miniature busts of Vladimir Lenin.

"This doesn't look like two million zlotys."

"They're gold. Be smart when you sell them, you'll get more than that."

"The deal was cash," Hryczuk said.

"It's the best I can do. Thank the chief of the Volgograd militia. Tokens of his visit in eighty-one."

Hryczuk hesitated, but pocketed the pins.

"You get a doctor to see your head?" Kosinski asked.

"Hospitals are for dying in."

Kosinski whacked the newspaper against the step. "Okay. Then what happened?"

"Mrs. Baraniec, apartment four thirteen. She spoke with your hooker. Cornered her the day she moved in, invited her over for tea."

Baraniec, Krystyna Krol's neighbor, was a sixty-four-year-old widow. "Lonely and talkative, right?"

"Yeah," Hryczuk said.

"I interviewed her myself. Why didn't she tell me she spoke with her?"

"Because you didn't threaten to hold her head to the stove."

Kosinski gaped at him. "You didn't."

"You wanted results, right? She says your hooker told her to fuck off, said she wouldn't be around long enough to make friends. Did you know your girl was leaving the country?"

"Yeah? For where?"

"Didn't say. Just that she was catching a flight. That was the only time Baraniec saw her."

"Baraniec hear anything the night of the murder?" Kosinski asked.

"Loud music and a disturbance. Like a husband-and-wife thing, she said. Except I don't suppose hookers have domestic issues with their johns." Hryczuk thought the theory over for a moment. "She didn't tell the cops this because she was afraid the guy would come back."

"What guy?"

"Whoever it was that had the fight with her."

"And the other neighbors?"

"Zawada clubbed me, the rest didn't hear anything—or at least they said so." Tossing a rock into the river, Hryczuk moaned, "Fucking baseball bats. Things ought to be illegal."

"They are," Kosinski said, "in about a dozen municipalities." He pulled a photograph from his pocket and handed it to Hryczuk. "Look familiar?"

Hryczuk took in a mug shot of a dark-skinned man with a tree stump for a neck. He said, "Never seen him."

Kosinski had procured the photo after a confusing phone call from a *Gazeta Warszawy* editor named Wanda Borowska. Borowska gave him the name Oskar Ret, said the guy had assaulted Julian Krol in Cracow, and had been in possession of Krol's Security Services file. Krol himself had instructed her to call Kosinski with this information.

"Look closely," Kosinski said. "Be certain."

"I'm certain," Hryczuk said. "I never forget a face."

"Well, you and this guy have overlapping prison records. He was in the Wola the same time as you."

"What was his rap?"

"He got in a fight in the casino at the Victoria Hotel. He

stabbed a guy in the spleen."

Hryczuk narrowed his eyes. "Must have been on a different block. What is he? Georgian? Chechen?"

"Polish," Kosinski said. "His mother's Romanian."

Hryczuk shook his head and handed back the mug shot. "I was in the Wola for only two months. You're saying he's involved in your meth thing?"

"That's what I'm trying to find out."

Hryczuk picked up a twig and doodled a circle in the dirt. "Why are you so gung-ho about this?"

"What do you mean?" Kosinski asked.

"Why don't you do what you cops usually do? You need a perp, go find some bum who can't defend himself. Lock him up, move on. This meth dealer's really that important?"

A fisherman reeled in a finger-sized roach. He dropped the fish into a metal basket holding a dozen or so other fish.

"Why is it," Kosinski said, "that a cop can't simply want to do a worthy job well? Why does everything have to be corrupt?"

Hryczuk spat into the turbid water. "Maybe you should ask your pals at the komisariat that."

Kosinski looked long and hard at him. "Hryczuk, what are you doing selling dope for a living?"

"How long you been a cop?"

"I asked you first."

"Humor me."

"Thirty-seven years," Kosinski said.

"And how much money you have socked away?"

"That's none of your business."

"I thought so. Zip. And I know what your cop pensions are like. The papers keep telling me how they're 'adjusted' for inflation. You'll get nothing for your old age yet you'll stick to the job anyway. You're a do-gooder, a blind Samaritan. Like you're making a difference. In a year or two you'll be wondering if you can afford the sunflower bread or if you should stick to the rye. And I'll be sitting in my booth at the Bartek, doing business, living well. I won't worry about rent, won't worry about the next meal." He grinned as if he'd finally cornered Kosinski. "That's why I sell dope. Because it works."

Kosinski slapped a mosquito on his neck and took back the photo of Oskar Ret. "Funny," he said, "for a second there you sounded bright."

Hryczuk shrugged.

Kosinski asked, "You been checking on Walesa?"

"Gone," Hryczuk said, "a few months ago."

"Where?"

"Uganda. How should I know? Anyway, if your overdose was recent, you're probably looking for someone else. And no one on the street is talking about Angel Fire. At least, not to me."

Okay. Kosinski gained his feet and slapped the dirt from his trousers. "My friend, in the future, I don't want to hear your name come up in the precinct."

"Meaning this is good-bye?"

"Let's hope for good. My guys won't bother you, but if you don't keep your business small, I won't be able to help you."

"What's the rush? I just took a whack on the head for you. Sit a while."

"You lonely? Starting to like me?"

Hryczuk laughed. "Naw. Go ahead. Go clean up the streets."

Kosinski pointed to the newspaper. "If you believe what you read, they don't need cleaning."

"Oh?"

"No. Because 'the numbers work out just fine.' " He shook Hryczuk's hand and offered a piece of parting advice. "Be good, Fryderyk."

He returned to his car and drove toward Okecie Airport. There was a demonstration outside the Royal Castle, which meant a fifteen-minute traffic jam on Krakowskie Przedmiescie. While a pair of street children washed his windshield, Kosinski watched Warsaw shopkeepers mass for a march to the Presidential Palace. They would protest a new law allowing foreign supermarket chains to purchase Polish land with few restrictions. Another "anti-Poland" directive from the European Community.

Shops Equal Jobs, read one banner.

Polish land, Polish owners, read another.

The head of the Warsaw Shopkeepers Union promised through a megaphone that shop owners would erect barricades in front of new supermarkets. They would also storm the mayor's office, do as the disgruntled citizenry in proud villages once did, stuff the traitorous local bureaucrat into a wheelbarrow and push the bastard down the street for all to chide and deride. The union head thundered that the average Pole didn't mind having to shop at different stores for milk and bread and veggies. The average Pole demanded only that the shopkeeper be a countryman. The French chains were planning to colonize Poland through the proliferation of cleverly packaged foodstuffs.

The drive to the airport took almost an hour. At the LOT Airlines desk on the departures level, Kosinski flashed his ID and told the young man there to go find his boss. A few minutes later, Kosinski sat in an office with the Head of Ticketing and Reservations, a man named Wiktor Dutkiewicz.

Dutkiewicz scrutinized the police ID through sloe-black eyes. "Something we did," he asked, "or something a passenger did?"

"Neither. A peripheral bit of information."

Dutkiewicz tapped the desk with a pen.

"It's a murder case," Kosinski said. "I want you to check your records, see if there's a ticket in the victim's name."

"A murder case."

"The victim was planning to leave Poland. If you have a

reservation for her, your computers will have a notation on where the reservation was made. And how it was paid for."

"So you're after the purchaser's credit card number," Dutkiewicz said.

"That's right."

"You need a court order for personal information on customers. I'm sure you know that, lieutenant. And this airline has a strict policy. No disclosure of client information."

"The laws will be changed soon," Kosinski said. "I'm appealing to your sense of justice."

"I'm afraid that's not good enough," Dutkiewicz said.

"You're kidding."

"Do I look like I'm kidding?"

He didn't. He looked like he thought cops were walking garbage.

Kosinski said, "Law or no law, I can think of three judges offhand who would sign a compliance order. But the petition process takes time. I don't have that time."

"Think of my position," Dutkiewicz said. "Handing out names would jeopardize customer confidence. The least we can do is give our customers full protection under the law."

Dutkiewicz let out a cavernous yawn, locked his hands behind his head. That cops-are-garbage look grew even stronger.

"You know, lieutenant, my country house was broken into last winter. You guys didn't even dust for prints. You said there was no way you'd find the guy."

"Funny," Kosinski said, "I don't remember telling you that."

"Go get your court order. You'll need it."

Kosinski sat still a moment. When he gained his feet, he moved in slow motion, made a show of looking defeated. "Sorry for the trouble. I hope you've been a conscientious taxpayer."

"You what?"

"My petition will include a request for access to your bank records."

Dutkiewicz's eyes widened. "You would have to charge me with something."

"No, I wouldn't. That's another law they're still working on."

"But you can't just—"

"I can and I will. Borough prosecutors can use their discretion in authorizing searches. I know a few who have good discretion."

Four minutes later, Kosinski had what he wanted: Warsaw–Frankfurt–Lahore, July 15, under the name Krystyna Krol. One way. The ticket buyer had paid with a MasterCard at a Cracow travel agency on July 2. The payment was for one ticket and one ticket only, and the purchaser was listed as one Konrad Markat.

"Can I use your phone?" Kosinski asked.

Dutkiewicz muttered something and stomped out of his own office.

Kosinski picked up the receiver and called the komisariat, told the desk sergeant to do a record check on Markat. Then he headed out to his car. He was outside the terminal, passing through a group of German tourists, when all at once he realized he'd forgotten about—and missed—his job interview with the magazine distributor.

So much for selling *Wpost* and *Naj* and *Newsweek Polska* for a living.

Not that it mattered. It would take a few days until the urge to change jobs flared again. The desire came and went.

Chapter 18

Bullets for the Mauser would be at the apartment that the Hearts Companionship Agency rented for Teresa Nowak. The taxi driver was saying something, but Teresa was deep in thought. The man with the scar and his dark-skinned partner, they weren't just going to disappear. They were probably looking for her right now.

Teresa had a wealth of experience at feeling stressed and besieged. She'd been through both drink and drugs. She'd been beaten by dates and jailed by the police. Her mother had been an alcoholic prone to fits of violence; her father was in the Torun prison tower, locked away like Rapunzel for murdering a postman and stealing his cash disbursements for pensioners.

And she had pulled herself up from it all, taken the only livelihood available, survived the only way she knew how. Such a lifelong training course, she now told herself, watching the austere factories of southern Cracow fly by, should have taught her a little perspective. It should have made clear the merits of self-sufficiency. Count on no one. What kind of ploy was it to squeeze money out of a maimed and drug-dazed man who was suicidally bent on investigating his sister's murder? What kind of desperate stupidity was *that?*

It was the kind of thing Irena Platz would try. Irena, who had said she was going to Warsaw for the weekend, who had obviously been doing something else—something to bring the two men to Powisle Street. Irena was one blunder after another. She must have hatched some new scheme. Maybe she tried to horn in on Krystyna's smuggling business, scam something for herself. She'd certainly displayed interest in the job often enough, back when Krystyna was around to be prodded.

Teresa had the cabbie stop a block away from the Hearts apartment. She walked around the fourteen-story building and entered from the rear. Checking her purse for the gun, she climbed the stairs to the second floor. Apartment 209 was more of a bedroom than an apartment, two hundred square feet at a fairly priced two million zlotys per month. Only two other people had keys to the place. One was dead and the other was—Teresa had no idea where Irena was.

The door had a small nameplate and a gaudy iron heart at eye level, the only markings to distinguish it from the building's two hundred and twelve other apartments. Working the lock, Teresa heard footsteps from the other side, someone reacting to her presence. Her heart leapt into her throat. She drew her bulletless gun and pushed open the door. The two men she expected to encounter inside were not there. Instead, Irena stood next to the window, backed against the wall. Her clothes were rumpled, grass-green. A dark red line circled her wrist and her blonde hair fell into tangles at her shoulders. There was no longer makeup to cover her bruised eye. Her face was wet.

Teresa lowered the gun and sat on the giant red heart on the bedspread. "You see what happened to the apartment?"

"Yes."

"You owe me an explanation."

Irena dried her face with a towel. Water was running in the bathroom. She looked Teresa up and down. "Are you okay?"

"You got mixed up with Krystyna's smugglers, didn't you?"

Irena stepped into the cubicle washroom, splashed some water around. Finally, she said, "Look out the window. The maroon Mercedes."

Teresa crossed to the window and pulled back the curtain. It was the same car from yesterday, and no doubt inside it were the two men from yesterday. She stepped to the drawer, found the box of bullets. With trembling hands, she pushed the jacketed lead into the gun.

Irena kept talking from the washroom. "They worked with Krystyna on the import business. At least, one of them did. I don't know if they followed me or you. I just noticed them."

Irena stepped out of the washroom. Teresa studied her, saw that the bruise around her eye was starting to fade. "They came to the apartment because of you," she said. "What have you gotten us into?"

Irena pitched the towel at the bed and it landed on the floor. "We better get into this somewhere else."

She opened the door and Teresa followed her down the stairs and out the rear entrance. Looking back while they scurried forward, they crossed Lwowska Street and hopped onto a crowded streetcar heading toward the Old Town. They stood near the front, keeping other passengers between themselves and the back windows. Teresa peeked back between an army cadet and a young girl reading a William Wharton novel. She glimpsed the Mercedes creeping around a corner. The car caught up with the streetcar, followed it.

"Start talking, Irena."

"Krystyna's job, that interpreting—"

"For the smugglers."

"I've been checking into it."

"From what's happened today, I'd say you've been doing more than checking."

"They think Krystyna told us what they were doing before she killed herself."

Teresa paused. Irena sounded so sure of herself, so certain she had everything covered. There was a perverse kind of pleasure in now telling her, "Krystyna didn't kill herself. She was murdered."

The streetcar jerked and lurched. Teresa grabbed the rail over her head, saw that her roommate was, for once, speechless.

"Her brother came down from Warsaw. He says he has proof she was killed. These two guys showed up looking for you, then snatched him and beat the hell out of him. They did that because they thought he knew about their drugs."

"Their what?" Irena said.

"You didn't know they're running drugs?"

"No, I—"

"Then what have you been *doing,* Irena? How did you get someone so upset?"

She waited, but Irena only said, "Drugs?"

"Jesus." The car was still there, still just behind the streetcar. "Listen, what do you know about a garage? Lubon A-M."

Irena scrunched her eyes. "What?"

"Krystyna underlined its phone number in the phone book. And these two"—she pointed to the Mercedes—"it's the place they took her brother to work him over. Maybe they store the dope there or something. Krystyna tell you about the place?"

"No, never. What would a garage—"

"Krol also asked a lot of questions about Markat."

"Markat? He's mixed up in this?"

"I don't know. I just know Krol was asking questions."

"If Markat's involved," Irena said, "Krystyna would have told me."

"You're sure of that?"

"She never thought much of the guy."

The streetcar had stopped, taking on a group of Carmelite nuns. Martin Figur's Mercedes stopped too, but no one got out. Teresa checked the road ahead when they were rolling again. There wasn't time to grill Irena.

"The Kazimierz Komisariat is the next stop up. Tell them about the drugs, about these guys. Tell them to check out Markat, see if he's in on it like Krol says. Just don't mention my name."

"Don't what?" Irena said.

"I can't be around cops."

Irena gave her a searching look, but there wasn't time to explain.

"If I go into that komisariat, I won't come out. Something from a long time ago."

She watched her roommate eyeing the car. It wouldn't be unlike Irena to do something monumentally stupid right now. Like maybe try to talk to the two goons, think she could outsmart them.

"If you run straight to the komisariat," Krystyna said, "they won't catch you."

The streetcar slowed again. They pushed through the passengers, headed for the doors at the front.

Irena pointed to the car. "What if they don't follow me?"

"I've seen how much they want you. Don't worry, they'll follow." She added, "And I mean it, don't mention my name to the cops."

The streetcar stopped and Irena stepped onto the cobblestones. "I'll leave a message for you at Hearts."

She sprang toward the komisariat. Teresa heard the Mercedes' tires squeal, then saw the car launch after Irena, sending the streetcar's disembarked passengers diving for safety. When Irena reached the komisariat steps, the streetcar was moving again and one of the men from the Mercedes—the guy with the nice suit and the cut from eye to chin—was out of the car and sprinting over the cobblestones after her. He looked willing to follow her all the way into the building.

The streetcar clicked over the rails and turned onto Mala

Street. Teresa peered down the tracks, waited, and stepped off at the next stop. The street teemed with people. She walked past a catatonic beggar and a woman sweeping the sidewalk outside her block. She entered a milk bar, a dark place, windows covered by dusty shades. The daily special on the chalkboard was meatloaf and cabbage. Six or seven locals were eating. A few more were standing in line with trays. She pulled back one of the shades and looked outside.

Two or three minutes passed, and she decided that either the Mercedes had gone straight, missing Mala Street, or the two men had kept running after Irena only to back off once she reached the cop shop.

The Mauser, full of bullets, had a reassuring weight. She kept her hand inside her purse, maintaining contact with the cold, unyielding metal.

CHAPTER 19

With Platz inside the komisariat, Martin Figur rushed back to the Mercedes and backed it onto a side street with a narrow view of the entrance. From there, he spent almost an hour watching the komisariat doors. No cops dashed out. Platz did not leave the building escorted by cops. She was staying inside, and she knew his name, and Figur already knew how much she liked to drop names.

Sitting beside him, Oskar Ret watched the brick building in stoic silence. Figur took that as insubordination. Everything about Ret was an insult. The bullheaded half-breed was not exactly tortured about bringing Mirsk Industries all of this trouble, and he wasn't lifting a finger to reverse or mitigate it. He just tagged along while Figur worked. And he was wearing a three-piece Hugo Boss suit. The guy had made money somehow, but for the life of him, Figur couldn't fathom where. You needed energy to make money, didn't you? You had to make decisions, not sit there like a cripple, not simply wait for rewards to fall in your lap.

Figur checked his hair in the rearview mirror. "Hate to put you out," he said, "but we have to decide what to do."

Ret didn't twitch.

"Maybe she's not even reporting us," Figur said. "She *did* try to blackmail Mirsk. That's a crime. Maybe she's just using the komisariat as shelter."

Ret opened his door and stepped out of the car. "Let's call it a day," he said.

"That's the sum of your wisdom? Run?"

The Gypsy poked his head back in. "Learn when to cut your losses, Figur. It's over."

"Why doesn't this lack of ambition surprise me?"

"Kidnapping and aggravated assault. That's what we'll be charged with. I've already done time. It's not a fun thing."

"Not a single cop left the building," Figur said, "not since she went in. Shouldn't someone have at least popped out, taken a look around?"

"You need serious help, Figur."

The big man began to back away, so Figur drew his gun. "Stop making me come down on you. Get back in here."

Ret hesitated, lowered himself into the car, closed the door. Figur kept a relaxed grip on the gun, liked the feel of it.

"I came all the way down here to meet you," he said. "I was patient despite your principled-mute routine. And like you said, we don't have time to waste, cops might be coming. So I have few requests and I want to hear some answers."

Ret gave him an unpromising sigh.

"Number one, I want to see some of your blue jeans."

"I don't have any."

"Not a single pair? You said you moved tonnes. There'd be a pair or two somewhere."

"But I don't have any."

"I know you don't, because this kind of mess doesn't get started over blue jeans. What are you really running? Dope?"

Ret eyed the gun, then glanced at the komisariat. He seemed to gather that Figur wasn't bluffing, was capable of shooting him. "I've been handling transports," he said, "been doing it—"

"Explain 'transport.' "

"Been moving them for two years. Someone in Pakistan sets them up, someone else receives them. I make sure they get through Poland."

"Through?"

"To Germany. It's a transit job. I've been paid for some of the work, but they still owe me money."

"And you're getting paid through the Mieltor Salt Mine. Why?"

Ret eyed the gun. "Would you put that thing away?"

"You're partnering with someone at the mine?"

"I don't know why they're paying me there—I mean, at the mine rather than somewhere else. My boss fixed it that way. I don't work for Mirsk anymore. Haven't since I did security for him a few months ago. The man I work for—*he* works for Mirsk."

"Doing what?"

"Meeting bigwigs on behalf of Mirsk Industries. Ministry officials. Industry and Trade men."

"Why?"

"I was there for security, but my boss said he didn't need me for that, given it was ministry guys he was meeting. He put me onto the imports instead."

"You're very good at blurring the lines," Figur said, certain Ret was lying like he'd been with the blue jeans. "You forgot this little story back at the bar?"

"Back at the bar I wasn't staring at your gun."

"What's your boss's name?"

Ret paused. "Put the gun away, Figur."

Figur raised it even higher.

"His name's Konrad Markat," Ret said.

"Konrad Markat. And how can I reach him?"

Ret ground his jaw for a while, then handed over a business card. "If you're crazy enough to hang around, tell him I'm sorry I couldn't say good-bye."

Figur checked the card's two numbers. Both were for cell phones. "Doesn't he have a land line?"

"If he does, I don't know it. Don't be surprised if you get his voice mail."

Figur stared at the card. "So the smuggling has nothing to do with Mirsk, and this Markat is paying you through Mirsk's salt mine, and you yourself don't do anything for, with, or in relation to Antoni. Nothing apart from garden-variety security a while back. Am I getting this right?"

Ret nodded.

"And you have no idea why the mine would bestow upon Markat this generous favor of paying you?"

"Figur, as long as the money's in my bank account when it's supposed to be, I don't care."

"You weren't even curious?"

"Would you be? Would you go around asking questions and jeopardizing the payoffs?"

Figur still couldn't tie it together. Ret opened his door again and stepped onto the cobblestones. At first Figur didn't react. His memory ran a check on the name "Markat" and found no match. The mine wasn't paying Ret out of good will. Markat was earning the favor. Why hadn't Mirsk told him, Figur, this before sending him down here? Why had Mirsk given him that story about the Pruszkow Mafia?

When Figur looked up, Ret was almost to a taxi stand. Figur realized he was now pointing his gun at thin air. He pocketed it, scrambled out of the car, and caught up with Ret. Four bums near the taxi stand were playing chess on the sidewalk and debating whether the European Community leadership was composed of Freemasons or Jews.

"You still haven't answered the big one," Figur said. "What's your cargo? Drugs, guns, what?"

After a pause, Oskar said, "Afghani hashish."

Figur sagged. After all this time, all his suspicions, the final admission felt anticlimactic. Depressing, too.

"If a shipment gets stopped," Ret continued, "whoever's handling it gets locked up and possibly rolls over on everyone else involved." He pushed Figur aside and began walking. "I'm not going to be here for that."

Figur jumped around to the front, but Ret reached out and calmly shoved him aside.

"We're on a street," he said, "in broad daylight. What are you gonna do, shoot me?"

Chapter 20

Lieutenant Daniel Kosinski walked past Martin Figur's Mercedes on his way into the Kazimierz Borough Komisariat. The train trip south from Warsaw took only three hours, but that was enough time for his aging joints to stiffen. The creeping decrepitude reminded him of a song he'd learned while studying English thirty years ago. It was sung by another guy who was now a fogy, a big-lipped Englishman named Jagger—something about getting old—and how much of a drag it was.

Markat couldn't be reached from Warsaw—no answer at his phone numbers. The Kazimierz Komisariat had a file on him, though, and offered to send a copy to Warsaw.

"Not necessary," Kosinski had told the Cracow cop before boarding the train. "Just hold it for me. I want to come down and interview him."

Inside the komisariat he was met by a Lieutenant Sosnowski, a burly young cop who spoke as much with animated hand gestures as he did with his mouth. Inside Sosnowski's office, a place as cold and barren as Kosinski's Warsaw office, the Cracow cop spread out the Markat file and asked, with a broad sweep of his arms, how his humble resources could be of service.

"Homicide," Kosinski said. "A prostitute. Markat bought her a plane ticket just before she died." He added that he knew precious little about the man's background.

"Well, it's pretty much all here," Sosnowski said of the file. "Your man's a pimp. Has three companionship agencies and two other businesses—that we know of. He's slippery."

"Why isn't he locked up?"

"Because he has money and friends. Ministry friends. He was up for extortion last year, and for bribery once and assault twice. Word always came down to drop charges."

"Word from where, the prosecutor?"

Sosnowski nodded. "It doesn't take imagination to know why. His girls give companionship to men who value discretion."

Companionship. And Krystyna Krol had been a hooker. So she had worked for Markat?

"You said he has two other businesses," Kosinski said.

"There's the three agencies and a restaurant and a garage."

"The restaurant being Holst's, in the Old Town."

"You've done your homework," Sosnowski said.

"What about the garage?"

"He bought it from the commune government and closed it down. Hasn't done a thing with it, don't ask me why. It's one from the old Lubon A-M chain. Most of the other Lubons have been making money since being privatized."

Kosinski flipped back to the arrest record. Sosnowski hadn't been telling tales: there was indeed assault and bribery and extortion. But there were no charges relating to the sex trade. That seemed odd.

"A man like this, I'd imagine his assets exceed his taxable income."

Sosnowski shook his head. "He knows his bookkeeping. Most of his income comes through the agencies. He puts the money into cheap land. Bought a country house in the Drwinia Forest. He also owns a lot of farmland in Mieltor. Seems like everything on the Mieltor market, he puts in an offer for it."

"Why Mieltor, of all places?"

Sosnowski shrugged. The town, just south of Cracow, wasn't

much. It was known mainly for the thing beneath it, the world's oldest salt mine, a tourist magnet that had a restaurant, a museum and an endless labyrinth of subterranean tourist trails and chambers. It was the world's most-visited mine, and it was still functional enough to churn out quantities of salt that could supply a small country.

But the town above it was nothing, a place ravaged by hyper-inflation and structural unemployment.

In fact, it was worse than nothing—possibly the last place in Poland that any prudent real estate speculator would target. A good one-fifth of the town itself was sinking into the mine. Water had been leaking into the salt bed of an abandoned gallery for centuries. The more water, the more erosion. The mine installed pumps, but pumps could handle only a fraction of the deluge. Engineers tried plugging holes with slag and cement, but that was expensive, and with more than three hundred uncontrolled leaks, and more springing every week, they could never do it fast enough. The place was falling apart. Houses and roads were sinking. Every decade or so the train tracks leading out of town became so warped from the shifting earth that they had to be replaced. Real estate was selling for one-fifth of what it was in neighboring communes.

So it was cheap land, but it was cheap for a reason. And Markat was snatching it up?

Kosinski held up the file. "Mind if I take this to my hotel?"

Sosnowski said, "Sign it out. It can't leave the building for more than twenty-four hours."

"Thanks," Kosinski said. "I won't need it that long."

Irena couldn't believe her own nerve. She *still* couldn't get Canada out of her mind. She had been kidnapped and shot at. She'd gone home to Cracow running—home to a burnt-out husk of an apartment—and had been chased into this komisariat by men who had tried to kill her.

But *still* there were bedazzling thoughts of a clean, rich country and a chance at a new life.

Ale Kanada!

The great, good place. A broken record. A mantra that she knew she should probably lock in a trunk and drop to the bottom of the Baltic.

She sat at a bench across from the desk sergeant, a deep-voiced, no-nonsense cop who looked up from his paperwork and asked what her hurry was.

"No hurry," she said, "I'm waiting for a friend."

She needed time to think. Maybe she could tell the cops everything, admit she'd tried to con Mirsk, tell them Figur was armed and dangerous and going around torching apartments. Have the cops round up Figur and Ret and start checking into Krystyna's murder and that drug business that Teresa was so convinced about.

But something stopped her from doing that. Part of it was fear (would the cops arrest her for blackmailing Mirsk?) and part of it was puzzlement (how could she tell them this zany story without giving them Teresa Nowak's name? It was, after all, Teresa's apartment that had been torched).

And Canada. Canada refused to stop calling her. If she turned into a good citizen and confessed and shared everything with the cops, that would be the end of her hopes for a livable future.

And the end of hope would be the end of her.

There had to be an angle left—somewhere—a way of having all this turn out to her advantage. This wasn't a matter of greed; it was self-preservation. There were options out there, somewhere. There always were.

She stayed at the bench and wrestled with these thoughts for close to an hour. In the end, an image of her own death won out, an image of her lying in the forest somewhere, stiff, cold, being chewed up by warthogs. She walked over to the desk sergeant, who was busy writing something.

"This is gonna sound weird," she said, "but remember when I came in here and you asked me what my hurry was?"

The cop nodded.

"Well, I was running because I was being chased."

"Oh yeah?"

"By a couple men who tried to kill me. One of them smuggles dope. From Pakistan. The other one is head of security for a company called Mirsk Industries in Gdansk."

The cop stared at her as if she had three heads.

"I know," she said, "but it's all true."

"Mirsk as in Antoni Mirsk?" he asked. "The rich guy up north?"

"Yes," she said.

He looked her over, then looked past her, sought someone else in the empty room. "Sosnowski put you up to this?"

"You think I'm joking?"

"You were chased in here?"

"That's what I'm saying."

"So why sit on the bench and twiddle your thumbs for so long?"

That was a good question—one she knew would be hard to answer. The idea of being charged with blackmail kept her from saying anything.

"Tell Sosnowski very funny. I may be new here, but he'll have to do better than that."

The sergeant returned to his paperwork.

Another cop approached the desk. He was older, in his mid-sixties maybe, and he was carrying a folder. He showed the desk sergeant a Warsaw badge and said, "I want to remove this file from the building."

The desk sergeant leaned over and studied the folder. "Show

me the number."

"U-L-six-one-oh-three," the Warsaw cop said, "Konrad Markat."

He held the file out for the sergeant, just inches from Irena. It was so handy that she found it only natural to snatch it out of his hand and read the name for herself. Yes, she had heard right. Konrad Markat.

The desk sergeant snapped the folder back from her and stood up. "All right, Miss, enough's enough."

"I know that man," she told the Warsaw cop.

"Yeah?" Kosinski said.

"I mean, I've never met him, but I know him."

The desk sergeant said, "Never mind her. She's Sosnowki's cousin or something."

What was it Teresa had said on the streetcar? That Krystyna's brother thought Markat was involved in the murder?

"Any chance," Irena said to the Warsaw cop, "that you're here because of Krystyna Krol?"

The Warsaw cop took her to an office and introduced himself as Lieutenant Daniel Kosinski from Warsaw's Centrum Borough Komisariat. The way he asked questions—and gave her time to answer those questions—he struck her as genuinely kind, not a strutting, self-important pig who thought a badge was an aphrodisiac.

He told her yes, he was working on the murder of the hooker Krystyna Krol, and she replied that she'd been a friend of Krystyna's, said Krystyna had worked at one of Markat's companionship agencies.

She was ready to talk to this guy, to tell him what had gone down with Mirsk and Oskar Ret, to urge him to get that psycho Figur off the streets. He asked her for her home address, and she gave him something off the top of her head, said nothing about Teresa or the burnt-out apartment. She asked him how Krystyna died, and he said someone had poisoned her with methamphetamine and hashish.

Kosinski handed her some coffee. "How well do you know Markat?"

"I don't. I just know Krystyna worked for him."

"Did their relationship go beyond that of employer and employee?"

"Was he screwing her? No."

"Krystyna Krol was an educated woman," Kosinski said. "Did she work for Markat in any other capacity?"

Oskar Ret's trafficking operation came to mind, but that had nothing to with Markat. "If she did, she would have told me."

Kosinski sipped his coffee. "You two were close?"

"As close as was possible with her. Krystyna wasn't exactly a people person."

"Markat bought her an airline ticket for Pakistan. Do you know why?"

Pakistan. So Markat *was* in on the drugs.

But something sounded wrong here. Mirsk and Figur wanted her, Irena, quiet, but they professed not to be in on the drug operation. And she believed them. Markat now appeared to be in on Oskar Ret's business, but had no clear link to Mirsk and Figur. Confusing. And within the confusion lay a vivid possibility:

Irena. You fool. You went and blackmailed the wrong guy.

If only Krystyna had told her something—anything—to suggest Markat was involved in the smuggling. If only things had grown a little clearer before Krystyna moved to Warsaw. Irena could have gone after a small-time *alfons* rather than the daunting businessman Mirsk. She could have left the tiger alone and gone after the cub.

"Krystyna never said anything about Pakistan," she told Kosinski. "As far as I knew, Markat was just her *alfons.*"

Kosinski said delicately, "Are you, also—"

"Yes, I am."

"Krystyna moved to Warsaw three weeks before she died. She tell you why?"

"For a new start. To get out of the life."

"Yet she was hooking in Warsaw."

"Oh yeah?"

"You don't sound surprised by that."

"Because I'm not." She told him the Krystyna she knew didn't have the confidence to brave new conditions. You don't just stop hooking overnight. If you *could* do that, all the girls would walk away. There were always outside factors at play, conditions that dictated that this type of work continue to be done.

But Krystyna moving to Pakistan? That was a new one.

Irena fought to slow her thoughts. A new idea took root:

Maybe hold off on telling this cop about Figur and Ret and everything else. For now. Maybe first . . . work on Konrad Markat?

"Miss Platz?"

Kosinski was staring at her. She snapped out of it and he moved to less delicate questions. Did Krystyna ever take drugs? Emphatically no. Had she been at odds with anyone—serious odds? No. Depressed? No. Who owns the Hearts Companionship Agency? I don't know. Can I reach you there? Yes. The longer Irena sat there, the more convinced she became that Markat had a lot to lose by her getting cozy with the cops. Maybe she could go to him and find out just *how much* he had to lose. She could even help him put a zloty figure on it.

Kosinski wound up the interview with a confused look. "Miss Platz, why are you here?"

"What do you mean?"

"In this komisariat. What brings you here?"

She shifted in her chair. "It's a little embarrassing."

"You don't look like you blush easily."

"I was visiting a friend."

He nodded, thought it over. "You're not planning any trips in the next few days? You can be reached at the number you gave me?"

"I'll be around," she said.

She left the komisariat through a side door. Figur and Ret weren't there, so she walked the crowded street without fear.

Bear down, she told herself, there's one last shot, one last ticket to the great, good place.

Make the most of Markat.

CHAPTER 21

Martin Figur crinkled his nose at an awful stench. The smell was coming from right there in the car. He checked the passenger seat, but it couldn't be Oskar Ret, because the big guy was gone.

Garbage, maybe. Something rotting.

He rolled down all the windows and flipped the air conditioning on high. Then he knew the smell was coming from his own clothes.

Which mortified him.

Never in his adult life had he been two full days without a shower. His two-million-zloty broadcloth cotton shirt might be putrefied beyond cleansing.

He drove to Florianska Street, found a haberdashery next to the McDonald's. He stepped inside and told the sales clerk, "That one, the beige one, you have it in forty-three?"

The clerk brought him the shirt and he checked the label.

Wolczanka. Polish.

"You have any Enzo Dipiano?"

The clerk nodded, brought him a beige one and a white one. Figur bought the white one and took it next door into the McDonald's. The brand new fast-food joint had received bomb threats from haters of American junk culture, but it had the cleanest public washrooms around. Free, too, no need to dig out a couple thousand zlotys for a depressing old gatekeeper.

After scrubbing his armpits raw with soaped-up paper towels,

Figur trashed the old shirt and donned the new one. Then he removed his bandage and checked his hamburger face in the mirror. Not bad. The cut might not leave a scar, at least not a bad one. He returned to the car feeling invigorated.

Then he used his mobile phone to call the numbers on Oskar Ret's business card—the numbers to Konrad Markat.

There was no answer, not even voice mail, so he pushed auto-dial and waited for Antoni Mirsk to say hello from Gdansk.

"Why'd you send me down here?" Figur asked him.

"What do you mean?" Mirsk said. "Did you meet Ret?"

"Yes, I met Ret. But why'd you send me down here without telling me what the deal was at your salt mine? Ret says you have a man named Markat meeting government men on your behalf. You knew all along that Ret works for Markat. You could have told me that instead of feeding me that story about the Pruszkow Mafia."

"Easy," Mirsk said, "just calm down. What's going on down there?"

"Screw you, that's what's going on. What am I, your lackey? Dumb muscle you can dispatch when trouble starts?"

After a pause, Mirsk said, "I don't know any Markat. If I did, I'd have told you. Why'd you think I wanted you down there? To get information. What's the status with Platz?"

The question deflated Figur. "She got away."

"She what?"

"And things have happened that can cause us serious trouble."

"Martin, I *told* you not to act like a cowboy."

"It's what you didn't tell me that worries me."

There was a pause before Mirsk spoke again. "Look, this is hardly the time to be getting into this. Let's talk bottom line. What's the worst thing that can happen next?"

"Platz can talk to the cops," Figur said, "and you and I can get measured for prison-issue pinstripes."

"Then I suggest you get off the phone and get back to work. Go find her."

Sound advice had a way of hitting home.

"Whatever you're holding back," Figur said, "I swear, if I go down, I'll be taking you with me."

"I'm not holding—"

"My loyalty ends where prison starts. Try to remember that."

Chapter 22

Teresa Nowak was there when he woke up again, looking down at him with that same measured expression, the same caution. Someone had put him back in bed, rehooked the cast to the rod.

"Sorry," Julian told her, "I still haven't gone apartment shopping."

"The nurse said they found you on the floor."

"I was checking lino patterns for your kitchen."

She leaned in closer. "That stuff I said, that bit about you owing me, I was pretty upset."

She looked more attractive now, without the edge, without the protective mask of mistrust.

"I do owe you," he said. "I'll check around, see what I can do. In the meantime, if you need a place to stay, Krystyna's old room is still empty."

"You're kidding," Teresa said.

"If you have another idea, that's fine, too."

She appeared to think it over; there wasn't much choice.

But there was something else right now. Julian said, "I have to call a cop in Warsaw."

Which brought back the mask of mistrust. She said, "I figured you'd get to the cops. Just make sure you leave me out of it."

Julian tried to sit up but couldn't. "You said that before, but it would be hard, wouldn't it? It was your place that they—"

"Look, I'm going to tell you a story. So you understand."

"A story."

"There was this man, a date, back before I worked for Hearts."

"You don't have to explain—"

"How do you know what I have to do and what I don't?" She gave him time to respond. When he didn't, she continued. "His name was Waldek, and he was a cop. We used to meet at his apartment. He was always—"

"A cop?"

"Gentle," Teresa said. "That's what he was, gentle. I liked him, in a sad kind of way. Shy. Not a big cop, not one of those guys who lord it over you. We were in his apartment one night drinking mead. He was talking about work, about some drunk driver or something. He was like that. Never rushed into things. Believed in a kind of decorum."

"Some cops are big on procedure," Julian said.

"He was talking about—saying I can't remember what, and then from out of nowhere he asked if I wouldn't mind if his ex-wife joined us for the evening. This timid little man who shouldn't have been on the force. I hadn't even known he was divorced, wouldn't have cared if I had. I told him yes, I would mind, because I didn't do that kind of thing. I knew girls who did, but I didn't. And wouldn't."

"And how'd he take that?" Julian asked.

"Quietly, at first, as if he'd expected the answer. But then, a few minutes later, he said I didn't understand, the thing with his ex-wife had to happen with me, not with some strange girl who might've been sleeping with farm animals for all he knew. He said he thought he'd become something real for me, not just another date. We were turning into something."

Julian asked, "Does that happen often?"

She looked surprised. "You mean men getting territorial? Like clockwork. Men always expect to set the rules. When they fall for you they assume they've won some kind of power over you. I told him in case he forgot, he was paying me a million and a half a week for our special 'something.' My obligations started and stopped there."

"You said you liked him," Julian said.

"I like lots of things. He was a Tuesday night."

"So what happened?"

"At first the obvious. He sat there looking lovesick. You'd be surprised how many men get that way, Krol. You'd be surprised how breakable men can be when they understand they've been foolish with women. I knew right then, when I saw his face, it would be best to get out of there. When they start getting sloppy, they get unpredictable. I told him we shouldn't meet again for a while. I told him to snap out of it, be a man, take no for an answer. That's when he did it.

"He lost it. He grabbed me, started to choke me. There was murder in his grip, a kind of lost fury, another thing that's common with men. Women walk away when they've been beaten; men only accept loss if it's dished out by someone stronger than them. He hit me, and kept hitting me, wildly. I was certain he'd kill me. He stopped only when the doorbell rang."

"The doorbell," Julian said, getting an idea of where this was going.

Teresa lit a cigarette, used a pill cup for an ashtray. The nurses would come running when they smelled the smoke, but Julian said nothing.

"It was the ex-wife arriving," Teresa said. "He'd invited her. Uncharacteristically confident of him. He hesitated when he heard the bell, and I picked up the mead bottle and hit him with it. I did it like you might stab someone—not over the head, but straight on, in the face. The bottle shattered and the piece of glass went deep into his face."

She cleared her throat and looked away. Then she pressed on, looking Julian in the eyes. "I got out of there. I walked right past his ex. When I got outside I heard her scream and saw lights go on in other apartments. I took a taxi home and waited for the cops to come. But they didn't. I'd never told Waldek my real name, and the neighbors had no idea who I was."

"But they knew your face," Julian said. "And they were sure to figure out what you did for a living."

"Which was why I didn't leave my apartment for a month. I told a friend I had *grypa,* had her do my shopping. Then I moved and took the job at Hearts. I'm sure I left something at his apartment. Fingerprints or something. And I'm sure there's a composite sketch of me in every komisariat's files." She paused, let the story sink in. "So, Krol, *that's* why there can't be cops. You want to phone your cop, I can't stop you. But do me the courtesy of letting me know about it first. Give me time to get out of the way."

Maybe it was too late for that. The talk with Wanda yesterday . . . by now, Milewski would have phoned Lieutenant Kosinski. Kosinski would be casting a net for Oskar Ret and Konrad Markat and whoever else those file checks unearthed. But "Teresa Nowak," maybe *that* was a fake name, an on-the-run name.

"I'll call the cops later," Julian said. "Tell me what you know about Markat."

"What's that mean? I already told you, back in the apartment."

"You didn't strike me as forthcoming."

"You know what your problem is, Krol? It's not that you have no tact, which you don't. It's that you think you can read people when really you can't. You grasp at things. You *hope* that certain things will be thus and so. What I told you yesterday, it was the truth."

"I've been wondering," Julian said, "how many *alfons*es own restaurants and run drugs? I need to see what they're using Lubon A-M for."

Her eyebrows jumped. "Haven't you had enough of the place?"

"They're using the office. Maybe they keep dope there. Maybe they—"

"It's an abandoned garage, Krol."

"Then why did Krystyna keep the address? If they're running drugs, it's a transit point. Maybe they're—"

"You are unbelievable."

Julian couldn't stifle a sad chuckle. "This whole thing is unbelievable. My thumb is unbelievable. And if Markat's goons think I've been scared off, that can only work in my favor."

"Then call the cops," Teresa said, "anonymously. Why go there?" She dropped her cigarette into the pill cup, let it smolder. "I broke you out of the place. I'm not breaking you back in."

"You don't have to," Julian said. "All I want to do, I want to watch the building, see if anyone comes or goes. Then I'll back off and make the call. Anonymously, like you said." He indicated his useless arms. "You can drive, I can't. You know where the place is, I don't."

"I don't have a car," she said.

"We'll take a cab. We'll just sit there. Watch."

She missed a beat, which was a good sign. Julian did his best to look wounded and at her mercy.

She said, "There's the issue of your health."

"I'll be fine," he said.

"They said you'll lose your thumb if you're not careful."

"I'll take the chance. Will you take me there, or should I call my cop?"

He sat up—this time he had the strength—and unhooked his cast from the metal rod. She wavered a moment, then muttered something about him being typical, and went to find his clothes.

With the nurses watching TV down the hall, he probed the unit desk's drawers for painkillers. There was a box of meperidine, hoo-ha pills that killed pain but produced a bit of a high. He knew of a soccer player who'd taken it after knee surgery. He pocketed the drugs and hoped Teresa would have no trouble finding his clothes. Maybe she'd have to bribe a nurse or a janitor. She had the resources to do that. She had his wallet.

She returned with the clothes a few minutes later, and they left the hospital like leaving a cinema, joining a line of people and walking slowly.

Outside, the sun blinded him. His thumb throbbed against the cast. He held it gingerly to his chest, and they hopped into a taxi, which bounced them over a potholed road. The streets were crowded. Women and children lined the road selling blueberries and mushrooms. Horse-drawn hay wagons held up traffic. Every railway crossing brought a wait for cars and peasants and their cows. Julian swallowed a meperidine pill, and when the taxi stopped at the Okay Bar across from the garage, Teresa paid the fare with money from his wallet.

"Lunch," she said, "is going to be on you."

Chapter 23

Konrad Markat looked for a parking spot. A space opened up right outside the ministry building, but a small Fiat zipped in to fill it.

"Thanks," Markat said, and kept driving. He thought back to his meeting with Julian Krol. Krol had seemed determined. He would learn (if he hadn't already) that Krystyna had worked for Markat through Hearts. Krol was a reporter. He'd have no trouble digging it up.

And he would take it to the police, who in turn would start looking for him, Konrad Markat. They might even see him as a suspect.

No, they wouldn't. Krystyna had died in Warsaw, while Markat had left plenty of footprints around Cracow the day of the death. The alibi was strong.

Another parking spot opened up. He had the angle on the BMW beside him, so he gunned the engine and lurched into the spot and parked.

And told himself to calm down. One more day—that was all he needed. One more job, one more transport. After that, everything ended. Krol could do whatever he liked.

Still, striding into the office of the Industry and Trade Ministry, he felt a little off. Dizzy, maybe, like too much was happening too fast. Walking the corridor, he checked his cell phone log. Six numbers were listed, none of which rang a bell.

Ignore them. Avoid the unknown.

He found the door he wanted and walked in. A receptionist behind a desk looked up at him. Markat told her, "I'm here to see Deputy-Minister Mrozow. The name's Konrad Markat."

She flipped through a desk calendar. "I don't see an appointment."

"I don't have one," Markat said. "Just tell him I'm here. He'll want to see me."

She hesitated, then picked up her phone and said something sotto.

"He'll be with you in a minute," she said.

He'll be with me now.

Markat crossed in front of her desk and entered Mrozow's office. Inside, Deputy Industry Minister Edward Mrozow looked up from behind his cherry desk. Taking in Markat's presence, he shook his head sadly—and Markat had a good idea of what he was thinking. To Mrozow, Markat was a puppy who'd just chewed a slipper or peed on the rug.

"We have to talk," Markat said.

"Do we?"

"Afraid so." He almost added, *you moron.* Markat had never liked Mrozow, and he knew the feeling was mutual.

"Let's go somewhere," Mrozow said as Markat sat down. Markat just stayed in the chair until Mrozow, too, took a seat. There was an abstract painting on the wall. Markat wondered what the attraction was.

"I thought I told you," Mrozow said, "you are never to come to the office. I decide when and where we meet."

"Then try returning my calls," Markat said. "I don't work for you. I work for Antoni."

Mrozow snorted. "Good for you."

"Yes, good for me. Very good for me."

"How'd Mirsk hook up with a guy like you, anyway?"

"What exactly is a guy like me like?"

"Excuse me?"

"I'm curious. You seem to know."

Mrozow sat back and sighed. "Let's not do this."

Markat leaned over the desk. "No, I want to know. I mean, I know what a guy like Antoni is like, but what is a guy like me like?"

Mrozow began fidgeting with a pen.

"Well?"

"Leave," Mrozow said. "I'm not going to—"

"Listen," Markat said, "you're new to government. You don't know how things worked in the old days."

"How did they work in the old days?"

"Men worked together. They had respect. Someone stepped out of line, he was set straight. To get things done, people relied on each other."

"So that's what I'm doing?" Mrozow said. "Stepping out of line? You hear that bit in a movie?"

"You're feeling good," Markat said. "You're sensing your place in the hierarchy. But there is no hierarchy. There's only business, tasks to carry out. You either do the things that can be done or you don't. Either way, you don't go around and bitch, because you have no right. You've put yourself in the spot you're in. Understand?"

Mrozow nodded, but it was clear he had no clue what Markat was talking about.

Forget it. He'll learn the hard way.

"Antoni wants to start building next spring," Markat said.

Mrozow's eyebrows jumped. "That soon?"

"He wants to use the tax relief now. You know he—"

"Relax," Mrozow said. "He won. The SEC permit was sent to him three days ago."

"I didn't see anything in the papers," Markat said.

"A press release was sent to the Polish Press Agency. Maybe

they didn't run it." Mrozow fumbled with the pen again, this time in a hurry. The pen clattered to the floor. "I have to tell you something, just between you and me."

"You see?" Markat said. "That's what I was just talking about. *All of this* is just between you and me."

"When the trade people set up their customs office in Mieltor, I can't do a thing for Mirsk."

"I'm sure he knows that," Markat said.

"Those guys are clean."

"Unlike you."

Mrozow paused only briefly. "Everything has to be aboveboard."

"That's Antoni's problem," Markat said. "Far as I'm concerned, I've done my job. I just needed to know how things turned out."

He stood up to leave.

"Wait," Mrozow said.

"Don't take this the wrong way," Markat said, "but I don't want to look at you anymore."

"I got a call from Interior yesterday."

Interior. Heat rose in Markat's cheeks. He sat down.

"A friend of mine pulled an old Security Services file for a man of yours a few days ago, a man named Oskar Ret. The file was on a political named Krol."

Mrozow grinned, enjoying the discomfort on Markat's face. "My friend says you owe him for pulling the file. I told him I'd tell you that."

"Good of you," Markat said.

Mrozow leaned in closer. "Konrad, people have made sacrifices. I did a lot of arm-twisting to get Mirsk into that zone. If something's putting his permit at risk—"

"Nothing's at risk."

"I get nervous when reporters get involved."

"Krol isn't in this for a story. For him, it's a personal thing."

"So why is his personal thing happening in the place where we do business?"

"He doesn't know we've been getting Mirsk into the SEC. The only way Mieltor can fall through is if someone leaks it. That would make it your fault, not mine. Your office has more holes than a Polituro policy speech."

"I hope you're right," Mrozow said.

"I have to be right." Markat stood again. "I can't afford not to be." He started toward the door, turned before leaving. "And you can't afford to be such an asshole. In order to go along, you have to get along."

"Another movie?" Mrozow said.

Markat left before he throttled the guy. In the lobby, he noticed a copy of *Kurier Krakowski* on the coffee table. He ignored the secretary, picked it up, and scanned the front page as he walked down the corridor. A photo of a balding man with three chins looked up at him.

The headline: *Newspaper Editor Disappears*

He read the first few paragraphs and saw that the editor, an ex-Solidarity leader named Henryk Milewski, had vanished. He had left his newspaper, *Gazeta Warszawy,* on the evening of July 17. The last his paper knew of him, he was on his way to Gdansk, to interview one Antoni Mirsk.

Mirsk.

Gazeta Warszawy.

Krol's paper.

Markat pulled out his cell phone, switched on the ringer, and dialed Oskar Ret's home number. The phone rang a dozen times, but no one answered. He checked his call log again. Of the six numbers displayed there, none were Oskar's.

And Ret was supposed to have called in by now.

Chapter 24

Get out of Poland. While you still have a chance.

Oskar Ret rushed home, slapped what he could into a travel bag, and left his rented, one-bedroom apartment without locking the door or looking back. The phone began to ring before he stepped out, but he didn't stop for it.

Outside the building, he paused only briefly, telling a nosy neighbor that no, he wasn't packed because he was going on a trip; he was packed because he was going period. The leaving produced a feeling of release. The decision was long overdue.

But there was also doubt—a kind of doubt he couldn't name. That was troubling because his whole life he'd been able to understand the things that motivated him. He'd soaked up enough harassment growing up to write a treatise on the subject. Having his Romanian mother's dark complexion and his Polish father's slight frame—at least until a prodigious growth spurt in high school—he suffered at the hands of fair-skinned Polish bullies, grew up reviled as a "Gypsy" and a "*mieszaniec,*" or half-breed, because being so dubbed made so many of his tormentors feel better about themselves. They bullied him and beat him, but never did he lash out in revenge. There were other ways of getting even, ways that didn't involve violence.

He became what they expected—sullen, guileless, criminal—turned their preconceptions against them. He began with petty thievery and burglary, hitting the homes of his tormentors, and found the work easy and gratifying, a victim getting revenge. He graduated to robbery and black-market profiteering, but he never set out to physically harm people—never any violence. A knifing four years ago had earned him three years in prison, but what the courts saw as a crime he saw as self-defense. A minor mafioso had called him a flea-bitten Gypsy dog and had pulled a blade. Oskar simply took the knife from the man and handed it back to him sharp end first. It felt good, standing up for himself.

But he was growing tired of being the outcast, the fated villain. There was too much rationalizing, too much "they deserve it" in his thoughts. There were consequences to his actions, weren't there, and once his actions piled up and repeated themselves, he began to understand that. It was time for a change. He wished he could just leave everything where it was, run off somewhere, be a harmless, careless nobody.

For years he had dreamed about Romania, a land he'd never seen and hardly even knew about. He dreamed about trying his hand at farming (of all things), or at *anything* legitimate—in Romania. But from what he gathered, things were awfully hard there, worse than in Russia even. It would be a new world, different, harder, not necessarily better.

Today, after all that had happened with Figur, the dreams of Romania felt like relics of a bygone era—despite the contradictory fact that he was now, at last, going to make them a reality.

The whole thing didn't compute.

He drove to a used car lot and sold his old Skoda for an ultra-cheap but necessarily fast eight million zlotys. Then he found a *kantor* and changed all of his zlotys into U.S. dollars. Maybe "leaving" wasn't the right term for this. Maybe "running" was closer to the mark. And "running" was not the bravest thing a man could do.

Maybe Figur had been right. Maybe Oskar was a coward.

That was why he felt like a husband confessing an infidelity to his priest.

He pushed these thoughts aside and took a taxi to the Central Bus Station, where he boarded a shuttle bus for Ustron. The tiny mountain city on the Czech border was a tourist town, with hot springs and health spas and nearly bankrupt company retreats for thousands of coal miners. It was also the best place for anyone who wanted to leave Poland without showing a passport.

He kept his travel bag in the seat next to him on the bus, looked out at Cracow for the last time. Brick houses and black rooftops flashed by. The blocks and factories of the suburbs gave way to coal mines and fields of sugar beets, which in turn soon became the lush green Beskidy hills surrounding Ustron. There was no sentimental regret, no sense of nostalgia. When the bus finished its hour-long trip westward, Oskar found a sidewalk bar near the station and ordered a vodka and pork knuckle. He drank the former and ignored the latter.

Running.

This wasn't a good word to have bouncing around his mind.

He sat at the table longer than he wanted to. Ten feet away, traffic crawled the potholed road that bisected the town center. The cars pushed a pall of fumes into the crisp Beskidy air. The cafes and bars had sticky, exhaust-stained walls. Ex-miners staked out the beer bars. The lucky among them now worked in the hotels as janitors and bartenders. Others scrounged for work in the shops and on construction sites. Many of them drank more than they worked.

Oskar fingered a dull pain under his ribs. Lugging around the travel pack had stirred to life an old knife wound. He untucked his shirt and massaged the scar tissue, his mind flashing back to the day he suffered the injury. While lying on the sidewalk, while clutching at the gash as the pack of skinheads fled, while watching the indifferent faces—no, the *gratified* faces—of local passersby, he felt disgust for everyone and everything Polish. The old men in their half-century-old *Leninowki* hats and the stout old ladies carrying their bags full of potatoes and kohlrabi—the lot of them somehow managed to ignore him while staring right at him. He was different and therefore dangerous. He was a trespasser, a suspect person.

He checked his watch, then pushed his plate away and decided he could put this off no longer.

It was a short walk to the Czantoria, a ski hill that in the summers doubled as a picnic retreat for local tourists. Forty thousand zlotys bought him a ticket on the rickety ski lift that ran halfway up Czantoria Mountain. Once off the lift and safely into the forest, he hiked a well-marked trail over the verdant peak into the Czech Republic, crossing an unmarked border.

Two hours later, he stepped into the town of Jablunkov, where he knew he could catch a bus to Ostrava, then a train to Prague. Then he would hole up somewhere, find a way to cross into Slovakia, Hungary, and, finally, Romania. He had no passport, but he did have money, and money was what mattered. All he had to do was stay east of the expensive West.

At a kiosk, he bought a package of Prince cigarettes, paying with two American dollars. Then he sat down on a bench to rest up. He tried to dream of the future, of better times in a new place, but instead his thoughts drifted back to that one word:

Running.

Stop that. None of this is your fault.

At least, not much of it. He wouldn't be doing this if not for Konrad Markat. "Come work for me," Markat had said. "You're too bright to be babysitting Mirsk's managers. Move a few trucks for me, in one end of Poland, out the other. Simple. No risk unless you do something stupid."

Good thing he hadn't rushed to phone Markat once the

trouble with Martin Figur and Irena Platz started. Markat would have no problem sacrificing the help if things started to sour.

Oskar was the first passenger to board the bus. Exhaust leaked up through the floorboards. Only a handful of windows opened, so the fumes began to gather inside. He chose one of the open windows and looked out at a kiosk, at two drunks pestering an old man for spare change.

Running.

"Get over it," he muttered under his breath.

But he couldn't. The word would stick with him, a scarlet letter or an albatross.

So he stepped off the bus and asked one of the drunks in Polish, "Where's the nearest phone?"

The drunk gave him a blank stare.

"Telefon. Gdzie?"

The second drunk pointed, and Oskar bought some tokens at the kiosk and crossed the street to the phone. He dug Martin Figur's number from his wallet and dialed the number.

Figur sounded surprised to hear him. "I thought you'd be in Aruba by now."

"So the cops haven't caught you yet."

"Sorry to disappoint you," Figur said. "They won't catch me, either."

"I'm glad you're so confident."

"Well, I just called the Kazimierz Komisariat."

"The komisariat?" Oskar said. "What for?"

"To see if Platz or Krol reported us. And I don't think they did. I told them I was Krol's uncle, said I thought he was in trouble. No one had received any reports on or about him."

"Because he's terrified," Oskar said, "But Platz—you tried to shoot her. Why wouldn't she report us?"

"I'd like to ask her that," Figur said. Phone-line static filled a brief silence before Figur continued. "Why are you calling me, Ret?"

"I want you to meet me. Tonight."

"Why?"

"Remember that restaurant near Lubon A-M?"

"The Okay Bar."

"Be there at eleven."

Figur waited before asking, "Why so late?"

Oskar looked up at the hills. Hiking down Czantoria Mountain had been easy. Climbing back up would be a marathon. "It'll take me that long to get there."

He tried to hang up, but the phone wouldn't stay on its perch, so he let it dangle.

Figur's energy could not be doubted. Figur would show up at the bar flush with anticipation, probably get there at nine, scope the place out, not trust Oskar one iota.

Which was okay. His trust wasn't important. The important thing was getting back to Poland and making sure this thing ended in the best way possible. Even more important was the simple act of seeing it through.

The word *running* had to be erased from his vocabulary.

Chapter 25

Irena had never been to Krystyna's companionship agency, but she knew where it was. She stopped at a side-street cafe and bolted a sandwich and burned her lips on a cappuccino. Then she cut a path through the summer tourists, past the Czartoryski Museum and Jagiellonian University, to the border of the Old Town, where there were no more crowds, no greenery or cobblestones or expensive restaurants. Here there were decrepit gray blocks, quiet streets, the occasional, well-stocked fruit or newspaper kiosk splashed with graffiti. There were things functional, but little else. Offices occupied ground floors of blocks, and two years into the free market, many of their owners had yet to embrace the concept of advertising. The Only You agency was the one business on its block to have more than a nameplate on the door: it had a small wooden sign, a pink silhouette of a man and woman entwined in a passionate embrace.

First thing she would do in Canada: buy an apartment. They said Toronto and Vancouver were expensive, so maybe she should try a smaller city, something in Quebec, maybe, which they said was more European than the rest of the country.

Now, was Markat any less dangerous than Mirsk? The question felt important.

Krystyna had told her a few things about Markat. For example, he was almost dwarfishly short and he liked to lecture girls on how to behave, on how things were different in the "old days." But there was no way to build a strategy for dealing with him. She would have to win his trust, get him to like her, to take her for granted. Then he'd be hers.

As she stepped into the Hearts Office, a stocky, bug-eyed man at the desk looked up at her and she knew he was Markat. He was going over some papers.

"Can I help you?" he asked.

"I want to work for you," Irena said from the doorway.

She saw a kitchenette with a small fridge and two hotplates. A woman was in there rinsing a teapot.

Markat looked Irena over. "Just like that?"

"Yeah."

"Why me?"

"Why not you? I've heard about you."

"From where, Miss. . . ."

She chose a name: "Sowinska." She moved to a cheesy burgundy sofa, losing the sightline to the kitchenette. On the wall to her right, she saw the gaping maw of a mounted pickerel. The fish was a good match for the *alfons.* Both creatures had cartoonishly large eyes.

"One of my dates told me about you," she said. "You have a couple agencies, right?"

"And how'd you know where to find me?"

"I called. Your secretary said you come in on Tuesdays."

The woman stepped out of the kitchen. "Back in ten," she said. "Want anything?"

"Where you going?" Markat said.

"Vietnamese."

He shook his head. When she was gone, he glanced at the call register, a notebook of longhand scribblings detailing which companion had been sent to which client at what time.

"Again," he said, "why me? What makes me special?"

"I've had problems," Irena said, summoning a tone of the

downtrodden. "Bad dates. I heard your girls get protection."

"They're not 'my girls.' They're employees. Are you a police officer?"

"What? No."

"I had to ask. The girls, some of them get in trouble because they bring it on themselves."

"Mr. Markat. What would be expected of me here?"

"You move pretty fast," he said. "That's not always a good thing."

"It's not bad, either. You want to make small talk? Something about the weather? Want to waste time with a cultured chat about nothing?"

Irena! What are you doing? Don't get your back up.

But he only laughed—heartily, as if she was a riot. He said, "You would clearly be more trouble than you're worth."

"Trouble how?" she said. "I do the work, they give me money, I give some of it to you. I know how it works."

"There's more to it," Markat said.

"Like what? Want to put a brand on my ass?"

Oh, girl, no. You want him to like you or not?

"For one thing," Markat said, "you *act* like a hooker. The things you say, the things you do, you're a girl who's cruising for a comeuppance. And I don't handle girls like that. In fact, I don't handle 'hookers.' What I run are companionship agencies, legal entities. The girls who work for me, they're mindful of that."

"I can be, too," Irena said.

"Are you a cop?" Markat shot back.

"You already asked me that."

"Are you?"

"Do I look like a cop?"

He crossed his arms and sat back in his chair. "See how easily you spook? You're a bit of an idiot. Sorry."

"No," she said evenly, "I am not a cop."

"How long you been in the life?"

She told him, didn't even make any of it up. She'd been doing this for six years, since she was eighteen. She worked mainly in Cracow, but had spent a year in Poznan, just before the Berlin wall came down, when new westward traffic flowed in. She added that if he didn't want her, that would be too bad, but it would be his loss, because she didn't do drugs and she didn't get ideas of going back to school and she didn't put on airs. She was who she was, and she wouldn't try to be anyone else. Low-maintenance, despite her big mouth.

This appeared to strike a chord. Markat leaned over the table, chin in hand, appeared to give it some thought.

"The thing is," he said, "I'm getting out of the business." His hands swatted away bees. "I mean, not right now, but soon." He exhaled—nervously, it seemed—as if he'd almost let something sensitive out. "Sooooo," he said.

This was going nowhere. The woman who'd stepped out for Vietnamese food would return soon. There was that desk. All those papers. Something with Oskar Ret's name on it. Something linking Markat to Mirsk? Or to Irena?

Something he would pay to keep from being handed to the cop from Warsaw?

"My throat's dry," she said. "You have anything to drink?"

He smiled, which made her nervous. "Like what?" he asked. "Water? Tea?"

"Tea," she said. "I'd appreciate it."

He got up and sauntered into the kitchenette, kept talking, his voice far away. "Just tea? Green tea? Anything in particular?"

"Plain's fine."

"I'll have to heat some water."

Good.

She scurried behind the desk and slid open the top drawer.

Doing so, she kept the conversation going. "What'll you do when they make these agencies illegal?"

"I'll live," he said out to her. "Anyway, like I said, I'll be . . . elsewhere."

Her hands worked furiously. There would be an address book. Something with a Pakistani name. Something about Krystyna. Anything.

"But when Parliament passes the bill," Markat said from the kitchen, "they'll do it in typical government fashion. There'll be loopholes. The men still in the business will cope."

The top drawers held pencils, paperclips, other office supplies. She opened two lower drawers and pushed aside some staples. She heard him opening cupboards.

"And if they *do* get it right," he said, "then that's the nature of the beast, Miss Sowinska. You have to spread yourself widely but not thinly. Depend on only one thing, you can get imprisoned by it. I've seen it happen."

Don't stop there. Keep talking.

"So what are your other businesses? You mind my asking?"

The lowest drawer held a thick black address book. She jammed it into her purse.

"Yes," Markat said, "I mind. Let's just say I try to stay agile. And so should you. So should anyone."

She flipped through another notebook.

"Anything interesting?" he asked.

She was on a second row of drawers.

"I said, you find anything interesting?"

She peeked up over the desk, saw him in the doorway holding a tea tray.

Hot fear. Sudden fear. Like when Figur had pulled his gun on her. She slid the drawer closed and stood up.

"Maybe we should start over," he said. "My name's Konrad Markat. What's your name?"

She swallowed a lump and glanced at the door. The exit looked a long way away. He could cut her off if she bolted. This had to be turned around on him.

"My name's Irena Platz," she said. "And I've come here to give you a choice, Markat."

" 'Markat'?" he said.

"The cops are showing more than a passing interest in you."

"Oh? About what?"

"And I have information that can help them put you away for a long, long time."

Markat crinkled his nose. "Are you wearing a wire?"

"No," she said, "I'm shaking you down."

He stiffened, then approached the desk and slid the tea tray onto the blotter.

"Shaking me down," he said, getting it straight.

"You can afford it."

"How much?" he said. "And for what?"

She looked to the ceiling, did some foreign-currency math.

Don't make it exorbitant, but do more than cover the plane ticket.

"Say fifty million zlotys."

"And what does fifty million buy me?"

"Freedom. It keeps you out of prison. You and Oskar."

She studied him, certain the dropping of the name "Oskar" would start him trembling.

But he didn't flinch, and he looked nowhere near impressed with her.

"Because of your drug shipments," she added.

He thought it over and shook his head sadly. "I was right about you," he said.

"How's that?"

"When you first opened your mouth, I told myself, 'Here's a girl who probably shoots herself in the foot every day of her life.' I was bang on about that."

He crossed to the door, kept his eyes on her every step of the way. Coolly, with a *thwack* that sounded louder than a jet engine, he slid the deadbolt closed.

"Who," he said, "told you I was moving drugs?"

Chapter 26

Business was slow in the Okay Bar. Julian decided that was a good thing. He sat at a window table with a good view of the garage, watching.

Across from him, Teresa looked jumpy, ready to get up and leave.

"The place is dead," she told him, fiddling with a fork. "How long you want to keep this up?"

Lunch had been pear-filled pierogi and chilled beetroot soup, an unfortunate combo. The cast pinched Julian's hand. The meperidine didn't stop the swelling and didn't do much for the pain, either. The hand throbbed all the way to the elbow. The odd car passed by out front, but still—no action at the garage.

Thoughts of Krystyna rolled through his mind as if on an assembly line, bits and pieces being welded on every few seconds.

"She was at the top of her class," he said. "She was a scholar. It didn't matter what she studied, she absorbed it, A to Z. She didn't learn things like you and I do. How she could end up. . . ."

"As a hooker," Teresa deadpanned.

"How she could end up *changing.* I'm sure the question occurred to you, too. I half-wonder if maybe the cops weren't right. Maybe she did get into drugs."

Teresa gave a loud *tsk.* "She was a babe in the woods, Krol. That was her problem, not drugs. She was trying to start over—every day, it seemed. She was trying to get by in a place she had no training for."

"She was smart enough to—"

"Smart has nothing to do with it. She had the wrong kind of knowledge, no trust or faith in anything. A lot of people, Krol, they can't forgive themselves when they see they can't live up to the things they think they ought to be."

So failure explained it? No, it wasn't that simple. Krystyna hadn't failed. She'd dropped out because of an abortion—in part because she couldn't admit that abortion to her brother.

"I see what you're doing," Teresa said. "You're trying to take credit for her tragedy." She motioned toward the garage. "You want those guys to finish you off this time? Is that supposed to even things up?"

"This can't ever be evened up."

"Oh?" she said. "What I'm thinking, I'm thinking that your oh-my-god-I-can't-live-with-this-guilt thing hasn't even hit you yet. You're willing yourself toward it, but you're not really there. *That's* what really bothers you."

Julian didn't respond. The whole conversation was moving away from the point. "It's getting dark out," he said.

"So?"

"Let's find out what they're using the garage for."

"Sure. Let's."

"A fast peek in the office. It'll only take a second."

She glowered at him.

"What?" he said.

"At the hospital, you said we'd only watch the place. You said you—"

"I lied. I needed you to get me back here. If you want to leave, leave. We can meet up tomorrow."

She laughed. "And just how would you break into the place? One hand's in a cast, the other you can hardly lift to feed yourself."

"How did you get in there?" he said.

"I pried a wooden plank off a window."

"Then there you go."

He looked through the window. It was dark enough now.

"I'll meet you at noon tomorrow," he said, "at the clock at Cracow Central. I'll get you some money then."

He rose and hobbled out of the bar. Outside, the smell of coal from local ovens filled the air. Roosters crowed. A faraway dog strained at its chain and howled. The nearest barn held little of use, only a shovel in a feed cubicle overflowing with oats. Carrying the shovel wasn't hard. Hooking it over the crook of his arm, just above the cast, he marched toward the garage.

Teresa caught up with him as he walked.

"I can't believe I'm doing this," she said.

"You don't have to."

"Yeah. And have you on my conscience."

So she was admitting it—at last. She did care about Krystyna.

He handed her the shovel and she grabbed it a little roughly, sending a lightning bolt up his arm.

She checked the windows. Someone had nailed the wooden plank back up. Thick-headed nails. A lot of them. No way to slip the shovel between plank and wall. Julian jiggled the doorknob. Locked.

"What now, Sherlock?"

"Over here." He motioned toward the bay door. "Jimmy it up. See how far it goes."

She jammed the shovel between the door and the ground. Pushing down on the handle, she worked the tool as a lever. The big door rolled up a few inches, then hit a snag. Something blocked it from inside.

"Maybe you can fit under," he said. She stared daggers at him, but lay down on the oily ground, slid in under the door—and got stuck just past the shoulders.

"Push the shovel under," she said, and he did so with his feet. She took it up on the other side and he heard some clanking.

"What's happening?"

"Just a minute."

A chain link was slotted into a steel bar. On the fourth swipe, a clank of metal against metal sounded and the pressure of her body pushed the door up a few more inches.

Julian lifted the door with the top of his foot and ducked under as it rolled up. Teresa rolled it back down and left the chain where it was. Leaving the light off, she followed him past the tool bench and the same engineless Trabant that he'd seen the last time. It took five good whacks with the shovel to open the office door—and to see what was inside.

Food. A wall lined with cans of beef and chicken luncheon meat and two knee-high boxes of canned sardines. Also fat bags of dried bread and plastic plates. A desk with a MacIntosh Classic sat next to the door. Beside it, a half-empty box of urinal salts.

"If you're hungry," Teresa said, "we've come to the right place."

He stared at it all, couldn't put it together. Then he switched on the computer. Once it was ready, he checked some folders on the hard drive, but found only garden-variety home office programs.

"Check the drawers," he said, his eyes on the screen. "Floppies."

"What are floppies?"

"Diskettes."

She started on the drawers, and he saw an icon indicating Internet software. He had used the Internet at *Gazeta Warszawy.* It was all the rage in the West, but it sometimes took forever to find websites in Polish, and unreliable Polish phone lines made transmission a bit of an adventure.

He tried to open the e-mail program and was greeted with an "enter user name" message. So he typed in "Lubon A-M." The computer blinked and denied him, so he typed in "visitor," and the computer whirred and let him in.

There were two messages in the In box.

"Read these with me," he said.

"Why?"

"You might recognize something."

She leaned in close and watched him open the first message.

The sender's e-mail address contained no name, and the subject prompt had been left blank. The message was in English.

All well, left Smolensk this morning.

Six words.

"What's in Smolensk?" he said.

Teresa shook her head.

"Krystyna ever go there?"

"Far as I know, she never left Poland."

He opened the second message. It was from someone named Nawaz, and the address had a "pk" ending. It, too, was in English:

> *Truck come tonight in Poland as schedule. We ready and next transport. 120 men have pay, and we wait for vehicle in Lahore. Say when we expect vehicle.*
>
> *You agree translator to come five days ago. She not come. Why?*
>
> *Nawaz*

Julian reread the message, then recalled Krystyna's letter. Interpreting for Pakistanis. Only one kind of Pakistani crossed borders in a truck one-hundred-and-twenty at a time. Julian glanced at the food again. Everything there was nonperishable.

"They're running illegal aliens," he said.

"They're what?"

Gazeta Warszawy had run a feature on alien smuggling just two months ago. It was a booming business in the Asian republics. Men from South Asia—Pakistan and India, mainly—gave their life's savings to Russian "guides" for transportation to Germany, where they could either live illegally or take their chances with the immigration process. The Russians packed them into trucks, ferried them up through Tajikistan and Kyrgyzstan, through Kazakhstan and Uzbekistan, depending on which border guards had been paid. They housed them in rural shacks in Russia until the time was right to take them to their destination.

Or at least that was what the men were told. Sometimes the human cargo ended up in Moscow or Budapest or Kiev, sometimes in Bratislava or Bucharest or even Arkhangel'sk, on the rim of the Arctic Circle. The men were told they would have to work to pay off their debts to the guides. Many became indentured for life; others eked out hard livings, illegal-alien existences, not much better off than they'd been in the factories of Hyderabad or Colombo. The lucky ones earned or stole back their freedom and settled somewhere in Central Europe, keeping an eye out for anyone who smelled official. Few of them ever made it to Germany.

"That zakat," Julian said, "that 'tax' you told me about. Markat must be running trucks through Afghanistan. He's paying for safe passage."

He printed both e-mail messages, then opened a new file, typed a few words, and sent a message. Then he grabbed a wrench from the window sill and thrust it through the cathode-ray tube. Sparks shot out. Smoke spiraled upward from the crushed screen.

Teresa jumped back. "Is this your way of getting even? Breaking their stuff?"

"They'll know I was here, but they won't know I was reading. Or sending." He began rifling through drawers.

Teresa stepped back toward the pitch-black mechanic's pit, groped her way toward the bay door. "Krol," she said back, "you know what this is about now. You know why they were using Krystyna. Let's get out of here."

He kept at the drawers. Then:

"Krol, there's someone in here!"

He sprinted toward the pit. Something *whished* in the darkness behind the Trabant. Something else clouted him in the jaw.

Julian lashed out, but hit only air. His assailant grabbed him, swung him around, pawed at his face with a bitter-smelling rag. Julian shook it away, pulled at the man's arm, which was now around his neck, holding him close. But the rag returned, tight as skin. Julian clamped his mouth shut, held his breath, but then found himself having to breathe. The rag tasted light and airy, a little bitter.

He felt his muscles relax and his hands fall from the attacker's arm. He heard the dull sound of an approaching vehicle, wondered briefly where Teresa was, and thought, oddly, of Krystyna. Krystyna standing there in the office, watching this but doing nothing. Krystyna a ghost, both present and absent.

The light from the office doorway faded to black.

Chapter 27

Markat wasn't answering his cell, and a waiter at Holst's Restaurant told Lieutenant Daniel Kosinski the boss wouldn't be in today. That left the companionship agencies and the Lubon garage.

No one answered the phone at the garage, so Kosinski donned civilian clothes and headed for the agencies. Sosnowski offered to send a car instead, pick Markat up, but Kosinski wanted to talk to Markat, not spook him.

Only You was the closest of the three agencies, so Kosinski went there first, arriving near midnight. He knocked on the door and a woman inside said to come in. The place was a disaster zone. The desk had been knocked on its side. Papers littered the floor. Even a trophy pickerel on the wall was crooked. A woman was down on her knees scooping up pencils.

"What can I do for you?" she asked.

"What happened here?"

"Disagreement."

"Some disagreement. Are you okay?"

"The boss," the woman said. "It was his disagreement. What do you want? You been here before?"

"I'm looking for the boss," Kosinski said.

She trickled the pencils into a coffee cup. "You're not alone. I don't know where he went. I got back and he was gone. Left me a note saying to clean up."

"Where'd he go?"

"I don't know."

"I've been trying to reach him by phone."

"Leave the message with me," the woman said. "He'll call you if it's important."

Kosinski scanned the room again. "Is this normal around here? Fights in the office?"

The woman stared at him. "You sound like a cop."

Kosinski showed her his I.D. "What's your name?" he asked.

"Judyta Korowska. We're perfectly legal."

"I didn't say you weren't."

"So what are you looking for, a date?" She gave him an acid smile. "You wouldn't be the first officer of the law."

Kosinski walked to the kitchenette and glanced inside.

She said, "You think I'm hiding him in the cupboards?"

"Will you do me a favor?" Kosinski asked. "Will you tell him to call me the moment you hear from him?"

He gave her his card and stepped over some papers on the way out.

"Sure," she said, and he knew she wouldn't do it.

Two hours earlier, dusk had settled into darkness on the Baltic Sea. A Gdynia cod trawler switched on its winch and began rolling in its net. An anemic catch of undersized seafood slipped aboard, bringing a stream of obscenities from the captain. The trawler's owner, a loss-making state-owned cannery, would sell the boat for scrap metal if the poor catches continued. Knowing his days were numbered, the captain stopped swearing and instead muttered an under-the-breath prayer to the Virgin Mary to watch over him and his family in the coming years.

Then he saw something near the end of the net, something bleached and bloated. Eyes narrowed, he hollered at one of the hands to kill the winch.

It was a man in the net, a very fat man, stiff and bloodless.

His hands and feet were taped together. Part of the back of his head was missing. Flecks of skin were gone, too. The fish had been feeding on him.

Chapter 28

"You want what?" a familiar voice asked.

The words were clear but tinny. Julian tried to move but couldn't. Anesthetic again, that same you-can-move-your-tongue-before-you-move-anything-else feeling.

"Let them go," a second voice said. "I want to let them go."

Now the first voice laughed. Julian recognized it: Armani Guy, the guy who'd crushed his thumb.

"I give you Markat's cargo here," said the second voice, "and I set up a meeting with him. You and he can work things out. But we leave these two alone—and Platz, too. That's the deal."

Julian forced his eyes open. Above him was a dull fluorescent light attached to a low wooden ceiling. He was in a parked truck, a semi-trailer, surrounded by men in white Pashtun garb. The air was thick and rank with sweat and urine. Armani Guy was pacing the trailer, stepping over the odd outstretched Pakistani leg.

"Is that why you wanted to meet me," he asked, "to give me this truck? Which, by the way, you earlier said was drugs?"

Oskar Ret had his hands at his hips. "I called you so you and Markat can settle things however you want to," he said. "You both have interests in this; I don't. I didn't know Krol and the hooker would show up. But now that they're here, they're not going to get hurt."

"Ret, we just frigging chloroformed them."

"Better that than let you play with vises."

"You seriously want to send them on their merry way?"

Julian tried to sit up, but thought better of it. He lay still, listening. Teresa was a few bodies down, still unconscious. The Pakistanis ignored her and everything else. They were gaunt and drawn, filthy. Most of them ignored the argument. The few who watched it looked too tired to care what the two Poles were saying.

Armani said, "Why'd you give me those stories about jeans and drugs?"

"That's all you needed to know, that this business is illegal. It wasn't any of your business."

Armani chewed on that and said, "It doesn't make sense. I get to grill Markat about the dead girl and Platz, Platz and these two get left alone, but what about you? What do you get?"

Ret looked embarrassed. "Peace of mind," he said. "I go away knowing no one got hurt, not counting your little Tarantino scene back in the garage."

Armani paused before responding. "Not that it matters, but what is it about me that rubs you so wrong?"

"You're right, it doesn't matter. We have a deal or not?"

Armani stepped closer to him. "You're weak, Ret, that's what you are."

"Stop using my name, Martin Figur."

Julian silently repeated both names—and was thankful he'd chosen to remain "unconscious."

"A guy like you," Figur said, "it's a miracle you're not incarcerated. We let these two walk away, I'm as good as arrested."

Julian shifted slightly for a better view. Oskar Ret looked weary, broken.

"So that's how it's going to be?" Ret said. "You're not gonna do it?"

"Tell me where Markat is," Figur said. "I'll find him anyway.

These two, we'll decide on them later."

Ret shook his head and started toward the door. When he passed Figur, Figur reached out, grabbed an arm. "You don't want to test me."

Ret brushed the hand away and stepped out of the truck. Figur paused a moment, appeared to go over his options, then followed him out.

When they were gone, Julian sat up and studied the Pakistanis. They looked anemic. Germany, that land with fridges and clean washrooms and drinkable tap water—it wasn't to be.

At least they were alive. They didn't know the stories Julian knew. Last summer a truckload of Sri Lankans had been abandoned outside Budapest. When the police pried open the doors, the bloated corpses of thirty-eight men spilled out. The dead men had wooden splinters under their blood-black fingernails; they'd tried to claw through the plywood lining the truck walls.

Julian dragged himself over to Teresa and shook her shoulder. She didn't stir. His thumb strained against pin and plaster and his shoulder ached. He shook her again and she felt soft and relaxed, nowhere near conscious. He sat beside her, leaned back against the wall, and closed his eyes. Despite his size and strength, Oskar Ret had looked like no match for Figur.

Because Figur was going to kill Ret. This could not end any other way.

Where was Platz? If Figur hadn't known about the alien smuggling, chances were he wasn't the one who'd killed Krystyna. If Ret wanted to play Samaritan, let Julian and Teresa go, he wasn't a murderer either. That left Markat or Mirsk. Or Markat and Mirsk.

New questions zigzagged through his mind. Drowsiness descended, an invitation to shut everything away. Julian shook his head vigorously and gave Teresa another nudge. He asked down to her if she could hear him.

The rig's engine rumbled to life and the vehicle started to move.

CHAPTER 29

Konrad Markat felt slightly sick to his stomach while he watched the maroon Mercedes steam toward his country house. The car sent plumes of dust up from the gravel road.

Keep going, car. Do not stop here.

There was a woman in the house, handcuffed to a water pipe. The last transport was on Polish territory right now. And in only three hours, Antoni Mirsk would be throwing a party at the Mieltor Salt Mine to celebrate his SEC permit. Konrad Markat had a plan that would make it the most important party in either his or Antoni's lives.

The other country homes along the road were bursting with people on summer holidays. The Merc was no doubt destined for one of them.

But it stopped at his gate. The license plate was from Gdansk, and through the window the driver looked like a well-dressed man with a red laceration running from his eye to his jaw.

A Pakistani man pattered out of the house, held out a drink for his master. Before taking the glass, Markat measured his bow tie around his still-unbuttoned shirt collar.

"Something more for you?" the servant asked.

"Do we know that car, Zulfikar?"

The servant mistook the question for a command, scampered to the roadside to pry open the gate, then pattered back over the grass to the house. Markat rose from his deck chair and soon the guy from the Merc was walking in a most-determined, most-unfriendly manner toward the patio. He wore an expensive suit, dressed to kill.

"Konrad Markat?" he said.

"Who are you?"

"Name's Martin Figur. I'm head of security at Mirsk Industries."

Figur stopped walking, kept his distance, looked like he wanted to crumple Markat into crumbs.

"What can I do for you?" Markat said.

"I've got your truck. It's a few klicks down the road. I got it from your man Oskar. If you want all those slaves back, you'll have to play nice with me, okay?"

"You've got my truck?"

"And the slaves."

"They're not sla—what are you talking about?"

"Let's not dance around it," Figur said. "I'm not in the mood. Exactly what is it you do for Antoni?"

Markat looked down the now-empty road. What was all this?

"You've been having a bad day," he said.

"Fuck you, that's how bad it is. Antoni sent me from Gdansk to handle a problem, a problem that has become a *problem.* He didn't tell me you were the Grand Wizard of Paki Smuggling. And I'm guessing he didn't because he didn't *know* about it. But since he isn't telling me what it is you *do* do for him, I'm feeling a little nervous about trying to keep a lid on everything."

"Look, Mr. Figur—"

"No, you look. Frankly, I don't care if you and Oskar go down for those slaves. But Antoni can't go down. And I *won't* go down. What I will do, I'll back off, allow you to keep living. But only if you tell me what it is you do for Antoni."

Covering his tracks. Fine. At least the man was not behaving irrationally. Markat pulled his untied tie out of the loop of his collar and sagged into a deck chair. "You're not sending me a

Christmas card this year, are you?"

Figur pulled a gun, laid it on the table, far enough away from Markat not to be grabbable.

"You only get so many wisecracks," Figur said.

"How'd you find me?"

"You've been tabling bribes for him, haven't you?"

Markat thought, *Under different circumstances, maybe I could have hired this guy.* Instead, he said, "That's an outrageous accusation," and reached into a bowl on the table, popped a cherry into his mouth. "He's paying me to pay the ministry for a SEC permit. You know what that is?"

Figur sighed, put his head in his hands. That made the gun hard not to consider lunging for.

Markat said, "Mirsk is starting a salt-processing company. He wants to site it next to the mine, cash in on the tax relief. That's all. It has nothing to do with my transports." He added, "So you can tell me where my truck is, and you can go home to Gdansk and take it up with Antoni."

Markat glanced at the house. Zulfikar was watching from a window.

You know what to do, Markat thought. *Get the gun from the kitchen.*

Figur shifted in his seat. "And what about the dead hooker?"

The dead hooker. There was no point trying to look surprised by the question.

"She worked for you," Figur said. "She—"

"She has nothing to do with anything."

"Meaning you don't know her? Or meaning you killed her but you want me to go away and forget she ever existed?"

"I kill so many people," Markat said. "It's hard to keep count."

"Funny," Figur said. "You know what's also funny? Her brother and her roommates. They're a howl, running around trying to figure out whodunnit. Hilarious, right?"

"I didn't kill her," Markat said.

"Yet she was your girl. High-class trim for important people."

Markat glanced at the house again. Zulfikar was still at the window, still watching.

"She was a junkie," Markat said. "She took too many brain bonbons."

"You're saying she killed herself?"

"Maybe Mirsk killed her."

"Maybe *what?*"

"You really don't know which way is up, do you?"

Figur took a deep, calming breath. He also glanced back at the house. Zulfikar wasn't at the window.

"Where's the guy who opened the gate for me?"

"Inside."

"He alone?"

"Yes."

"It's funny," Figur said, "how much you can dislike a guy you've just met."

"I'll try to grow on you," Markat said.

"Call your manservant outside."

Markat began to tie his tie again. "Zulfikar!" he shouted, "come out here!"

Two crows lighted from the roof and flapped away. Zulfikar appeared on the steps, hands on his head, offering surrender. He stepped onto the grass and stood deathly still.

Markat sagged. "There's a banquet today. For the SEC permit. I have to be there."

"I doubt you'll be missed. Mr. Zulfikar, you go over there, stand with your boss."

The servant shuffled to Markat's side, kept his hands on his head. "Please," he said. "I do nothing. I go away. Say nothing and nobody."

Markat couldn't look at him. *I don't want to die like this, beside a man who's about to wet himself.*

Then he saw it. A gun peeked out the back of Zulfikar's pants. The damn fool had had brains enough to grab it, but couldn't muster the nerve to use it.

"There are thirty-eight men in that truck," Markat said.

"Are there?" Figur picked at some fingernail dirt.

"All like Zulfikar here. They'd be perfect for Mirsk's mine. Work them in the low levels, pay them immigrant salaries. And I'll send you more later."

For a moment, Figur looked as though he was considering it. Then: "Do you realize which century we're in?"

Markat glanced at the gun again.

"No," Zulfikar said through quivering lips. "No shoot. I go away. No shoot." A lateral step removed any chance of grabbing the gun. The next steps took him away from both Markat and Figur, toward Figur's car. Zulfikar was starting to cry.

Figur trained his gun on him. "Relax, man. No one's getting hurt here."

"No," Zulfikar said, "I no do things. No hurt me."

"But I no hurt you," Figur said, "if you no run. Don't be stupid."

He turned and trained the gun on Markat, who reached down and plucked another cherry from the bowl. Turning the fruit over in his fingers, he said, "So what now? You shoot the two of us?"

The question was hardly out before Zulfikar, hands shaking and eyes screwed shut, jerked the gun from his belt and shot Martin Figur in the back.

Figur stutter-stepped, looked more surprised than hurt, and pitched forward and hit the ground at about the same time Zulfikar tossed the smoking gun. For a moment, Zulfikar stood there frozen, gaping at what he'd done. Then he gathered up both guns and pointed one of them at Markat.

"Relax," Markat said, "take a deep breath."

"No more," Zulfikar said through clenched teeth. "I don't want more of this." Reaching down, he pulled Figur's wallet from his pocket. Then, walking backward, he found Figur's car and climbed in, keeping his eyes on Markat.

"Be reasonable," Markat said. "You've never driven a car. You told me so."

"I want to go home. No more with you. I want my family."

"Zulfikar, it's a *long* drive home."

The servant managed to start the engine and find a gear, but the car hiccupped and stalled. He flung the door open and said, "I want woman, Mr. Markat."

"You have your choice of demands and you ask for a woman?"

"Woman inside. To drive. Give me her or I shoot you. I promise you I shoot you."

"Come on, my friend. Let's slow down. Let's—"

Zulfikar pulled back the hammer.

"Okay," Markat said, "you want woman, you get woman."

He stepped inside to the hooker. Irena Platz looked up from an awkward sitting position beside the radiator. He uncuffed her ruggedly, towed her outside, shoved her toward Zulfikar. She had trouble walking, stretching the kinks from her legs. She appeared to take a while to understand what was happening.

"For the record," Markat told her, "if you try anything foolish, you will pay."

She stared at Figur, tried to put everything together. "When I heard the gun go off," she said, "I hoped it was you."

"I'm disappointing everyone today."

Zulfikar was still pointing the gun in all directions. He started toward the passenger seat. "We leave now."

Irena opened the driver-side door. Before climbing in, she gave Markat a cool look, one that he pictured her practicing in front of the mirror.

"I'll be in contact," she said.

She closed the car door, punched the gas, spun the car backwards out of the driveway. Zulfikar kept the gun on her. Just off the property, she pulled up along the fence and stopped and rolled down the window.

"If the cops don't get you for Figur," she said out to Markat, "I'll call you in a few days. I, myself, won't be going to the cops."

"Okay," Markat said.

"But the price is now two hundred million zlotys."

She hammered the gas and he watched the car disappear. Then he stepped into the house and punched auto-dial on his cell phone. When his man picked up at the other end, he said, "We're leaving sooner than planned. Is everything in place?"

". . ."

"Good, I'll need a man out here, send me one. I'll be there after the banquet."

". . ."

"Yes, I'm still going to the banquet."

The banquet was the last place he wanted to be. But without the banquet, all did not end well.

He cut the connection and, at long last, tied his tie. He crossed to the kitchen window and swept open a drape. Dead men on the lawn made for an uneasy feeling. As did the fact that Oskar Ret had let the shipments become known. Ret must have had his reasons for handing Figur the transport, and for pointing Figur toward the country house, but they weren't reasons that Markat planned to listen to.

Oskar Ret must have known that by acting like he was acting, he was signing his own death warrant.

Chapter 30

A message awaited Lieutenant Daniel Kosinski at the Kazimierz Borough Komisariat. Lieutenant Sosnowski handed it to him. It had been phoned in from a cop at Warsaw's Centrum Borough Komisariat. Someone had called the komisariat from *Gazeta Warszawy,* an editor named Wanda Borowska. She said she had received an e-mail from a sender named "Lubon" in Cracow. The message read:

> *Konrad Markat and Oskar Ret are smuggling illegal aliens from Pakistan. Krystyna knew, they killed her. Call Kosinski, Centrum Borough.*
>
> —*Julian*

Chapter 31

The trailer air crawled the skin like jungle moisture. Water was a harsh craving. Dizzy spells flared. Dehydration. A plastic bucket and a urinal salt occupied one corner. Four men sat close to Julian in a ragged circle, talking listlessly, looking like a poker game without cards.

Poker game. An odd memory flaring. Twelve years ago. Three Solidarity activists in Julian's living room, men who thought they knew one another, who thought they were friends. Julian feeding them vodka and cleaning them out at cards. And at the end of the evening, one of them stumbling into a coat rack, sending jackets flying, and hats flying, the drunken laughter of four men filling the room.

And popping out of one of the coats: a red-striped Security Services card, face up on the floor, mocking their bourgeois little game of chance.

The four men stared at one another and left the card where it was. No words were spoken. The three visitors pulled their coats from the pile, marched out of the apartment, and never met again.

The following day, a dark-eyed Security Services agent knocked on the door and demanded the card. Julian handed it over and resigned himself to the likely fact that he would never learn just which of his "friends" was the agent.

"You'll find out who it was," Krystyna told him afterwards. "I just get the feeling you will."

Turned out she was right—or almost right. Julian would never learn which friend was the rat, but he *would* see again the man who had come to collect the card—the same agent who, two years later, sat in the shoe factory in Poznan. The same man who Julian locked eyes with, stared at, but couldn't quite place, just moments before the riot police burst in and put Julian in prison again.

If you'd recognized him, what difference would it have made?

None. The tale was simply a reminder that Julian tended to arrive at his destinations a fraction of a second too late.

He turned to the men beside him, asked in English if the truck had moved much in the last few days. They looked, they blinked, but no one understood. Teresa was awake now, but listless, eyes closed, sweat glistening on her face. She had a melancholy, dignified look, a look of resignation.

"I didn't want this to happen to you," he told her.

The eyes stayed closed. "What would you do?" she asked. "If they let you out of here, what would you do?"

"Drink all the water in Poland."

"Would you go back to Warsaw? Go back to your life?"

An image of Krystyna flashed in his mind: Krystyna on the gurney, ash-white, a statue, the overhead light flickering. "I'd track down Markat," he said. "I'd have to know if he killed her."

She nodded. "Then don't take my suffering on your noble shoulders. There's no room for it."

She ran a hand through her hair, locked eyes with him. For the first time, she smiled, a smile of sad communion. It wasn't much, but it was something.

"You still have that scrap of paper?" he said.

"What paper?"

"The phone book."

She tugged the scrap from her pocket and handed it to him.

Julian glimpsed the Urdu inscription, then passed the paper

to the man to his right. The man looked at it and his eyebrows jumped. He jabbered an excited question.

"I don't understand," Julian told him.

The man handed the note to a spindly teenager to his left. The boy went over it, said something, and passed it on. Some of the men passed the note without reading it, but the ones who read it found it to be of great interest. By the time the last man received it, the readers were filling in the nonreaders. Three arguments started. One man shoved another man. All of them were coming to life.

Julian looked at Teresa.

She said, "I guess it's not a simple shopping list."

When the big door rolled up again, sunlight and swarming summer bugs spilled in, mixing with the pungent air. Oskar Ret stood in the doorway and surveyed the scene. He had food with him, a crate of canned sardines and a bag of dried bread. He also had a gun, Teresa's Mauser.

Some of the Pakistanis had crept forward, their eyes fixed on the gun. They were frozen in half-advance.

"You speak the language?" Oskar asked Julian. "You been talking to them?"

"If I could, they wouldn't believe me."

"Get out of the truck," Oskar said.

Julian rose to his feet. Teresa began to follow, but Oskar said, "One at a time. Slowly."

Julian jumped down from the truck. They were on a dirt road, secluded. The air was cool and inviting.

"Leave her out of it," Julian said. "She can't hurt anyone."

"You get out too," Oskar said to Teresa, and she took her time crossing to the trailer door and hopping down.

The Pakistanis stayed where they were. "What'll happen to them?" Teresa asked.

Oskar hoisted the food into the trailer and rolled down the

door. Then he told Julian and Teresa to step around to the front of the truck. They did that, and he pointed up the road. "Start walking that way," he said, and they did, Oskar walking behind, Julian worried that Oskar had had a change of heart, would now kill them.

"Where's Markat?"

"Looking for this truck, I imagine."

The road arced left and Julian saw an idling taxi in the distance.

"Stop walking," Oskar said. "Look at me."

They did. He lowered Teresa's gun, looked at them for a moment, then shook his head sadly and tossed the gun into the tall grass beside the road.

Then he reached into his belt and tossed his own gun into the weeds.

"I'm sorry about your sister. I never really knew her. She didn't talk much."

Julian glared at him. The guy had no right to offer condolences or request absolution. The deed was done. Krystyna was gone. This man, too, deserved to be gone.

Oskar Ret couldn't look Julian in the eyes. He wore shame poorly, like something he wouldn't shake for a while, if ever.

Julian said, "Markat killed her, didn't he?"

"He moved her to Warsaw," Oskar said. "After that, I don't know what happened."

He opened his mouth to say something else, but then shook his head; the guilt was getting to him. He turned and started toward the taxi.

"Where's Figur?" Julian asked.

"Go home, Krol. You can't do anything else." He added, pointing over his shoulder, "There's a highway a couple hundred yards that way."

Teresa said, "You're going to just leave those men there?"

"Leave the door open," Oskar said. "They'll figure out they're on their own soon enough."

He scrunched himself into the taxi and the driver folded his newspaper and jostled the rearview mirror.

"Wait," Julian said. "Where's Markat?"

Oskar gave him a long look.

"I'll find him anyway," Julian said.

Oskar cocked his head, gave Julian time to waver. Finally, he said, "There's a party. At the Mieltor Salt Mine. He'll be there."

"When?"

"This afternoon."

He told the driver to go, and the taxi chugged forward, shooting up a plume of dust. A few yards down the road, Julian ran into the brush, fished the two guns from the weeds, and gave the Mauser back to Teresa. Then he started back toward the truck, thinking, *Mieltor. This afternoon.*

"Why'd he let us go?" Teresa asked.

"How far's Mieltor from here?"

"No," she said. "No way. What we do, we have to deal with those men back there. It's the end of the line."

At the truck, Julian rolled the door up and did what he could to show the Pakistanis that this was the end of the line. They shuffled nervously, took a while to catch on. One of them asked a question. There would be more questions, too. Julian knew the main points. They had no visas or IDs. Their guide, a white man who had parted with them at—where, at the Pakistani border?—had taken whatever belongings they had brought with them. Their only real option was a return trip to the homeland, courtesy of the Polish government.

One by one, they climbed out of the rig. Five or six stayed where they were, their backs to the truck wall, eyes staring into space. Julian and Teresa started walking, and the Pakistanis followed. He motioned for them to stay where they were, to wait, and they backed off while Julian and Teresa kept going.

The direction felt like north.

"So Mieltor," Teresa said.

"I have to. You can bail out once we hit a town."

"Right."

"What's that mean?"

"Who keeps you from getting killed?"

Who indeed. If he continued on with this, his life would be in danger. That mattered, but not as much as other things.

Chapter 32

Irena Platz and Zulfikar Sindha were halfway through Brzesko when the argument started.

"Cracow," Zulfikar said, "not this way. We go police in Cracow."

The guy wouldn't budge. He'd been holding the gun on her since they'd left Markat's house.

"What's your name?" Irena asked, slowing the car for some traffic lights.

"Zulfikar."

"Well, Zulfikar, we're not going to Cracow. We're going to Rzeszow."

"Rzeszow?"

"We're going to stay out of sight for a few days, then make a few phone calls. Put the gun away. I never did anything to you."

"No," Zulfikar said, "Police. Now."

"I'm earning us some money, dummy. Your boss'll pay to keep—"

"No money. Home. Police."

"You just shot a man. The only place you're going is jail—unless you listen to me. Now put the gun away. You're making me nervous."

Zulfikar poked her in the ribs with it. "Police," he said. "You do not talk this way to a man."

"A woman doesn't talk this way? Listen to me, you little—"

He swiped at the steering wheel. The car swerved and Irena

elbowed him in the chest and pulled the car back on line.

"Idiot! You want to kill us?"

"Police. Now."

He was set on it. She watched him watch her right back. An hour out of servitude and he liked giving orders.

Fine, take a more traditional path.

She shifted her body toward him. "Let's go to a hotel, talk it over." She moved her right hand to his thigh, started it on a climb northward. "There's no point rushing things. I mean, let's get to know each other. Before we make any decisions."

Zulfikar froze, caught in the new dynamic. His expression melted to doubt, so she let her hand reach its destination, where it started a slow, if perfunctory, massage. He pulled back the gun, still appeared to be weighing his options, then, flustering doubt closing on him, he burst back to life, lashing out with the gun and crying, "I want to go home!"

The car swerved just far enough to plow into a Ruch newspaper kiosk. Papers and magazines scattered through the air, sending the kiosk attendant diving for safety.

To Irena, the crash happened in slow motion, every millisecond, every crinkle of the car vivid and audible. Metal and plastic settled into a new position around her. She sat still for a moment, heard faraway voices outside. Someone called out to her, asked her something that seemed irrelevant. The Mercedes dashboard pinned her legs to the seat and dug into her left arm. There was no pain, no real concern of any kind, only a hot, helpless feeling that kept her apart from herself, a bystander to her own calamity. She glanced over at Zulfikar. His head rested against the dash. His eyes blinked twice before closing. She hoped he was unconscious. If he was dead, it wouldn't do anyone any good.

CHAPTER 33

The banquet would be 410 feet underground, in the Mieltor Salt Mine's Koszalin Chamber. The only way to get to it, apart from an elevator that was off-limits to anyone without an invitation, was by walking three snaking sets of stairways and hiking through nineteen museum chambers. It was a two-hour walk, and you could make it only with a guide and a group. Unguided visitors were not allowed; they got lost in the subterranean maze and then complained that they shouldn't have been allowed to go down there in the first place.

Two miners at the elevator checked invitations. Julian and Teresa bought tour tickets at the *kasa* and waited on a bench for more tourists to show.

Teresa said, "What's the plan once we get down there?"

"We break from the group at the third or fourth chamber."

"No, I mean what'll we *do?*"

Fair question. "Find Markat," he said.

"There'll be security at the Koszalin Chamber."

"I would imagine."

He rose from the bench and crossed the floor to a kiosk, where he bought a map of the mine. The tourists trickled in, in twos and threes. Julian went over the map, studied the mine. It was immense. The salt chambers and chapels, some of which dated back to the Renaissance, were linked by two miles of trails.

Some of the tourists were staring. Julian and Teresa had eaten in Cracow, had also washed and bought painkillers that didn't work any better than the meperidine. He studied his reflection in a window: badly slumped shoulder, a cast that he wore like a club. He looked like a guy who'd just left a hospital, not a man interested in tours or banquets.

There were enough people for a tour at two o'clock, half an hour before the banquet. The guide was a miner who'd escaped the back-breaking work in the lower levels for the leisure of leading gaggles of tourists through the chambers. There were fifteen people in the group, all of them Poles, most of them retired. The guide looked pained by the demographics. Young foreigners tipped, older Poles didn't.

The wooden stairs of the Danilowicz Shaft took them down to the first level, two hundred feet down, slowly, with the visitors pausing to taste salt from the walls and to snap photos of petrified support beams. Julian and Teresa stayed at the back of the group, unobtrusive. It seemed like a long way to go to get table salt.

At the bottom, the guide led them into the Casimir IV Chamber, a small room with a salt statue of the king. The guide said Nicholas Copernicus visited the mine in 1495, and the statement somehow triggered a click-click of cameras. Julian clutched Teresa's hand, led her down the pathway and into the next chamber.

"Keep walking," he said. "Someone calls out, we don't stop. They won't come after us."

They raced through a chapel and four or five more chambers. At a small chamber near the end of the first level, they caught up with another group. They waited in a ventilation shaft, a cold draft blowing down on them. The group entered a chamber and Julian tugged at Teresa to get moving again.

There were no groups in the other chambers. The mine's biggest draws, the ornate St. Adalbert Chapel and the subterranean

Witolny Lake, a shimmering brine pond that made the cave walls sparkle like the aurora borealis, were empty. Julian's mother had once made him pray at the St. Adalbert altar. During a school tour, a classmate had fallen into the Witolny Lake, shoved by another student from the narrow wooden passageway.

Julian twice rapped his head on the low salt ceilings. He wasn't walking fast, he was now running. Teresa fell behind until he slowed his pace near the stairs down to the third level. Just around the corner was the Koszalin Chamber, with sounds of classical music and smells of food rich with marjoram and mushroom sauces. Teresa paused, and Julian knew she was stuck on the music, likely thinking it was forever since she'd last heard it.

And now that Julian thought of it, everything in his life—likely everything in her life, too—was from an entirely different existence. All that was left now was today. All that mattered was what happened in the next couple of hours.

He peeked around the corner, saw two stone-faced security men, no doubt moonlighting cops who made more money in a night of door-watching than in a week of policing. Both had truncheons. Both wouldn't be moved by heavy ordnance.

He glanced at the people inside. The men were in dinner jackets and bow ties, the women in dresses and shawls that kept the cool mine air at bay.

"Come on," Julian said, and he led Teresa around the corner as the music stopped. Someone on the stage spoke into a mike, welcoming everyone to the "new" Mieltor Salt Mine.

One of the security men held up a hand. "Invitation," he said.

Julian flicked out his press card—*"Gazeta Warszawy"*—and started past him.

With a loping stride, the second security man blocked his way. "No press, not without accreditation."

"I missed the press conference. I was invited by the Industry Ministry spokesman. His name's Konowalczyk."

Konowalczyk was as good a name as any. Any reporter would be wearing a blazer and have a notebook and maybe a camera. But the two guards didn't look like that mattered. They looked bored and testy, paid to be disagreeable.

One of them said, with a slight yawn, "No entrance without an invite or accreditation."

"The spokesman has our accreditation."

"He didn't leave it with us. Good-bye."

Julian looked past them. The man at the mike was still warming himself up. He was pleased so many people were here. He hoped the success flowed as freely as the champagne.

"I'll give you a million zlotys," Julian said.

"No you won't."

"Then make it two."

The second security man cradled his chin with his hand. "You look like a homeless guy. Even if I wanted to, I couldn't—"

"I don't care if they're wearing tutus," his partner said. "A million each, right?"

"We'll be in and out," Julian said.

"What happened to your hand?" the first security man asked.

"A police dog. Outside Parliament. I was covering a demonstration."

"Farmers?"

"Steel workers. The dog got me. In and out, five minutes."

The first security man said, "Someone stops you, say you lost your cards. You look like you ran here."

"We did. We're late."

"The washrooms are to the left. Go clean up."

"Thanks," Julian said, and he paid them the money and tugged Teresa through the entrance and into the crowd.

"I said go wash up," the guard said, but they kept going. The speaker was reading a monotoned tribute to a man named Antoni Mirsk.

"What now?" Teresa said, but Julian didn't answer. He still had her by the wrist, pulled her toward the stage. His shoulder burned.

"Krol, you're hurting me."

He released her at a spot close to a wall. It was also close to the stage, had a good view of the crowd. There must have been three hundred people here, perfume and aftershave mingling with salty air. Some of the guests stared at the strange man with the cast and the wild eyes. Teresa rubbed her now-cold arms, half-listened to the speech. Julian scoured the sea of faces for Konrad Markat.

The speaker was saying, "When Antoni Mirsk bought into the Mieltor Salt Mining Enterprise . . ." and Markat was nowhere to be found. Few people listened to the speech. Many had their backs to the stage, talking about debt restructuring or equity swaps or whether Andrzej Golota would get a title shot against Riddick Bowe. It was hopeless, searching for Markat in this crowd. He could be anywhere.

And then there he was, across the room, sandwiched by two security men. He was watching the speech, but he looked distracted.

The speaker said, "Ladies and gentlemen, I give you . . . Antoni Mirsk." Polite applause echoed off the chamber walls.

Teresa said something. Julian heard her voice but not the words. Markat was close, maybe thirty yards away. Mirsk spoke into the microphone and his message was a faraway buzz, the same honeycomb drone that had accompanied news of Krystyna's death. Julian found himself moving toward the target.

"What are you doing?" Teresa said.

"Wait here."

"What are you—"

"No, don't wait, go to the surface."

She reached out for him, but he broke away. He knew what she was thinking. After all of this, after being chased and maimed and almost killed, he was going to walk across a crowded floor and ask Markat why he had killed Krystyna?

Walking, Julian glanced back and forth between Markat and Antoni Mirsk, the latter a fit-looking man who spoke with confidence. Mirsk was talking about his special economic zone, something he'd made a reality thanks to the visionaries at the Ministry of Industry and Trade. One of Markat's security guards locked eyes with Julian, nudged the guard beside him. Both men fastened their gazes on the man with the blood-sopped cast. They zeroed in on Julian and he saw them and kept walking anyway, nudging people, making them spill their drinks.

Maybe twenty feet away, Julian lengthened his stride, then stopped dead when a scream rang out. Mirsk stopped speaking in mid-sentence. People turned their heads, searching for the screamer. An uneasy murmur started to spread.

Then a gunshot rang out. People scrambled. Someone slammed Julian to the ground. He scrambled to his feet, but it wasn't easy with people now darting in every direction. Up on the stage, Mirsk had been shot. He was leaning on the lectern, pressing fingers to his neck. The people closest to him scattered in time to miss a second shot, which put him flat on his back. His body quivered and fell still.

The shooter was at the far end of the chamber, high on the salt wall, behind wooden support beams. Julian caught sight of the rifle barrel before it withdrew into the wall and the shooter retreated into what had to be a ventilation shaft or an old passageway. The guests stampeded toward the exits. Security guards had guns out, but didn't seem to know where to point them. Julian broke through a wall of people and continued on toward Markat.

But Markat was gone, lost in the crowd. So were his bodyguards. Julian spun around, tried to take in everything at once. He glimpsed bodyguards pushing Markat through the crowd at the north exit.

Teresa, too, was gone, no longer back at the wall, maybe in an elevator. Maybe she would make it to the surface before the cops showed up and stopped people from leaving.

He vaulted for the north exit, squeezed between people, smudged them red with his leaking cast. He pulled out Oskar's gun, and when people saw it, they parted for him—or tried to. The crush at the elevator was apocalyptic. Too many people were inside; too many were trying to push their way in. The doors wouldn't close. The elevator operator shouted for everyone to step back, to wait their turns. Women screamed. Men started punching one another.

Julian paused near the elevator. Markat and his men had either turned left, down to the third level, or right, back up through the chambers between here and the Casimir IV Chamber. The third level had only two more chambers, no elevator or stairway to the surface, so it was an unlikely choice. Julian tucked the gun in his pants and turned right, pushed his way through a crowd doing the same.

Soon the crowd in the tunnel thinned. The Beskidy Chamber and the Cracow Chamber were teeming with dinner guests-turned-refugees, people who felt safe in the enclosure and who would wait for someone to come and say it was safe to leave. It was a wise move. There were too many corridors, too many ways to get lost, and who knew what nasties were roaming the trails?

Julian kept moving.

When he reached the fourth chamber, there were no more people. Near the fifth chamber, he stopped at an intersection, then continued on. In the Staropolska Chamber he saw the same group of tourists he'd passed on the way in; they were standing around a monolithic Communist-era sculpture of miners.

"Anyone come through here?" he asked the tour guide.

"Three men and a woman."

"A woman?"

"Yes."

"How long ago?"

"Just now. What's going on?"

Julian raced in the direction of the Witolny Lake.

Three men and a woman.

Soon he neared the entrance. At the corner that would open onto the lake, he heard a splash and an echo, as if someone had dived into the water. He stopped, pulled Oskar's gun, peeked around the corner. Teresa was standing on the pathway over the water. She was sifting through a wallet, counting money. She had her Mauser in her left hand and a second gun tucked under an armpit.

In the water below, clawing at rocks and pulling himself out, was one of Markat's security men.

"Seven million," Teresa said. "You shouldn't keep so much cash on you, not in this day and age."

Seeing Julian, she fumbled the wallet and trained her Mauser on him. Then she retrieved the wallet as quickly as she'd dropped it.

The bodyguard climbed out of the water and huffed and puffed as he gained his feet.

"Hands up," Teresa told him. Then to Julian: "Markat's a few feet ahead. He's still got one guy with him."

"What happened?"

"Markat and his men made for the same exit as me. They picked me up. They're in an awful rush."

"And him?" Julian pointed to the bodyguard.

"Markat told him to . . . he said he'd wait for him in the St. Adalbert Chapel." She turned to the bodyguard. "But no one bothered to frisk me, right?"

"Listen," the goon said, "you'll never—"

"Since you've had your swim, get out of here. And I mean run."

She motioned to the path back to the Koszalin Chamber. The bodyguard took a tentative step, kept his hands in the air. "I can't run when I'm wet like this."

"That's why you went swimming, Einstein. Now go." She raised the gun in her hand, and he turned and jogged off. Julian and Teresa watched him disappear, heard the sloshing footsteps grow faint.

"That wasn't smart," Julian said, "making him run back there."

"Why not?" she asked.

"Because that's where you're going, too."

"With pleasure," she said, "after he's had a head start. We have to get out of here, Krol."

Julian peered down the tunnel. "How long ago was Markat here?"

"Snap out of it. It's like I said, he's in a hurry. He said something about charges."

"What do you mean, 'charges'?" Then his muscles—his knotted back and neck, the pain in his hand and his shoulder—everything loosened up all at once. Charges. That topped everything.

"We have to get to the surface," Teresa said.

Julian peered down the path that led to Markat. "Why would he blow it up?"

"The guy with him, he's got one of those machine guns, those things in all the American movies."

"Go to the surface," Julian said.

And pushed her in the water and began running toward the St. Adalbert Chapel.

She might try to follow, but she wouldn't catch up.

At the entrance to the St. Adalbert Chapel he heard more voices. A vision of the bodyguard's gun flashed in his mind: an Uzi, a newfangled machine pistol, a Gatling-Glock-Thingama-whatever. He crouched low and poked his head around the corner. Under the ornate chandeliers and up near the salt altar stood the same tour group that he'd entered the mine with. The guide was telling the tourists about the New Testament stories that were carved into the walls. Markat wasn't around, wasn't waiting for his Teresa-disposing guard.

Seeing Julian's gun, the people lunged for cover that didn't exist. He began down the next passageway, but then stopped. If the tourists had seen Markat and a gun-toting bodyguard, would they be standing around discussing New Testament tales? Markat had left the route somewhere.

Julian dashed back through the chapel. Again the tourists cowered. On the other side of the entrance, a ventilation shaft blew cold air down the main tunnel. Julian looked up into the freezing darkness. Iron rungs led up to another level. The crawlspace looked claustrophobically narrow.

Julian tucked his gun under his belt and started to climb.

A few feet up there was no more light. He climbed with both hands, finding the rungs with his cast and clutching them with his good hand. One miscalculation and he would fall and shred himself on the rungs and jagged cave walls.

The wind chilled the sweat on his face. He climbed quickly, soon saw a dull light above him. A minute later he poked his head over the lip of the tunnel. He was at a higher level, one closed to tourists. The passage was just high enough to let him stand up straight. He began walking, then heard a click.

It came from behind him, only inches from his head. He

raised his hands and turned around slowly.

A fat man with a crew cut held a machine pistol at eye level—sideways, straight out of those American movies. Markat stood beside him, looked neither excited nor concerned.

The guard tugged Julian's gun away. "Turn around," he said, which Julian did. "Now walk."

Markat didn't add anything to that, so Julian started walking. Bare bulbs on the cave walls provided the light. Wooden signs held sector and level numbers. They were in 2G, whatever that meant. Other signs warned against unauthorized personnel. Julian waited and then looked back.

"Tell me why," he said.

Markat stayed silent a few seconds, then, finally: "Because she wanted out."

"So she could go work for your business partner in Pakistan. That much I know. Is that a reason to kill her?"

Again Markat went silent, surprised, maybe, that Julian had put this much together. Nawaz, the man from the Lubon e-mail, had promised Krystyna what she said in her letter she needed. Distance. A chance at a new start. But how had any of that threatened Markat?

"I know most of it," Julian said. "She interpreted for you. Nawaz couldn't speak Polish, and wasn't handy with English, either. She was a translator, nothing more."

Markat said, "If you've got it all figured out, why ask questions?"

"Because I don't know everything."

"She made us a lot of money," Markat said. "Not zloty money, dollar money."

"It's a relief to know she was killed for hard currency."

Markat didn't respond to that.

"So why not just send her away?" Julian asked. "Send her off to Pakistan? Couldn't trust her? What did you do, tell Nawaz she was coming? Let her talk to Nawaz, let her get excited about the move?"

"I did make her happy," Markat said. "I bought her a ticket. She fell in love with the idea."

Julian lowered his hands and stopped walking. The fat man with the gun didn't object.

"Then why'd she end up in Warsaw?"

Markat seemed to mull something over before saying, "Distance."

The bodyguard poked the gun into Julian's ribs. "Stop stopping," he said.

Julian resumed walking. Maybe he could swat out a bulb, run, take his chances with the gun. They came to another vertical tunnel, another set of iron rungs.

"Stop," the bodyguard said, and Julian looked down into the darkness.

Markat stepped forward and shared the view with him. "Can you guess what I want you to do?"

"Jump?"

"It's two hundred feet to the next level. I'll give you a minute to get there. After one minute, Stefan here sprays down some bullets."

Julian stared at him and thought, for the briefest of moments, that now he knew what made this man tick. Markat was not mad or greedy or sadistic. He was evil. He had gone too far in life unimpeded, had let his own success quash any questions he might have asked of himself. He'd never seen the need to apply the brakes.

"Better go," Markat said.

Julian stepped back from the opening. "Why destroy the mine?"

Markat's eyes widened. Words failed him.

"You're in a deal with Mirsk, but Mirsk shafted you. Or vice versa."

Now Markat looked perturbed. "Krol, nothing gets done without a reason. I couldn't care less about Antoni. He's not dead out of principle."

"Then why is he dead?"

"Because he was shot," Markat said. Then, maybe a little embarrassed by the trite sarcasm, he added, "Because he knows delicate things about me. And because shooting him was the best way to get people out of the mine before it blows."

"So you don't kill a lot of people?"

"So I don't kill a lot of people."

"And that," Julian said, "helps you delude yourself into thinking you're *not* evil?"

Markat laughed, but there was a hitch in it, a bit of tension. Maybe there was, after all, some humanity there—something.

Markat said, "There's more to it. What's the one thing that matters when the mine goes?"

"Plenty of things matter," Julian said. "Chief among them is human life."

"Another of those 'plenty of things' is real estate."

"Real est—what do you mean?"

"Every farm and disused lot within ten kilometers. Land that's ripe for appreciation."

Now it made sense. With the mine gone and the ouskirts of the town gone with it, federal money would help the surviving areas above ground. There would still be a Mieltor, after all, a good-sized town that would need a school and town hall and all manner of infrastructure. Real estate would stabilize—no more threat from the slowly sinking mine—and a speculator who had shown foresight and had made copious purchases would earn some real money.

Markat would wait a year or two or five, watch the new Mieltor develop, then start building or selling his land from abroad. And Antoni Mirsk would not be around to cause problems.

Markat gave the bodyguard an eye signal. The bodyguard said, "Get in the hole."

Julian didn't move. The bodyguard leveled the gun at him.

So he started down the rungs. On his way down, he waited for bullets. He heard something, a muffled, faraway explosion, then a rumble, growing louder by increments. He heard the earth above him start to shake, then saw it coming down, slowly at first, in bits and pieces, then in one fell swoop, bringing houses and schools and restaurants with it. He looked up at Markat, saw him standing there, looking down at him. The rumblings had been in his mind.

He increased the pace, went down as fast as he could, felt the wall for overhangs, any kind of cover. He found a rock bulging out maybe eight inches, pressed himself flat against the wall beneath it. He was cloaked in darkness, but when he poked his head out, he could see them looking down at him. He pressed his face against the wall, tasted salt.

"Okay," he heard Markat say, "that'll do it."

The bodyguard cocked the gun and pulled the trigger. Salt-rock chipped off of the wall, pelted Julian, but the bullets missed him, thudding into the salt rather than ricocheting. He hugged the wall until the shots stopped, then stayed put in case Markat's gunman shone a flashlight down the hole for signs of life.

Then there were gunshots from far away, different shots, hollow-sounding.

Julian peeked out around the rock. Markat and his bodyguard were looking to their right, the fat man aiming his gun at someone aboveground. A voice cried an indecipherable command and more guns went off. Soon the bodyguard was no longer at the hole.

Markat was still there, though, standing unsteadily, clutching his stomach. He teetered, and Julian felt something drip on him.

Then there was more echoed shouting. Markat raised his hands halfway—surrendering, but too late. He slumped forward and plunged into the hole.

He bounced off the walls and rungs, shredding himself. Julian pressed his body hard against the salty rocks, but knew he would be a wedge. When Markat hit, the blow was crushing. Julian slid to his side, heard Markat gasp.

Julian pressed out from the wall, tried to keep him there.

"How'd you do it?" he said. "How'd you get her to take the drugs?"

"Help me," Markat croaked.

"I'll drop you if you don't tell me."

"Hashish tea," Markat said. His hand searched the wall for something to grab.

"The meth?" Julian said.

"Water . . . funnel . . . please. . . ."

He clutched at Julian, so Julian pulled back slightly, slid his body to the side. Markat dropped down a little farther.

Someone aimed a flashlight into the hole. The glare blinded Julian.

"Don't move," a voice said from above. "We're coming down."

Cop voice. Julian shifted his body again, and again Markat slipped a few inches. One more movement was all it would take.

The cop's light shone on Markat's half-closed eyes, a face black with salt-rock and a fast-ebbing pain. Markat had a hand on one of Julian's ankles. The other clung limply to a rung. His feet hung against the tunnel wall. Julian locked eyes with him, told him wordlessly that he was now about to kill him. Markat only blinked.

"Hold him," the cop said. "Grab onto him."

Julian hitched his cast farther over a rung. He slid his legs to the right. There was a crisp sliding sound and Markat bounced down into the gloom. The sound lasted for a good nine or ten seconds, longer than Julian expected it to. He followed the cop back up.

Climbing onto solid ground, he saw Lieutenant Daniel Kosinski. The Warsaw cop was standing over the bodyguard, holding a gun on him.

"I got your e-mail," Kosinski said as Julian gained his feet. "You want to tell me about it?"

Julian peered down the hole. Something had been lifted, but not much. A weight was still there, and would be for a while.

"We better get to the surface," he told Kosinski. "The mine is wired to blow."

Chapter 34

Twenty kilometers to the west, Oskar Ret again hiked down from the Beskidy hills and into Jablunkov. This time the bus was waiting and running when he got there. This time the scar tissue on his hip didn't hurt. There were no second thoughts. Whatever happened in Romania, whatever work he found or didn't find, whatever trouble lay in wait, he would meet it head on. He felt good now, decent, or at least not guilty. For once. Maybe he didn't deserve happiness or peace of mind—maybe not yet—but there would be time to work on that. There were a lot of things that needed undoing.

There were also a lot of things that needed to be left behind.

Chapter 35

Julian sat on a bench in the hallway of Brzesko Hospital. Shaking out a copy of *Kurier Krakowski,* he glanced down the hall. The unit clerk had told him Irena Platz's room was the last one on the left.

A girl of five or six bounded out of the room and shrieked a joyful challenge to a nurse, who followed close behind her wearing a scowl. The girl was naked from the waist down, a punishment meant to keep her in bed. She vaulted past Julian, and the nurse gave chase, promised a spanking.

Some of what *Kurier Krakowski* reported was now ten days old, but Julian was reading everything he could find on the events. There had been two bombs in the mine, and both had been defused. Antoni Mirsk's murderer had not been caught, but the police were investigating Konrad Markat's role in the crime. Investigations had also been started into the murders of Martin Figur and Henryk Milewski, the latter in Gdansk, with rumors that Antoni Mirsk himself had ordered the hit after the editor set up an interview with Mirsk through his secretary. The cops were also checking the whereabouts of Oskar Ret, an alleged alien smuggler who had vanished, and the papers wrote that the murders and smuggling were linked to the killing of a Warsaw prostitute named Krystyna Krol.

Over the last ten days plenty had also been written about Julian. The papers identified him as the prostitute's brother, an ex-Solidarity activist (an expired description that didn't do much for his sense of identity). They said he was a hero and a question mark. A Warsaw doctor had reattached his left thumb, and he had police-surveillance orders not to travel abroad while the cops sorted the affair out. Krol, the paper said, had contradicted reports of a mystery woman named Teresa being with him while everything unfolded. He'd never met such a Teresa. She was a figment of his press colleagues' lurid imaginations.

He folded the newspaper and left it on the bench. He walked down the hall and entered Irena Platz's room.

She was in a hospital bed. A bandage hid half of her forehead. Plaster casts encased a broken left tibia and a shattered right ankle. She had a freshly blackened right eye to take over for the almost-faded bruise under her left eye. Bluish patches on her forearms gave her the look of a heroin addict.

Still, she was undaunted. She looked able to leap out of bed, march down the hall, broken legs and all, and hike to the nearest Tatra peak if she so desired.

Teresa Nowak sat next to her. When she caught sight of Julian, she gasped audibly. She rose from the chair, but made no move to greet him.

"How'd you get here?" she asked.

"I called him," Irena said. "I couldn't resist, not after all those stories in the papers. We had a nice chat. I called him your boyfriend. He didn't seem to mind."

"You look terrible," Julian said.

"A kisser like this, it pretty much forces a career change."

Teresa folded her arms and waited nervously. He knew what she was thinking. Three times he had brought her close to the brink. She had evaded a sad end each time, but there was still the future to deal with. Dodging the cops would be a full-time job, for a lot of years, and she had neither a home nor money. The arc of her young life was now taking a steep turn toward the ground.

"How's Markat's servant?" Julian asked.

"Keeps asking to go home to Pakistan," Irena said.

The girl-pursuing nurse poked her head into the room, her huge chest heaving from all the double-speed walking. "She come back?" she asked, and Irena shook her head, sending her on her way again.

Teresa finally spoke: "Everyone from your newspaper went to Torun. For your editor's funeral."

"My doctor wouldn't let me go," Julian said.

"It's a waste," Teresa said. "All those people dead and for what? Who got anything out of this?"

Julian knew of one person who would get something, but he didn't know quite how to say it.

"Remember Krystyna's note?" he asked. "The thing in Urdu?"

Teresa nodded, had been asking herself about it ever since the Pakistanis read it.

"The cops checked it out. It said 'They're selling people,' just those three words. That's what got those men in the truck so excited."

Teresa only shrugged, something else clearly bothering her. "That offer," she said, "that bit about Krystyna's bedroom being free. . . ."

"It still stands," Julian said.

"I was thinking a week or two, unless you have cops dropping in. I wasn't thinking about money. I don't need you to pay me anything. I just—"

"Money?" Irena said, ears perking up. "There some kind of transaction here?"

"We made a deal," Julian said. "We—"

"Forget it," Teresa said. "I'll get a job. They're always saying Warsaw is the only place in Poland where anyone can find a job if they have to."

The optimism sounded good. "Maybe I'll test that theory, too," Julian said. "I could use a career change."

"You're a hero," Irena said. "You can go on TV, make money telling everyone how you tamed so many bad guys."

Maybe he could. In the new and improved times, celebrity was marketable.

"It's funny," he said, "the papers call me a hero. And meanwhile you"—to Teresa—"can't go near the cops, while you"—to Irena—"have five weeks before you can even walk again."

Which made him feel good about what he would do now.

"Henryk had no family," he said. "He left his nest egg to me."

"His nest egg?" Irena said.

"It's a saying in English. It means money he saved. It comes to a hundred and twenty million, and it'll clear the tax office and reach my account in about a month."

"You want to give us your dead friend's money?" Irena said.

Julian focused on Teresa. "It's not much, I know, but it'll get you on your feet. And. . . ."

"And what?" Teresa said.

"My apartment needs a little work. I'd like to borrow a little, fix the place up. The rest I'll put in a new bank account. It belongs to you two."

No one said anything for a while. It wasn't the kind of news you could celebrate. The looks on the two women's faces were hard to nail down. Beneath their conflicting emotions was the fact that life could continue. There could be a future.

Irena looked at Teresa. "You thought we'd never see him again. You thought he was gone."

Julian watched Teresa try to smile. It was a poor effort, but an effort nonetheless. It was hard for her—for him—to feel truly good. But it was nice to at least start thinking about tomorrow. The first steps were being taken in three new lives.

"Truth is," Teresa said, "I knew I'd see you. Krystyna and I, like I said, we weren't all that close. But I guess I can see a little of her in you."

ABOUT THE AUTHOR

Hard Currency was inspired by **Steven Owad**'s experiences as editor of an English-language newspaper in Warsaw, Poland, after the fall of communism. Steven now lives in Calgary, Canada, with his wife Aleksandra and his daughter Sara. His previous crime novels include *Bodycheck* and *Brother's Keeper.* He can be found on the Internet at *www.stevenowad.com.*